MURDER
AT FROG'S HOLLOW

DR HAMISH HART MYSTERIES
BOOK THREE

Printed in Australia
First Printing: November 2022

Shawline Publishing Group Pty Ltd
www.shawlinepublishing.com.au

Paperback ISBN 9-781-9228-5077-5
eBook ISBN 978-1-9228-5082-9

A catalogue record for this book is available from the National Library of Australia

MURDER
AT FROG'S HOLLOW

DR HAMISH HART MYSTERIES
BOOK THREE

KAREN THURECHT

To Christine for always being there.

ACKNOWLEDGMENTS

I'd like to acknowledge the traditional owners of the land on which Brisbane is now located, the Turrbal and Jagera peoples, and pay respect to Elders, past, present and emerging.

I would also like to pay my respects to the Chinese immigrants who came to the colonial frontier of Brisbane Town and who worked so hard to establish a thriving economy for the future.

CONTENTS

PRELUDE

A shadowy figure remains tucked into itself, crouched in the rafters of the old warehouse, knees drawn up and chin low. Stockinged feet grip the wooden beam beneath while the upper beam presses down on the figure's back. Breathing is shallow. The figure listens carefully to its own breath, controlling the flow, in... and out... The figure watches.

A middle-aged Chinese man can be seen through the glass windows at the far end of the warehouse. The shadowy figure watches as the man extinguishes the gas light and blackness descends on the office. Breathing is steady. This is not the time to let the pulse rate increase. Steady... steady... the figure feels blood pumping through every limb. Energy is building, slowly, controlled, stored, coiled.

The Chinese man emerges into the workshop revealing an expensive European suit and short hair, no pigtail for this fellow. He is what he appears to be, a businessman. The shadowy figure clenches its jaw, every muscle held tight while watching the merchant stack rattan chairs on top of one another. The merchant moves toward the door. One more step, one more step... breath in... hold it... Then the figure releases a torrent of stored energy and leaps from the rafters landing directly in front of the merchant. Legs are immediately steady, apart and slightly bent at the knees. Eyes lock and the figure acknowledges the startled and terrified eyes of the merchant. A sword slips from the sheath soundlessly releasing a glint of light before the figure plunges the long blade upward hard and fast under the merchant's ribcage. The merchant's eyes roll back.

'One can forgive murder ...' he croaks as his body slumps to the floor.

Blood flows freely and the shadow sees a small amount mix with the sawdust. The figure leaves the sword where it is. It is done.

CHAPTER ONE

Just about 500 yards in a beeline from the Breakfast Creek stands a peculiar-looking building. It is the new Joss House and for some days past, the fever of anticipation had settled upon the usually cold-blooded Chinese of Brisbane, for the building was approaching completion and they at last were to have a respectable place wherein to conduct their strange rites and mysterious ceremonies.

The Queenslander, Brisbane. Saturday 30 January, 1886

Doctor Hamish Hart stepped onto the deck of the crowded carriage and held out his hand to support his friend Rita, who, without accepting his help, leapt into the throng and wriggled into a gap between himself and Wallace. Everyone was in a good mood, despite the tram car being scandalously overloaded. Men and women, young and old, jostled against one another, happy for the contact and looking forward to what promised to be an exciting evening. At first, the horses couldn't move; the carriage was so full. Hamish stretched his neck to look above the heads of the crowd and saw two surprisingly small horses swaying back and forth on the track. How would those creatures pull an overladen double-decked carriage?

All at once the collective mass of passengers making up the lower level lurched forward as one. The shouting and whipping of the coachmen had finally forced the horses to move and the whole contraption jolted into motion. Hamish fell onto Rita, who lurched into Wallace. Laughter and cries of delight reverberated through the crowd while individuals disentangled limbs, feathers and fancy hats. The poor horses lumbered up the hill, past the Valley Church and down toward Breakfast Creek. The conductor shouted that no one should expect to alight before the completion of the journey as he could not guarantee the horses would resume movement again. Couples on the street hailed the car in vain as it passed them by.

The excitement was palpable as the carriage drew to a halt about five hundred yards from the Breakfast Creek Bridge. Individuals from all walks of life – men, women, children, workers and businessmen stepped out of the carriage and stared in awe at the building before them. Hamish took hold of Rita's hand so he didn't lose her in the crowd and Wallace kept close behind. Rita gasped. Hamish, who had lived in the Ballarat Goldfields as a child had seen many such buildings. Still, the splendour was not lost on him. In the context of Brisbane in 1886, an unremarkable town in its architecture and largely homogenous in its demography, the newly constructed Joss House was both exotic and majestic.

The building itself was a simple rectangular structure about forty-five feet in length and twenty-four feet wide, with walls reaching over twenty feet in height, whitewashed, cement-rendered brick. There were no windows, save one small square at the back to let in light. But the triple roof was breathtaking. And essentially Chinese. The tiled roof supported pipes that carried water into four great earthenware fish which discharged the flow through gaping mouths. At the front of the roof were scenes of Emperors and Warriors, and pretty courtesans waving fans. At each gable end there was a porcelain female figure gracefully playing a flute and at their feet, a fish with an enormous tail and fins curling into the air. In the centre of the roof, between the two fishes, was a spire holding up a small painted globe.

'It's magical,' whispered Rita as she gazed up at the red, gold and green roof.

'It's small, as Joss Houses go,' said Hamish.

'But splendid.'

It was almost seven o'clock and the moon was rising behind the woodlands beyond when a group of Chinese musicians formed an orchestra and started playing. The sounds were quiet at first and foreign to the European ear. There was a gentle tapping and clapping coming from drums, a pan-gong and a pair of large cymbals. Gradually the sound became louder and the instruments came together in one deafening, prolonged crash. The beating heart of the crowd quickened with the noise. Exotic smells filled the air. The atmosphere was intoxicating.

People continued arriving.

'They must be coming from all over Brisbane,' shouted Hamish over the din, 'curious to see the new building.'

'Even people who have no interest in architecture or culture have come to see what all the fuss is about,' said Rita.

Hamish, Rita and Wallace managed to work their way through the crowd to the entrance of the joss house, the doors of which stood open welcoming the curious to enter. The place was ablaze with light from lanterns, lamps and chandeliers. Hamish watched as Rita placed her hand to her mouth and gasped again. There were tables adorned with silver vases filled with flowers made of golden tinsel and peacock feathers. A terrible dragon-headed monster stood on a gilded altar at the back. The altar also had niches holding objects covered in crimson paper. Hamish saw the expression of awe on Wallace's face.

'Surely you have seen such places in your travels,' laughed Hamish. 'Having sailed across the world many times.'

'Seen them, certainly but I have never entered such a place,' said Wallace.

Two Chinese men came from the back of the building pushing at the spectators with outstretched hands.

'They want us out.'

Hamish held Rita's hand tightly as the Chinaman ushered them from the building with the throng of other Europeans staring, faces upward, at the glistening decorations.

When they were outside, the door closed shut.

'They'll be carrying out their preparations,' said Hamish. 'They want us out of the way.'

The visitors milled around outside in anticipation, while word went around that something exciting was going to happen. Speculation and imagination ran rife. Meanwhile a cool breeze kept them all comfortable and cheerful under the starry sky. Entertainment was scarce in Brisbane and numbingly unvaried. This was something different and the population was not going to miss a moment. Hamish immersed himself in the pulsing sea of colour, Chinese men and women in traditional embroidered tunics of red, green and gold silk. Like driftwood floating dull against sparkling fish, Hamish spotted the occasional Chinese man wearing a European suit. Each man wore the long, braided pigtail, a foot in each camp, Hamish supposed.

What a difficult way to live. Hamish was reminded of the Chinese festivals he attended as a child in Ballarat. There, the men did not wear splendid colourful costumes or European suits. Rather they wore the trousers and shirts of the worker.

As his mind had wandered into memory, it was not surprising that when Hamish noticed one man slightly taller than the others, his neck held high, his eyes scanning downward across the crowd, he was immediately put in mind of his childhood friend, Ah Tay. Ah Tay had been taller than the other Chinese boys in Ballarat. And this man had a similar air: a stance that was proud and unsure at the same time. But this was not Ah Tay. This was a grown man, with an expensive suit and short hair combed carefully back from his high forehead. No pigtail. From this distance, and after twenty years apart, would he even recognise Ah Tay if he saw him? Hamish laughed. He thought how strange it was that the people in one's memory didn't age. In his mind, his friend was still a child, thirteen, fourteen, no more.

Hamish reached across to place his hand over Rita's arm linked through his. Her smile brought him instantly back to the present, the jostling crowd and the excitement of the warm summer evening. The smell of incense in the air was intoxicating and the sounds of chatter, English and foreign excited the senses. There was a collective expectation. Anticipation held by so many, it was exaggerated tenfold by each individual. Something unexpected was going to happen. The excitement kept people there, waiting, exuberant, for far longer than they would have imagined.

At half past one, a thundering noise made the crowd jump. A rope of fireworks lit up the night sky and exploded around them. Hamish, Rita and Wallace stared upward watching as the heavens erupted in colour. Tiny droplets of light fell from eternity. Hamish shifted his gaze to see the lights reflected in Rita's eyes, her face glowing pink, then green, then diamond white as the display above played out in her eyes. A tangy smell of gunpowder descended on them with the falling lights and clouds of smoke. The spectacle lasted longer than the senses could take it in and Hamish slipped into a trance before the din ceased and the last of the lights fell.

The crowd had barely finished gasping and applauding the fireworks display when the doors to the Joss House swung open. While they were distracted, a group of Chinese had assembled themselves into a formation. At the head was a man adorned in red and gold beating a gong. He was followed by two Chinese noblemen bearing a half-rolled banner. Over their heads was a canopy of richly embroidered and embellished cloth and over that was suspended a leaf-shaped fan made from the same material. Next came an elderly Chinaman with sunken cheekbones, hollow jaws and eyes that didn't reflect the light. He wore a red flannel robe with chintz borders and a rural scene painted on the back. A black cap sat on his head with a golden knob at the crown. He was beating a circular plate of iron. Following him the rest of the procession was made up of ordinary Chinese men beating drums and gongs.

The parade made its way through the entrance to the Joss House and proceeded to the altar where the noblemen unfurled the banner and hung it in front of the dragon monster. Chinese men broke ranks and tore away at crimson paper that covered niches in the altar. As the paper tore, bronze idols were revealed and the men fell to their knees, bowing their heads, touching their foreheads to the floor. One old man, who must have been a priest, dipped a branch into an ornate bowl and sprinkled water on the altar, the idols and the building, mumbling to himself in his own language as he did so. A man then brought in a cock with its comb bled and the Priest anointed the idols with the cock's blood. The Chinese continued bowing.

'What are they doing?' asked Rita.

'They are warding off evil spirits,' Hamish explained. 'Life enters the idols through the hot blood of the living cock. See the priest tossing wood into the air? He is asking whether the Gods will protect them.'

A group of Chinese gathered around the wood each time it fell and examined the pattern on the floor. At the seventh try, the Priest nodded and the Chinese cheered their thankfulness.

'They have had success,' said Hamish. 'The temple has been blessed by the Gods. The Joss house is now officially open.'

Hamish noticed that three whole pigs, roasted and greasy, waited at the front of the building and there were tables with plates of rice piled high, as well as other plates and bowls of Chinese foods. Another table was covered with cups of spirits and tea, and plates of pastries.

The formalities complete, the party could begin and the Chinese tucked into their feast. While the visitors were welcome to join them, few of the European inhabitants of Brisbane accepted the offer of crisp chicken feet or the other strange delicacies on offer.

Around three in the morning, when the night was at its coolest, the last of the observers climbed into the trams to return home. Tired but exhilarated they chatted on about what they had witnessed. Hamish, Rita and Wallace were among the last group to leave. Although they were standing in the crowded carriage, Rita rested her head on Hamish's shoulder and closed her eyes. His heart rate increased a little as he placed his chin on her head. He felt content. Catching a knowing glance from Wallace, Hamish wanted to tell him to 'shut up'. But Wallace hadn't said anything and to speak would spoil his mood.

CHAPTER TWO

It is evident that for some time past, the Customs authorities have been on the lookout for Chinamen who arrived in this colony, for the purpose of imposing the poll tax of ten pound upon all that have not previously been resident in Victoria. Every steamer that has arrived from Hong Kong has been most carefully scanned but no direct instance of imposition has been so far ascertained.

The arrival of the steamer Afghan this morning, however, has been most anxiously looked for by the officers of the department as it was evident that information had been received and duly authenticated that close upon 200 Chinese were on board, who intended to evade the poll tax. The vessel arrived shortly after nine o'clock and according to instructions issued by the department, no one was allowed to leave or board the steamer until a thorough examination and overhaul of their effects and papers had been made by the chief officer and the customs. Consequently, the Afghan was anchored well out in the stream while several officers were put on board for the purpose of minutely examining the credentials of the new arrivals.

It is alleged that out of this large number on board, over one half have had their naturalisation papers sent over by Chinamen, who at the present time, are residents in different parts of Victoria. Some of the papers had the appearance of having travelled the ocean several times.

The Herald. Monday 25 January, 1886

The following morning, Hamish descended a dark staircase to the basement of the Royal Brisbane Hospital. It was already stifling outside, though it was barely seven o'clock. Hamish placed his hand on his forehead where his fringe had already fallen moist and limp over his eyes. He pushed the hair back and it stood upright, a mass of wet curls on top of his head. If anyone had been there to see him looking unkempt, he wouldn't have cared. The late night combined with an early message from Sergeant Bellamy to join him at the morgue had dulled his wits. His fingers touched the scar on the left side of his face; it was often itchy in the heat. The scar was the consequence of a fall down a mineshaft when he was eight years old, in Ballarat, where his days were a mirage of heat and dust and creek beds, traversed, explored and written into adventures in his mind, by himself and his friend Ah Tay. He scratched at the scar, stopping himself when it stung.

Hamish made his way down the stone staircase into the basement, appreciating the cooler air that prickled his skin and taking in a deep breath as he landed in the coolest part of the building. The morgue was not his favourite destination and it was beyond him why Sergeant Bellamy had sent for him but he was thankful, at least, to be out of the heat. He had conducted a necropsy at the sergeant's request once before but that was twelve months ago and the hospital had engaged a doctor with experience in the field since then.

Hamish noticed Bellamy through the double doors leading into the morgue. He was talking to an older man with longish grey hair and bushy eyebrows of a similar colour and texture.

'Good Lord, it's Inspector Scratchley,' said Hamish, surprised to hear the words spoken out loud.

'Good day to you, Hart,' said Scratchley, barely moving his eyes from the sergeant as he spoke. 'I want this matter cleared up as a priority,' he said directly to Bellamy. 'With all the excitement around the opening of the Joss House last night, emotions are high. The Celestials will be worked up about this.'

Bellamy had his chin down resting on his chest.

'I mean it, Bellamy. Don't be distracted by these bleeding hearts on this one.' He glared sideways at Hamish. 'Clear it up fast.'

With that, Scratchley left them, bounding up the stairs two at a time.

'I take it he means me,' said Hamish.

'He's not forgiven you for getting the Kanaka off last year.'

'We solved the case though, didn't we? Kaelo didn't do it.'

'Yes, we solved it and illuminated a scandal within one of the colony's wealthy landowning families. I swear, Scratchley would have preferred to see the Kanaka hang.'

'So, why have you sent for me now? Since we're at the morgue, I assume there is a body.'

'Of course, there's a body. I want you to examine it.'

'Where's Doctor Simpson?'

'He's away. Family responsibilities down south. I'm afraid you're next in line.'

Only a few months earlier a medical examiner had been appointed to the colony, causing Hamish great relief as he no longer had to fear being called in to act in the role. He felt ill equipped having had no prior training or experience in the field when he first arrived in Brisbane.

'Right then,' said Hamish. 'Best get on with it.'

He pushed the doors open and looked down at the man on the slab.

'Where are his clothes?' asked Hamish, alarmed.

'Over there.' The sergeant pointed to a pile on a table pushed against the wall.

Hamish blinked his eyes rapidly, as though trying to understand what he had heard.

'Nothing should be moved before the examination,' he cried.

'You'll be disappointed to know he arrived with the weapon still stuck in his torso, then,' said Bellamy. 'It has also been removed. It's over there as well.'

Hamish rubbed his forehead and shook his head. He walked over to the table and examined the ornate silver sword covered in blood. Turning his attention back to the sergeant, he said, 'I would have expected everyone to know the importance of leaving the body and associated paraphernalia intact. In fact, I should have been called to the scene.'

'This is how Simpson works,' said Bellamy with no sign of apology. 'We bring the bodies in, the orderlies prepare them, then Simpson does his part.'

Hamish shook his head again and muttered his disapproval under his breath.

'I beg your pardon?' asked Bellamy leaning in to improve his chances of hearing.

'Nothing,' said Hamish who had returned his attention to the corpse before him.

Hamish reminded himself he had a general practice to maintain and that was enough. There was nothing to be gained by objecting to the methods of the new medical examiner. If he was called upon to help, he would do what he could. Beyond that, it was none of his business if the police constables stomped all over the murder scene and the body wasn't examined *in situ.*

The man before him was small in stature and Chinese. As Hamish let his gaze settle on the man's face, a lump formed in his throat and his pulse quickened.

'We brought him in earlier this morning,' said Bellamy. 'The workers found him when they showed up at the factory.'

Hamish tried to steady the growing sensation of confusion in his mind.

Bellamy began, 'His name is …'

'Ah Chit,' finished Hamish.

'Do you know him?' asked the sergeant.

Hamish didn't answer.

'He was found this morning in his warehouse. He makes furniture, or his workers do – that rattan stuff that is so popular. Agatha wants to replace a comfortable settee …'

'Yes. I know him.' Hamish recovered his voice.

'He worked for my father on one of the mines in Ballarat. When my father sold his claims and returned to Melbourne, Ah Chit purchased his own mine. He grew quite wealthy, I heard, bringing in his own Chinese workers and expanding his claim. I also heard he had returned to Melbourne and set up a furniture factory in Lygon Street. But I had no idea he was in Brisbane.'

'What else do you know about him? Anything that would have a bearing on his untimely end?'

'No,' said Hamish. 'As I said I didn't know he was in Brisbane. He has a nephew, two years older than me. Ah Tay. We used to play together as children. Is he in Brisbane too? Does he know his uncle has been killed?'

'I don't know. Pennyweather is interviewing employees now to get background information on the Chinaman. Ah Chit, you say?'

'Yes. That's his name.'

Bellamy watched for a moment but Hamish was already peering into the wound in the man's chest.

'I'll leave you to your grisly work then.' Bellamy walked to the door then turned and said as an afterthought, 'Will you be able to carry out the examination, knowing him, I mean?'

Hamish's face was twisted in deep concentration as he sunk his finger into the wound.

Bellamy left.

'Stab wound produced by long, sharp, pointed object,' Hamish said to himself. 'Not exactly a revelation, given the murder weapon is laid across the table.'

Hamish examined the margins of the wound and the angle. He measured the space between the margins. The wound edges were well approximated; he was seeing a slit rather than a gape. The weapon had entered cleanly. Hamish went to the table and picked up the sword recovered from the man's body: a Chinese sword, a *Jian*. The blade was long and thin, consistent with the wound, and it was coated in blood almost to the hilt. He could expect the wound to be deep. Hamish went back to the body and rolled it over. He was not surprised to find that the wound perforated the man's body exiting through his back. The exit wound was at least six inches higher than the entry point. The assailant had thrust upward, from beneath the ribs and with such force, the weapon travelled right through his body.

Hamish checked the clothing piled on the table for blood. There was surprisingly little. He noticed a patch around a slice in the fabric that would have been at the entry point and a slight pooling at the back. Surely there would have been more blood from such an attack? Hamish examined the man's hands and arms. There was no sign he had attempted to defend himself. Surely, he would have raised his arms to cover himself or tried to hit out against the assailant? But there was nothing to indicate he did so. His skin was clean apart from the wound site. No abrasions, no bruising, in fact, not a hair out of place. He must have known his attacker – or been completely surprised by the assault.

Hamish began the internal investigation. He followed the passage of the wound with a long needle. It appeared to slip by the heart without piercing it. How could Ah Chit have died without losing more blood? He wrote in his notepad, *perforation of body from right to left, upward and from front to back.* He took his scalpel and cut a four-by-four-inch window in the anterior aspect of the chest wall. The heart sac was opened anteriorly so that the pericardial cavity could be filled with water. When the heart was submerged, Hamish used a needle to puncture the right atrium. Bubbles escaped and floated to the surface confirming the presence of an air embolism in the heart. This explained how death might have occurred rapidly without extensive blood loss. A large vein had been severed by the sword. The heart kept pumping and created a vacuum effect sucking large volumes of air into the vein. The result was instant cessation of blood flow.

Hamish restored what dignity he could to the body and cleaned up.

When he went upstairs, Bellamy was in the foyer waiting for him, leaning back in a faded armchair set against brown wood panelling. Hamish always found the room dark and oppressive, uninviting as an entrance hall to the medical school building. Bellamy stubbed out his cigar when he saw Hamish approach.

'Do we have to talk here?' asked Hamish.

'No. I have a cab waiting.'

'There's something I need to do before we talk.'

'Can I drop you somewhere?'

Hamish followed the sergeant to the waiting police cab. 'The post office,' he said. 'I need to send a telegram.'

Bellamy watched the younger man carefully for a few moments before he spoke. 'You'll tell me what you find out?' he said.

'Certainly,' Hamish answered but for some reason he could not explain, he was unsure that he would.

Seated comfortably in the cab, Hamish flicked through his notebook for his father's details. He hadn't been home or even spoken to his father in three years. He had letters from his mother so he was aware of their move into smaller accommodation in recent months. She told him it was difficult managing enough servants to keep a large home running, now they were getting older and their needs were few. There was no shortage of money, as far as Hamish was aware.

Prior to making money from gold in Ballarat, they had lived in a tent alongside the Yarra River, so Hamish imagined his parents would be comfortable during their autumn years in a more modest home. Hamish's father had been a set price bookmaker for the past twenty years. Perhaps the horses were not paying as well as they used to. Hamish shook his head. That seemed unlikely. He composed the telegram in his head as the cab rattled on. When they reached the post office in Queen Street, Hamish thanked the driver and let him go. Bellamy provided the cab to take him home but Hamish wasn't ready to return to his house yet.

Hamish wrote out the message already formed in his mind.

> *Making enquiries about Ah Chit. Has turned up in Brisbane, deceased. Murdered. Do you know anything about his move north? Did Ah Tay come with him? Do you have contact details for Ah Tay? All well with me. Practice busy. Hope you and Mother are also well.*

Hamish read the message again before handing it to the postmaster. It seemed succinct for the first communication in three years. But what else was there to say? He had barely spoken more than a dozen words to his father in the years prior to moving to the 'frontier', the label his father had given the northern colony.

After sending the telegram, Hamish considered his next move. He needed to know if Ah Tay was in Brisbane. He and Ah Tay had been close as boys. It was surprising he had not contacted him if he was in Brisbane with his uncle. Hamish walked toward town with no clear plan in mind. He thought if he visited the warehouse belonging to Ah Chit someone might be able to tell him if Ah Tay was in Brisbane.

Hamish arrived at the warehouse to find that Constable Pennyweather and his colleagues had not long left. The Chinese workers made clear their tolerance for questions from European men was extinguished. If the local constabulary believed themselves to have authority over the Chinese workers, the assumption was not shared by the Chinese but the young doctor had even less chance of gaining their confidence. They ignored Hamish's presence as though he were not there. When he asked a question, they simply kept working. When he moved in front of them, they stepped around him as though he were a piece of furniture left in the walkway. He felt frustration rising but any expectation of gaining information from these men was fruitless. The Chinese workers were as calm as he was anxious. And they were not going to talk to him.

Nonetheless, he was not ready to give up. He walked several blocks to the Roma Street markets where the Chinese community sold fruit and vegetables. When Hamish last had contact with Ah Tay, he had a garden and was selling his produce in the markets of Melbourne. Surely, if Ah Tay was in Brisbane, this is where he would be. Hamish wandered up and down the street observing the stall holders. The very young and the very old were all represented and the stalls were busy with customers haggling for the best prices in their various dialects. One or two European women, servants rather than ladies, were also bidding for fresh vegetables at a good price.

An elderly man with a conical-shaped hat and no teeth caught Hamish's attention, selling Chinese herbs from large baskets. When Hamish stopped, he scooped a pile of the aromatic dried plants into a paper bag and offered it to him.

'For cough,' the man called out to Hamish.

He held out the open bag. Hamish hesitated and leaned in toward the offering but the smell was overwhelming. He staggered backward, rubbing his nose.

'No cough.'

As he turned to move on, he caught sight of a man close to his own age standing at the end of the line of stalls. The man stood still, staring in Hamish's direction.

'Ah Tay?' Hamish whispered to himself. He picked up his pace and moved quickly toward the figure. But as quickly as Hamish headed in his direction, the figure disappeared.

He stopped and looked around him. Chinese men and women moved back and forth between the stalls in front of him and behind him but none of them were dressed in European suits and none of them were like the figure he had seen.

Hamish forced himself to breathe evenly. A flush appeared on his face and neck, and he scraped his hand through his hair, then cupping the back of his neck with his hand, he compelled himself to focus. There was no reason to believe it was Ah Tay he had seen. He had no reason to believe Ah Tay was even in Brisbane. He should wait to hear from his father. His father would have remained in touch with Ah Chit, at least until a few years ago. Maybe he would know something. Hamish turned toward home.

As Hamish walked, images of Ah Chit flashed through his mind. The man he saw on the slab that morning didn't look that different from the image of Ah Chit in his memories, except that the man on the slab was dead. Ah Chit was a formidable man in his youth, as Hamish recalled him. Hamish had known him as a leader within the Chinese community in Ballarat. On the minefields, the Chinese tents were in a compound separate from where Hamish and his family lived; however, Hamish spent a great deal of his time at the Chinese camp seeking the company of Ah Tay who was two years older but centuries ahead in maturity and experience. Ah Tay told Hamish he and his uncle came to Ballarat to escape the terrible poverty in Southern China. He said he learned English from a mission school in his province, his family believing this would help him become rich in the new world. His father and mother had both passed away, so he was sent with his uncle to Victoria to make his fortune. Ah Chit worked on Hamish's father's mine. He worked hard, according to his father, and he made sure the other Chinese workers worked hard as well.

Hamish also remembered how hard Ah Tay worked. He ploughed dirt that seemed more like cement, to make soil that would grow Chinese vegetables for the camp. He sold vegetables to the Chinese workers as well as to the European miners. As a child, Hamish would sometimes help him on his daily trip carting pails of water from the stream to the garden. Most often, to his shame, he skipped alongside his friend unencumbered while Ah Tay carried the water. He felt it was unfair, at the time, that his friend had to work so hard when they could have spent their days better fossicking for the glints of light on the rocks at the bottom of the creek bed or exploring the old abandoned mine shafts. He put his hand to his cheek at this memory. The old scar was still thick on his skin, tingling sometimes and breaking down occasionally, an intermittent reminder of the fall that left him cowering in the bottom of an abandoned mine shaft for twenty-four hours.

Forcing himself to shift his attention from that incident to the memories of Ah Chit, he tried to recall what had become of Ah Chit after he and his family left Ballarat.

Hamish remembered his father speaking about Ah Chit's success, investing his wages in other mines and finally purchasing stakes of his own. Ah Chit became quite wealthy according to the stories. Ah Tay grew into adulthood at the mines, while Hamish attended a private school in Melbourne from the age of twelve. Having made his fortune, Hamish's father moved the family back to Melbourne and established himself in betting. He could vaguely remember his father making reference to Ah Chit in more recent years. He knew Ah Chit and his nephew had also moved to Melbourne a decade later and his father remained in contact with Ah Chit but he could recall no more details than that. The clearest memories he had of Ah Chit were during those dry, hot, magical years on the Ballarat goldfields when he was a child.

CHAPTER THREE

The Chinese are certainly a peculiar people. But on the whole they are good, sober colonists. No matter what others may say as to their immorality, their opium smoking or their gambling propensities, I believe, as does the significant portion of our digging community, they (the Chinese) will compare favourably with the major part of our working population; and for hard work, thrift, honesty and sobriety, in my opinion, will far outstrip the thousand-and-one boosey specimens of humanity who hail from the land of civilisation and who may well be called by 'poor John' from China, barbarians.

Here in Ballarat, one portion of the local press would fain make you believe the Chinese were fiends incarnate, imps of the devil, the seducers of children and a thousand other extravagances but this is really going too far. Let us look at home and we will find that the crimes and atrocities of the English, Irish and Scotch mongrels who have emigrated to this colony will far outweigh the demonical tendency to be found amongst the poor despised Chinese.

A few evenings ago, we went on an exploring expedition through the Chinese Camp. We visited opium shops, gambling halls and cook-shops, pubs, dancing saloons and the Chinese theatre; and although seeing a pretty fair parade of vice and infamy, yet taking the European element away, very little that was objectionable remains. Every hall we visited had its scores of hobbledehoy gamblers – not Chinese – but the sons of respectable English fathers and mothers.

The Weekly, Melbourne. Saturday 7 January, 1871

Hamish was turning the key in the lock of his townhouse on Wickham Terrace when he felt a tingle in the back of his neck. He turned to find a man almost his own height with slick black hair and a handsome Chinese face staring back at him from such a close distance, he could feel the man's breath on his skin.

'Ah Tay,' he said quietly.

'Just so,' said the man.

Hamish struggled to reconcile the man who stood before him with his childhood memories. There was the same set to his jaw and the same intensity in his eyes. He looked more like his uncle than the boy Hamish remembered. He shrugged off his confusion and smiled as he took the man's hand in his and shook it firmly.

'I'm so glad to see you, friend,' he said. 'Please, please come in.' Hamish stepped into the hallway and gestured for Ah Tay to follow him.

'How long have you been in Brisbane? Why didn't you contact me?'

Ah Tay's expression remained serious and alert.

Hamish checked himself. 'I'm sorry about Ah Chit. I have so many questions. Join me upstairs and we can become reacquainted. If only the circumstances were different,' he said as he led Ah Tay up to the sitting room.

Hamish had converted the terrace house the previous year to provide consulting rooms for his practice. There was a kitchen downstairs and comfortable modern living quarters on the second level. Hamish motioned for Ah Tay to sit in his favourite blue velvet armchair while he settled on the settee. As they sat down, his man-servant Wallace reached the top of the stairs with a pot of tea and two small china cups. A wiry red terrier skipped up the stairs with him and stopped mid-leap when he saw a stranger in the room. The dog sat himself at Hamish's feet and glared at the visitor.

'Green tea,' said Wallace, placing the tray on the occasional table.

'Good Lord,' cried Hamish. 'How did you get that ready so fast?'

Wallace nodded to the guest and headed back downstairs without responding. The dog stayed put.

'I don't know how he does it. He knows what I need before I do. Is green tea suitable?' Hamish asked.

'Perfectly,' said Ah Tay politely.

His long tapered fingers curled around the cup, his hands almost feminine, not at all reflective of a man who spent his time gardening. Ah Tay had always had a slender frame but as a man he was elegant, moving with his back erect and his head held high. He wore a tailored suit in the European style and his immaculately combed black hair framed a face with angular features, high cheekbones and dark intelligent eyes. Was this really the child he had been so close to in Ballarat?

'I have been searching for you today,' Hamish began. 'Since I learned of the death of Ah Chit.'

Ah Tay nodded. 'I know,' he said. 'I saw you.'

'So, it was you. Why did you run away? Why didn't you speak if you saw me?'

'It is awkward.' Ah Tay spoke hesitantly. 'I know you work with the police from time to time and I didn't know if you were representing them in the market today.'

Hamish flushed. 'I see.'

'The Chinese community will not open up to me if they think I am talking to the police.'

'Is that why you didn't contact me when you arrived in Brisbane?' Hamish asked.

'I came to look into my uncle's affairs. I had an idea he was in trouble. I was focused on my uncle.'

Hamish didn't quite see how contacting him would have been a distraction – but he let it go.

'Why are you here now?'

Ah Tay took a sip of tea and crossed his long legs. 'I wanted to know why you were looking for me?'

'I was worried about you. I know how close you and Ah Chit were and I thought you might be in Brisbane with him. I expected you would be upset. I wanted to renew our acquaintance, perhaps even our friendship.'

Ah Chit showed no emotion on his chiselled face or in his dark eyes.

'You and I were friends as children,' he said. 'I was alone but for my uncle when we arrived from Kwangtung. Gold is easy to get, a close friend is harder to find.'

'Our friendship meant a great deal to me,' said Hamish. 'I was sorry to lose touch with you when I moved to Brisbane. I realise we didn't often have cause to meet in the years prior to that but we always kept in touch. Even if it was through my father and your uncle much of the time. Ah Chit spoke of you with great warmth. He was always proudly relaying your achievements to my father.'

Ah Tay didn't smile but there was a slight turn upward at the corner of his lip.

'Are you working with the local police on the investigation into my uncle's death?'

'No,' said Hamish truthfully. 'I was asked to carry out the necropsy. That is all. I honestly went to the Chinese quarter today simply to see if I could find you to offer my condolences.'

'Did you find out anything during your medical examination of my uncle?'

Hamish sighed. 'Not really, he was stabbed using a Chinese sword, a *Jian* to be precise. It was a clean wound, professionally executed, I would say.'

Hamish imagined he saw Ah Tay's eyes soften at this information but his facial expression did not change. Hamish caught himself wondering if Ah Tay cried when he heard of his uncle's death. There was no sign of grief in his demeanour now. Was he able to grieve? Everyone expressed grief in their own way and it was not Ah Tay's way to show emotion. He recalled the time when Ah Tay was nine and sliced his foot on an old pickaxe that had been left lying around, he didn't cry then either. He sat down in the dirt, removed his shirt, tore it into strips, then wrapped them tightly around the wound. Hamish watched on in horror as blood seeped through the makeshift bandage. But they walked the full mile across rocky terrain back to the camp while Ah Tay didn't flinch once nor did he flinch when old Doc Roper stitched up the wound. When Ah Tay next spoke, Hamish was jolted back to the present.

'Ah Chit was in some sort of trouble with the Chinese Societies. I was suspicious when he left Melbourne suddenly. He didn't tell me he was planning the move. He simply closed the warehouse one day and left. The workers came to find me when they found themselves locked out. There was an outcry over it, as the workers were owed their wages for the previous fortnight. In the end, I paid them.'

'It seems Ah Chit brought his problems with him to Brisbane,' said Hamish. 'What have you learned since you came here?'

Ah Tay didn't answer right away. Hamish shifted in his chair, uncomfortable that his friend didn't trust him. *We were as close as brothers when we were children. I would have trusted him with my life*, he thought.

Hamish leant down to place his hand on the terrier still alert at his feet.

'I have heard that you are … inquisitive,' said Ah Tay.

'What?'

'They say that once you are faced with a mystery, you won't stop until you find the answer.'

'Who says that?' asked Hamish.

Ah Tay looked into his eyes. His stare was compelling, Hamish felt bare but at the same time unable to look away.

'I feel sure you will continue to look into my uncle's death.'

'I assure you,' said Hamish, 'I was only asked to conduct the necropsy because the local man is away. That's it.'

'You will investigate,' said Ah Tay. 'I ask that you allow me to accompany you. I need to know what happened to my uncle. I need to know what he was involved in. I need to restore honour to my family.'

Hamish opened his mouth to object that he had no intention of investigating the murder. He was about to explain to Ah Tay that he was a family doctor establishing his practice in the colony and had no interest in intrigue and secret Chinese Societies. But the words didn't come. His old friend would see right through him.

'Just as a fence is built with pegs, an able person needs the help of others. I can help you,' said Ah Tay. 'I have access to the Chinese community that you do not.'

'I'm sure Sergeant Bellamy would be grateful for the assistance …'

'The police cannot be involved,' Ah Tay said forcefully. 'The Chinese community will not speak if the authorities are involved.'

'The police will investigate,' said Hamish. 'A man has been killed. They will interview everyone who knew him in the Chinese community.'

'Yes. But the Chinese will tell them nothing but lies. You and I can find out the truth.'

Wallace came up the stairs to take the tray and the dog left Hamish to greet his master.

'This is Red,' said Hamish. 'I'm sorry I neglected to introduce him earlier. Red is named for his political views. He is a committed socialist.'

Ah Tay stared at the terrier while the dog stared back at him. Neither was prepared to warm to the other just yet.

'Can I bring you more tea?' Wallace said.

Hamish glanced toward Ah Tay, who shook his head.

'Perhaps a whiskey instead?' suggested Hamish.

Ah Tay nodded.

'Whiskey, please, and three glasses. Why don't you join us?' Hamish motioned to Wallace.

Ah Tay's eyes flashed.

'Wesley Wallace is my closest friend,' said Hamish by way of explanation. Certainly, second best, he thought, a vision of Rita flashing before him. Then he realised he had introduced the dog before he introduced his friend. Had he come to think of him as a servant? He hoped not. After everything they had been through, he was more than that.

'Wallace, meet Ah Tay,' he said. 'We were friends as children growing up on the gold mines in Ballarat. There were very few children in the camps so we had to stick together.'

Wallace held out his hand and the Chinese man took it in his. Wallace raised a bushy brow in surprise. Hamish smiled in amusement that the slender man's grip was stronger than the stocky seaman expected.

'Wallace worked as a ship's cook for most of his life,' said Hamish. 'I believe he has sailed to and from Asia many times.'

'Where do you come from in China?' asked Wallace.

'From the Pearl River Delta in Southern China. My family are poor and… there was trouble with the French. My uncle and I travelled to Adelaide by ship and walked a long way to reach the mines in Victoria.'

'You walked?' exclaimed Wallace.

'We walked. It took many months and many men died.'

'How old were you?'

'I was eight when we left China.'

'Ah Chit, Ah Tay's uncle, found work with my father,' said Hamish. 'Father said Ah Chit was his best worker. Ah Tay used to grow vegetables and sell them at the camp. Do you remember the time the men chased you from the European camp but their wives would sneak out to the Chinese camp to buy your fresh vegetables? I swear my own family would have starved for want of fresh food if it were not for your garden.'

Ah Tay didn't smile.

'There is plenty of bad feeling about the Chinese in the colonies,' said

Wallace. 'I fear it becomes worse as time progresses.'

Ah Tay's face twisted into a sneer and he spoke quietly. 'We are called ignorant by people who have never been to China, people who know nothing of its moral, intellectual and cultural history.'

'Many men born in this land put down others out of fear of their own past catching up with them,' said Wallace. 'The majority of our citizens have parents who either came here as convicts or to escape some dreadful circumstance in their homeland. I believe it has resulted in a collective inferiority complex.'

Ah Tay's face relaxed. 'I believe that is so,' he said. 'Inferiority is overcompensated by a sense of believing one is superior.'

'Do you remember the Chinese store in Ballarat?' said Hamish.

'What makes you think of that?' asked Ah Tay.

Hamish was lost to his childhood memories. 'Ah Chit used to take us there,' he said. 'I'll never forget Loong Hung Pung sitting at the back of that dark store overlooking everyone who entered. He had a silk embroidered cap and robe, and a long pigtail that hung all the way to his waist at the back. Do you recall his moustache? We used to try to count the hairs. It was so sparse and there was that long thin tuft of beard that hung from his chin. I thought he was an emperor.' Hamish laughed.

'You enjoyed the sesame cakes,' said Ah Tay.

'Ha ha! You do remember,' cried Hamish, slapping the side of his thigh. 'Remember sitting outside on the grass, leaning against the weatherboards? That was the only time we experienced moist green grass. We were used to sitting in red dirt. The smell of grass freshly wet from the rain still leads me to crave sesame cakes.'

Ah Tay's face continued to relax by fractions but it by no means reflected comfort.

Hamish hoped that with time their easy friendship would return.

'I must go now.' Ah Tay stood. 'We should meet tomorrow to pursue enquiries,' he said to Hamish.

Hamish stood also. 'I have consultations until two o'clock. Then I am free to assist you.'

Ah Tay took a notebook from his pocket and wrote down an address in fine script. 'Three o'clock then,' he said as he tore the page and handed it to Hamish. 'I'll meet you outside this address. My uncle owns this property.

We may learn something there.'

Hamish saw his friend out. As he was about to close the door on his way back into the house, a young man skidded to a halt on his bicycle and handed Hamish a telegram.

My Dear Son, Ah Chit, left Melbourne for Queensland six months ago. Apparently, the move was precipitated by a business disagreement with other furniture makers. However, as Ah Chit ran several gambling houses, I am inclined to believe any disagreement will have its origins there. Ah Tay did not accompany his uncle at the time, though he may have followed later. Write to your mother. She is more inclined to take your long silences personally than I am. Clifford Hart.

CHAPTER FOUR

According to a report in today's issue of a meeting of the Woolloongabba Divisional Board, there are no less than four inspectors being employed night and day watching houses of ill-fame and taking down the names of those who visit there. I would ask why the many other well-known houses of ill-fame in the same division are not also being watched all night and day? If they were, instead of four, it would take forty quasi detectives to do the work. I should also like to ask whether the ratepayers are aware of the expenditure being incurred in making black marks against the names of persons who have as much a right to visit the houses in question as they have to frequent hotels and other well-known places, which are, of course, now largely resorted to for similar purposes.

Instead of licensing houses of ill-fame, to which women who are also licensed can go to meet the opposite sex and keeping such houses together in restricted and suitable neighbourhoods, these inspections have insisted on the keepers of these houses and the women frequenting them being hunted from place to place until they have become spread all around Brisbane. By the action of these well-meaning but foolish workers in the cause of social purity, a social evil is being rapidly extended and greatly increased, whereas by enforcing common-sense workable regulations it might be checked and decreased.

The Brisbane Courier. Monday 22 February, 1886

At three o'clock Hamish stood on the edge of the road in Albert Street staring at the address on the piece of paper Ah Tay had given him. A row of nine houses were joined under one roof, ramshackle in appearance and in poor repair. There was a narrow shopfront at street level to each of the houses, with accommodation at the back. Beneath the level of the road, each of the dwellings had a cellar, the ceilings level with the street. Hamish could make out a small, grated window, about fourteen inches square on the side of the cellar in the first house. The window overlooked a yard comprised of mud piled with old mattresses, food waste and excrement. Hamish wondered how anyone living there could stand the smell.

As he was pondering the lives of the people who must inhabit such a place, Ah Tay appeared beside him.

'The Nine Holes, they call it,' he said.

Hamish started. 'I didn't hear you coming.'

'On the planning documents it says Nine Halls. But the locals call it the Nine Holes.'

'I can see why,' said Hamish. 'This whole area must flood when it rains.'

'I believe so,' said Ah Tay. 'My uncle owns this property. He bought it recently. I want to believe he would have made improvements for the tenants if he lived.'

'Surely ...' said Hamish, grimacing at the smell.

Ah Tay began walking toward the yard of the first house, stepping into the grey-green mud. Hamish tried to hold his breath as he followed him. He felt the mud suck at his boots with each step. They picked their way between piles of rubbish to a small door at the back of the building. The doorway was embossed on either side with a Chinese sign and as they approached, a woman emerged. She was dressed in silk, faded but expensive. On the forefinger of her right hand was a ring with an inset of red glass and there was a sparkling brooch fastened at her snowy throat. It spoke of diamonds but Hamish assumed it was also glass. Her dress was rumpled and the back of her elegant hat was crushed in. She steadied herself with her right hand against the Chinese sign while she waved in Ah Tay and Hamish with her left hand.

When they entered Hamish had to duck, the ceiling was so low. The woman falteringly let go of the sign and half walked, half stumbled in behind them. The room was dark, the only light that could enter sneaking in through the grated window. As his eyes adjusted to the dark, Hamish made out a series of mattresses that covered almost the entire floor space.

A Chinese man sat in the corner, cross-legged on one of the mattresses. Beside him was a small lamp, over which was placed a diminutive glass bell open only at the top. The man dipped a silver wire into a small phial of opium. The resinous extract adhered to the wire and he held it over the flame of the lamp until the liquid evaporated and he was left with a solid mass. This he dipped again into the phial and a new layer of the substance was subjected to the same process. When he was satisfied, he transferred the mass into a peculiarly shaped pipe and proceeded to indulge in the enjoyment he had so patiently prepared. A few rapid whiffs of the pipe stem exhausted the entire supply. The man seemed oblivious to their presence.

Hamish felt nausea rising as he scanned the room but he could make out nothing other than piles of clothing everywhere. Then one of the piles moved. Startled, he fixed his gaze on the moving fabric. Gradually the shape of another woman formed. She leaned on one elbow and addressed Ah Tay.

'What you after, then?'

'Get up,' Ah Tay said. 'And bring your mother with you. We'll wait on the street.'

Ah Tay headed out the same door they had entered. Hamish took one glance back at the woman who flashed him a coquettish smile with her mouth, her eyes remaining cold. Hamish hurried after Ah Tay.

When they were back on the street, Ah Tay lit a European cigarette and took a long puff. 'These women work at the gambling house run by my uncle.'

'Opium.' Hamish shuddered. 'Is that why they live like this?'

Ah Tay didn't seem to hear him.

Within minutes, two women made their way through the stinking yard and joined them. The taller of the two was the youngest. She wore a faded gown that would have once been red but was now a dull maroon. It was low cut and revealed an ample cleavage. The gown was hopelessly crushed. As if she could hear Hamish's thoughts the woman patted down the fabric but it did no good. The dress had lost its shape. She had a heart-shaped face with large eyes and long eyelashes. She tried to sweep her dark hair into a roll and secure it with a pin, without success; it was already falling about her face.

The older woman was struggling to maintain a dignified pose while leaning on her daughter.

'May I introduce Mrs Daisy Walton and her daughter Miss Kate Walton,' said Ah Tay with a formality that contrasted with the fact he had unceremoniously entered their home and ordered them onto the street only moments earlier.

'How do you do?' Hamish bowed politely.

Both women curtsied.

'You have no doubt heard of my uncle's death,' said Ah Tay.

Daisy nodded while the younger woman stared.

'Doctor Hart is investigating the murder,' explained Ah Tay. 'I want you to tell him anything you know.'

'What would we know about it?' asked Kate.

'You work at the Pearl. You may have heard something,' said Ah Tay.

Daisy shuffled back a step. Her eyes were fearful. 'No,' she said.

Kate was twisting the lace that had come unstitched from her collar.

'Do you know anything of Ah Chit's death?' asked Hamish.

She shook her head imperceptibly.

'Why are you afraid?' demanded Ah Tay, in a tone that could only have heightened their fear.

'Hung,' said the older woman. 'He will own your uncle's businesses now, is that not so?'

'Who is Hung?' asked Hamish.

Ah Tay spoke quietly. 'It is so.'

'Then we work for Hung now. We have to work,' said Daisy. 'We know nothing of Ah Chit's death. We must go.'

'Ha,' said Ah Tay. 'It's not work you seek, it is opium. Go now.'

Both women curtsied once again and left them.

Hamish had so many questions swirling through his mind he couldn't decide where to start.

Who is Hung?' he repeated. 'And why will he inherit your uncle's businesses? I assumed you ...'

'We cannot talk here,' said Ah Tay and he began walking with a determined stride down the street. Hamish was left with no choice but to follow him. As they walked down Albert Street toward the river, Hamish saw a sign proudly displayed at the front of a grocery store. Hamish knew the grocer to be European but the sign was written in Chinese.

'What does this sign say?' he asked. His friend stopped to read the sign and smiled.

'Your people realise the value of Chinese patronage in their businesses,' he said. 'They hope to entice Chinese people to buy their goods.'

'How so?'

Ah Tay smiled even more broadly.

Hamish hadn't seen him smile properly since they had renewed their acquaintance.

'I doubt the shopkeeper has achieved his goal,' said Ah Tay. 'He has paid a Chinese man to write the sign for him and the man played a trick.'

'What does it say?' Hamish was determined to know.

'It says, *do not buy anything here; this storekeeper is a rogue.*'

Hamish fell backwards laughing. The storekeeper waved to them from inside and Hamish waved back. They continued down the street while Hamish laughed.

They turned into Charlotte Street and stopped at a shopfront with coloured Chinese lanterns out the front. The space inside was small with several sets of tables and chairs crammed in and no customers. Hamish and Ah Tay sat at one of the tables at the back of the room. A tiny Chinese woman in a white shirt and pants overlaid with a square black smock came to the table and bowed deeply. Ah Tay bowed back. He spoke in Chinese and the woman bowed again, then she left them. Hamish guessed refreshments were on their way. He was still suffering a lingering nausea from the smell at the cellar so he hoped his friend had ordered tea – green tea would be ideal.

Hamish asked again, 'Who is Hung?'

'My uncle owed money,' Ah Tay said at last. 'That is why he left Melbourne. He hoped to start again in the north. He told me he hoped to make enough money to pay his debts and restore his honour. But his rivals were anxious to take over his business. His position was weak and others were able to take advantage.'

'Do you think he was killed by his business rivals?' asked Hamish.

Ah Tay didn't answer.

'This Hung. Is he the one Ah Chit owed money to?'

'Not exactly,' said Ah Tay. 'My uncle will have left his business to me in his will; however, the debt to the Sheathed Sword is so great it will mean the business must be handed over to them. The will has not yet been read but it is a formality. Hung has already assumed the role of headman for the Society in Brisbane.'

'What is the Sheathed Sword?' asked Hamish.

'It is a Chinese Secret Society. There are many of them. This one has its roots in Southern China where we are from. These societies support the Chinese communities through providing benevolent funds for families who are ill or cannot work.'

There was more Hamish wanted to know about the Sheathed Sword but he decided to wait until Ah Tay was more relaxed with him to ask.

'Why do Daisy and Kate seem afraid of Sam Hung?' he asked instead.

'I am new in this colony. I don't know,' said Ah Tay with a tone of finality.

Hamish thought that Ah Tay knew a lot for someone new to the colony and he didn't quite believe he was unaware of why the women were afraid of Hung. But he accepted his friend's answer.

The tiny Chinese woman delivered a teapot with two small cups and poured steaming tea into each. Hamish took a sip and felt its warmth slip down his throat. The grassy smell made him feel better long before the tea could have had any real physical benefit.

'Can I ask how two European women came to be renting mattress space in your uncle's cellar?' asked Hamish after the tea had calmed him.

'They are prostitutes,' said Ah Tay matter-of-factly. 'They take opium daily to keep them sane and they work the gambling house at night. There are rooms at the back of the gambling house where they take clients. The cellar at the Nine Holes is where they sleep for a few hours between work commitments.'

Hamish had guessed the women's trade but to have it laid out so objectively jarred him.

'How could Ah Chit charge people money to stay in that filth? Surely they make enough money for proper lodgings?'

'They spend their money on opium,' said Ah Tay.

'And does that money also go to your uncle?'

Ah Tay was silent, which was his answer.

'We need to know more about Hung,' said Hamish. 'Where can we find him?'

'I only know he is at the Pearl most evenings.'

'The Pearl?'

'It's the gambling parlour behind the drapery store in Albert Street.

Entry is through the back door.'

Hamish shook his head. 'There's a gambling house back there? I've walked by that place a dozen times. I didn't know.'

'You are naive. You see only what you want to see.'

Hamish flushed. He didn't want to think of himself as naive. He felt an inexplicable shame at not knowing much about the seedy nightlife of Brisbane and the challenges those who live that life face.

'We should go to the Pearl and meet with Sam Hung,' said Ah Tay.

'Tonight, then?' said Hamish.

'Ten o'clock.'

Ah Tay stood and bowed deeply to the old woman who had rushed forward to remove the teapot and decorative china cups.

Hamish stood up as well.

'It is good to see you again after so long,' Hamish said. 'I hope we are able to spend more time together and recall childhood adventures.' He smiled.

Ah Tay nodded slightly but his eyes remained steady. He was staring through the entrance to outside. They both walked to the door and saw the rain falling heavily, already muddying the street. The smell from the yards was amplified in the heavy rain. Hamish felt his nausea returning. As they stood contemplating their next step, Hamish noticed a European woman struggling along the street in the rain. She was poorly dressed and already wet, her dress stuck to her skin. An infant was cradled against her chest, its small head tucked into her neck and another child clung to her skirt.

Ah Tay looked back into the tearoom and saw the old woman watching him. He nodded and she scurried into the back of the room returning with a large paper parcel. Ah Tay took it from her and hurried out into the rain. As he handed the parcel to the woman, the soggy paper fell away from the corner revealing two large blankets. They were of superior quality. Ah Tay turned immediately and re-joined Hamish in the doorway without saying a word to the woman. She hesitated for a moment to stare at them, then she continued on her way along the street clutching the blankets to the back of the infant.

'That was kind of you,' said Hamish.

'It was nothing,' said his friend quietly.

They stood silently in the doorway watching the rain form muddy pools along the side of the street. A brown horse, his mane limp across his eyes, trotted by hauling a dark carriage, then nothing. There was an eerie quiet in the street that accentuated the dull pounding of rainfall and rising smell of decaying offal and human waste. As soon as the rain eased to a drizzle, Hamish put on his hat.

'Tonight,' he said and strode out into the damp. He could wait no longer to escape the oppressive atmosphere and the smell.

Hamish plodded through the drizzle to the police depot at Petrie Terrace. He told himself several times he was not betraying Ah Tay by going there. He understood the need to maintain the trust of the Chinese community but he also felt a certain loyalty to Sergeant Bellamy who had proven a man of integrity and a friend over the past twelve months.

Bellamy was seated behind his large desk with papers piled high as well as scattered about the room on the sideboard and chairs. Hamish removed a stack of papers from a chair opposite the desk so he could sit down. Bellamy leant back in his chair and balanced on the back two legs, a pencil perched between his lips like a cigarette.

'Good day, Doctor Hart. To what do we owe this pleasure?'

'I have some information in relation to the death of Ah Chit,' said Hamish.

Bellamy sat forward in his chair, bringing it down with a bang onto all its four legs. His face became serious.

'I have made contact with Ah Chit's nephew,' he said. 'I told you he was a childhood friend of mine.'

'Well?' said Bellamy.

'He says that Ah Chit owed money. A lot of it. Now he is dead, a man named Hung will take over his businesses. They belong to some manner of secret society …'

'The Sheathed Sword.' Bellamy finished the sentence for him.

'You know about him?'

'Yes, we know him. He has been in Brisbane since '82. He was put out when Ah Chit arrived last year throwing money and influence around.'

'Ah Chit lost all his money in Melbourne,' said Hamish.

'Yes, it would appear so. Nevertheless, the Chinese Societies stand by their members. The Sheathed Sword paid out his debts and provided him a line of credit to establish himself in Brisbane. We don't know why he was enabled to surpass Hung, who has been trying to set himself up as Headman for years. Family ties have long roots that go all the way back to China. I can only assume Ah Chit had strong connections.'

'Why didn't you tell me all this at the necropsy?' demanded Hamish.

'I didn't know all of it then. In any case, I didn't want you getting involved.'

'I'm not involved,' said Hamish. 'I had to check on my friend when his only relative in this country was killed.'

'Ah Chit was not his only relative in this country or even in Brisbane.'

'What are you talking about?'

'Foong May runs a tea house in Charlotte Street. She's about a hundred years old by all accounts – she's Ah Chit's sister-in-law. They brought her over at about the same time Ah Chit arrived in Queensland, set her up in the tea house. It's owned by the Sheathed Sword.'

'What? That can't be true … I've heard of no sister …' Then he recalled the woman at the tea house. One hundred years old was a stretch but she was certainly old.

'I'm afraid it is true,' said Bellamy. 'Hamish, I'm warning you to stay out of this. These Chinese Societies do plenty of good for their own but they will have no qualms about killing an outsider who looks to threaten their operations. This one makes money from illegal activity – gambling, prostitution, opium. You need to leave this to us, I mean it.'

Hamish was not sure how to respond. He was still trying to process the information that the frail little old woman at the tea house was Ah Chit's sister-in-law. That meant she was either Ah Tay's Aunt or his mother. She couldn't be his mother because his mother died before he left China. When Hamish came to think about it, there was a certain familiarity, but why didn't Ah Tay introduce him if she was family?

'Hamish, are you listening?' The sergeant caught his attention and held his gaze. 'Do not become involved in this.'

'No,' said Hamish. 'That would be best.'

He took his hat and left Bellamy's office, still processing the information he had gained and planning how he would tell Wallace they would be joining Ah Tay at the notorious Pearl Gambling House that evening.

CHAPTER FIVE

On Saturday night, between the hours of ten and eleven o'clock, Ah Foo along with thirteen other Celestials was arrested for playing an unlawful game known as Fan Tan. Constable Lloyd together with five other officers of the law, who had been on alert, went into the house in question on Blane Street, where it was intended to apprehend them in the act. Lloyd, with two others, proceeded to the back and three others to the front door and before the Chinese knew what to do, they were surrounded. The fun continued for as soon as the unfortunate Celestials found themselves in such a predicament they carried on all sorts of antics, such as tumbling and vaulting over tables and chairs, and each other's heads. But this was soon put to a stop and the fourteen soon found themselves hors de combat. They were then tied safely with rope, as the handcuffs did not seem to suit their wrists. Indeed, they slipped off as soon as they were put on.

The prisoners were then marched to the police station and lodged in the cells, where they did not seem to fare badly by any means, as their countrymen supplied them with rice, which they demolished in their own peculiar fashion with chopsticks. The owner of the house was yesterday brought before the magistrate and charged with being the keeper of a common gambling house. The arrest was found to be illegal as a new Act now in place requires a warrant for such an arrest. The group of Chinese marched out of court seemingly very happy and were returned the money which had been appropriated by the police during the confinement in the cells.

Morning Herald, Newcastle. Tuesday 10 March, 1885

At ten o'clock Hamish and Wallace stood in the yard behind the drapery shop. It was dark with heavy clouds covering the moon, the last remnants of the earlier rain. They heard excited voices in the building but they couldn't see the way in. Ah Tay appeared silently alongside them. The man moved about like a ghost.

'This way,' he said as he led them to the far end of the back wall. He knocked twice and a crack appeared. When Ah Tay pushed against the door, light flooded out onto the yard. He shoved Hamish and Wallace through the opening and followed, closing the door immediately behind them. During a quick scan of the room, Hamish counted more than twenty Chinese men as well as nearly a dozen Europeans. The only two women were Daisy and Kate who were pressed to either side of an elderly European man tapping his feet, rapping his fingers on his leg and singing to music that could only have been playing in his head. There were several tables set out with men playing Fan Tan and there was one Chinese man at a table near the drapery door selling lottery tickets. This is where Ah Tay led Hamish and Wallace first. They handed over six shillings each for a card and Ah Tay showed them how to mark their choice of symbols.

'The winner will be announced at midnight,' he said.

'What's the pot?' asked Wallace, causing Hamish to raise an eyebrow.

'Usually eighty pounds,' said Ah Tay.

'Whoa,' gasped Wallace and he tucked his ticket into his pocket.

Ah Tay settled them alongside a Fan Tan table to watch the game and left them.

Hamish stared at the square board with each of the sides numbered one to four. The banker dropped a double handful of ivory buttons onto the centre of the board and covered them with a blue and white Chinese bowl which appeared to Hamish to be ancient. He had seen the Chinese men playing Fan Tan at the mining camps but he hadn't bothered to learn the rules of play.

'Each man bets on how many buttons will be left at the end,' said Wallace.

'The end of what?' asked Hamish as he watched the men place their bets on the numbers around the board. The banker then lifted the bowl and a second man used a small bamboo stick to remove the buttons four at a time.

'He's the *tan kun*,' said Wallace. 'When he has removed the buttons by fours until the last group remains, we will see who wins.'

'How do you know so much about it?' asked Hamish.

'Not much to do on the ships,' said Wallace.

'It looks harmless enough.'

'It's just a game. It's the gambling part that makes it illegal.'

Hamish noticed an immaculately dressed Chinese man leaning against the opposite wall. He was wearing a tailored European style suit that fit him perfectly and his hair was short and styled according to the latest European fashion. He oozed confidence and seemed to be overseeing the room. Hamish wondered if that could be Sam Hung.

Scanning the room for Ah Tay, Hamish finally spotted him behind the lottery table caught in a heated discussion with a slender Chinese boy. As Hamish watched them, he became uneasy; the boy's willowy frame and small features appeared wrong somehow but he couldn't put his finger on what was troubling him. The boy stood tall and held his chin high but his profile was delicate and soft.

'I think it's a girl!' said Hamish.

Wallace followed the direction of his gaze.

'It's a girl alright,' he said. 'She's wearing the loose shirt and pants of a boy but that is a young woman.'

'What are they arguing about?' asked Hamish.

Wallace leant forward as if the shorter distance between them would facilitate his hearing. 'I can read her lips,' he said. 'She is telling him, "No". She's quite adamant about it.'

'What is she rejecting?' prompted Hamish.

'I can't tell. I can't see Ah Tay's face from this angle. He's quite animated, though. He's desperate to convince her of something.'

'I'm going over there to find out,' said Hamish.

'It seems to be a private conversation,' Wallace pointed out.

Hamish took a step toward them regardless, then a rush of noise stopped him. Three police constables burst into the room through the drapery door and immediately set upon the man selling lottery tickets. At the same time, two constables burst through the back door and rushed toward the man Hamish assumed to be Sam Hung.

Hamish had barely processed the scene when three more men, European and not in police uniform, barged through the now open back door.

'Get out, yer yellow devils,' yelled the men, fists raised as they rushed toward the table closest to Hamish.

The first man threw a punch that landed in the face of one of the men playing Fan Tan. The other men at the table jumped from their seats and buttons flew everywhere. Infuriated that the Chinese man had been attacked while peacefully playing a game, Hamish swung his left fist forward and connected with the assailant's jaw. In return, one of the larrikins smacked Hamish over the head with the chair vacated by the Fan Tan player. Blood rolled down his forehead and into his eyes. He could see well enough to observe Wallace knock the man unconscious. Mopping the blood from his eyes with his handkerchief, he watched the room descend into chaos. Chinese men were tumbling and leaping to avoid the police, who were at a loss to hold on to their slippery and agile prey. Handcuffs were placed around the wrists of two Chinese men, who nimbly slipped their hands through them and ran. Through the blood dripping over his eyes, Hamish tried to locate Ah Tay but he couldn't see him among the men in the room. He had disappeared when the raid began.

Hamish noted the police were maintaining their hold on the man who he thought may be Sam Hung. He assumed this man was the real object of the raid. Three constables marched Sam Hung through the doors of the drapery. One of them was Constable Pennyweather, an acquaintance of Hamish. They had worked together on other investigations. He wondered for a moment if Pennyweather had seen him. The larrikins moved on to assault other Fan Tan players and the police were interrupted in their efforts to arrest the Chinese men while they attempted to detain the larrikins, all of whom were shouting in protest that they were there to restore law and order in the face of the yellow peril. Hamish noticed Daisy and Kate slip through the drapery door with the young Chinese woman. Still, there was no sign of Ah Tay. Wallace, who had been pursuing the mates of the man who attacked Hamish with gusto, returned to his employer's side, his face red and wet with sweat and furnishing a smug smile.

Ah Tay suddenly appeared behind them.

'Come on,' he said. 'We'll get you to the hospital.' He was looking around nervously as he and Wallace steadied Hamish and made their way onto the street where a cab was waiting.

Hamish was feeling increasingly foggy but he was conscious enough to note the driver was Chinese. He thought that must have been why Ah Tay disappeared, to bring transport to get them out of there. That was the last thought he could recall while at the Pearl.

KATE

Daisy and Kate hurried down Albert Street toward the Nine Holes. By the time they came within sight of the building, they relaxed their pace and were laughing hysterically at the scuffle they left behind.

'Did you see the look on that constable's face when the Fan Tan player executed a double somersault over the table to escape him?' said Kate.

Daisy traced the somersault in the air with her arms and the two women crashed into one another, laughing. The young Chinese woman kept up with them ducking gracefully to avoid their arms as they flung them wildly mimicking the actions of the men.

Suddenly, Daisy stopped short and Kate, whose arm was linked through her mother's, tripped and fell. A man had appeared out of the shadows and slipped his arm around Daisy's neck. A second man grabbed Kate by the shoulder before she landed in the mud. Instinctively, the Chinese girl slid sideways and put some distance between herself and the attackers. They let her go, intent on containing the two women they had. A third man joined them and ripped at Daisy's bodice, while the first held her with his arm tight around her throat. Daisy struggled and cursed as the third attacker uncovered her breast. Kate remained still for a moment before twisting her upper body away from the man gripping her shoulder and whipping herself behind him, throwing the force of her whole body against his legs. He crumpled and fell. Before he had time to register what had happened to him, she righted herself and brought her boot up under his chin, kicking him hard. His head fell back and carried his body with it. Within seconds he was lying face up in the mud, dazed and confused as to what had just happened.

Kate leapt onto the back of her mother's assailant and clung to him, her fingers gouging his face. He let go of Daisy and she slumped to the ground. Just as the third man was about to throw himself on top of her, the Chinese woman appeared, as if from nowhere, grabbed him by the hair and pulled him sideways. She slid a small knife against his throat. His eyes bulged.

'The stinking, filthy Ching has got Smithy,' cried the man who assaulted Daisy.

'Filthy sluts,' croaked the second assailant.

Between them, the men dragged their mate up out of the mud and disappeared down Albert Street toward the river.

Kate helped her mother stand up and gently rearranged her bodice to return her dignity.

'They were the same men as crashed the raid at the Pearl,' said Kate. 'The police will know who they are.'

Daisy spat blood onto the road. She had bitten her lip in the attack. 'We're not telling the police.' She coughed. 'Lucky you were with us,' she said to the Chinese woman. 'Kate can fight but we would have been outnumbered without you.'

'Miss Kate most certainly can fight,' said the woman.

She and Kate supported Daisy back to the Nine Holes.

CHAPTER SIX

This afternoon the Reverend introduced a large deputation to the Premier from the Social Purity Society and its object was to submit a Bill that had been drafted for the advancement of social purity and the better defence of young women against immorality, and of unprotected females against outrage. The Bill provided that young women should be under protection from seduction by law up to the age of 21, at which age they could marry without their parents' consent. It was also proposed by the Bill to punish owners as well as occupiers of houses of ill-fame. One member of the meeting pointed out that as a result of certain inquiries, it was found that many such houses in the city were rented from members of the Christian Church. It was decided more consideration of the proposal was required before a decision could be made.

Morning Herald, Newcastle. Wednesday 7 July, 1886

When Hamish next opened his eyes, he saw a dull grey wall opposite. He was slumped in a wooden chair. Gradually the smell of the place began to remind him of a hospital … 'Hospital?' he said out loud. He vaguely remembered Ah Tay saying something about taking him to the hospital. Where was Ah Tay? Where was Wallace for that matter?

A stern nurse appeared in the starched uniform they had recently taken to wearing. 'Come with me, Doctor,' she said.

Hamish tried to stand but as he did the blood rushed from his head and his vision was reduced to a pinprick of light. He fell back into the chair.

The next time Hamish opened his eyes, he was laid out in a hospital bed with Ah Tay leaning over him. Behind Ah Tay, he could see Wallace.

'How are you feeling?' came a female voice. Still groggy, Hamish registered that the voice did not belong to Wallace.

'Rita,' he cried.

Rita Cartwright moved forward, firmly pushing Ah Tay and Wallace out of the way.

Hamish instantly felt better.

'What are you doing here?'

'Wallace sent for me,' she said. 'What on Earth have you been doing?'

Rita touched the bandaged wound tightly around his head.

'I think there was a fight,' he said.

'Ha! A fight,' said Wallace. 'It was an all-in brawl. Hamish jumped in to avenge the dignity of a Fan Tan player.'

'It was a raid,' said Rita.

'Yes. That as well. But a bunch of larrikins decided to get in on the act when they saw the police enter.'

'Three,' said Ah Tay. Wallace stared at him.

'Only three men, other than the police,' said Ah Tay.

'As may be,' said Wallace, not to be deterred from a good story. 'But they created enough confusion for a dozen men. Bellamy won't be too pleased with how his raid turned out.'

'Speaking of Bellamy,' said Rita.

Ah Tay and Wallace turned their attention to the door in time to see Bellamy march in.

'Constable Pennyweather told me I'd find you here,' he said to Hamish.

'Blast,' thought Hamish, realising Pennyweather had seen him.

'What the hell were you lot doing at the Pearl?' He turned to Rita. 'Please tell me you weren't there?'

Rita shook her head.

'Is this what you call staying out of the investigation?' barked Bellamy.

Before Hamish could respond, Rita stepped between the sergeant and the hospital bed.

'The patient is concussed, sergeant. You may be able to speak with him tomorrow but not sooner.'

Hamish watched Bellamy's eyes grow dark and Rita's grow darker. Bellamy stood down.

'Very well, Doctor Cartwright,' he said, 'tomorrow then. Nine o'clock. And you two can come with him,' he said to Ah Tay and Wallace. 'You can explain what you were doing at an illegal gambling house and while you're at it, why I shouldn't arrest the lot of you.' Bellamy strode out of the room as seriously as he'd come in.

Hamish knew that as a qualified doctor, Rita could command a presence. She was well respected by the other medical doctors, even if they preferred she remain within her province at the Lady Bowen Lying-In Hospital dealing with women's 'problems'. Rita directed the nurse to remove the bandage so she could inspect the wound. She peered with interest at the split in the skin and the darkening bruise surrounding it.

'It will heal without sutures,' she said, 'if it is bound well.' She spotted a woman in a crisp uniform standing well away from the formidable group gathered at the doctor's bedside. 'Bring me a clean bandage,' she called out to the nurse. 'I'll bind the wound myself.'

The nurse scurried off and returned in seconds with a bandage and a tray of instruments.

'What's all that for?' cried Hamish.

Rita smiled at the nurse. 'Leave the tray over there,' she said, pointing to a table at the back of the room. 'I only require the sponge, water and the bandage.'

Hamish felt the pressure of the bandage like a vice around his head as Rita pulled it tight. 'Ow,' he cried.

'Stop whining,' said Rita. 'You know as well as I do the bandage is safer than sutures but it has to be tight to hold the wound. You'll be fine.'

Nine o'clock the following morning found Hamish and Ah Tay in Bellamy's office, seated among the stacks of unfixed documents and old newspapers. Bellamy continued writing for some minutes after they were seated. Hamish was well aware it was a gesture crafted to establish a power differential for the interaction. When Bellamy put down his pen, he leant back in his chair until it tipped onto two legs and his head rested against the wall. He clasped his hands across his chest and studied the men waiting silently on the opposite side of the desk.

'Where's Wallace?' the sergeant asked.

'At home,' said Hamish. 'I told him there was no need for him to attend.'

Bellamy stared at Hamish long and hard. At last, he said, 'I suppose you dragged the poor sod to the Pearl anyway. It's a good thing he was there – you might have taken a worse beating.'

Hamish adjusted the bandage around his head, pushing it up higher over his left eye so he could see. It had already loosened to the extent that its efficacy was questionable. Hamish grimaced as the drying wound beneath was disturbed.

'Who would like to start by telling me why you were at the Pearl last night?'

Hamish looked across at Ah Tay. His face was creamy wax. Not a muscle moved. Dark curtains had come down behind his eyes. It was clear Ah Tay would not be speaking anytime soon.

'I wanted to see Sam Hung,' said Hamish. 'I was told I would find him at the Pearl.'

'And what is your interest in Sam Hung?' asked the sergeant.

'I have formed an opinion he may have killed Ah Chit,' said Hamish.

'Based on?'

'He profits from his death.'

'What were you hoping to do when you saw him – accuse him of murder?'

'Of course not.' Hamish had no idea what he'd intended. He simply wanted to see him, as though that alone would have confirmed his guilt. He would come across as churlish if he didn't tell the sergeant the truth, so he leant forward across Bellamy's desk and spoke honestly.

'Look,' he said, 'Ah Tay is my friend and his uncle has been murdered. You called me in yourself to examine the body. It cannot surprise you that I am committed to finding out what happened. I have been involved in investigations in the past, as you well know, that bear no personal connection to myself.'

'I'm hardly surprised,' said Bellamy, 'But I did explicitly direct you to stay out of this case. These are dangerous people.'

Hamish glanced at Ah Tay with his face of wax. He didn't flinch.

'They have all been dangerous people,' said Hamish. 'The Chinese hold no monopoly on that account.'

Bellamy sighed and let his chair fall back onto four legs with a thud. He leant across the desk toward Hamish from his side.

'This is doing us no good at all,' he said. 'If you are determined to stick your beak into this matter, you had better at least keep me informed of where you are going. I may be able to prevent you ending up skewered on a ceremonial sword like your friend's uncle.'

'Fine,' said Hamish, noticing out of the corner of his eye that Ah Tay twitched slightly at the reference to his uncle's death. A thought occurred to Hamish that he believed may at last gain him the advantage in this interview. He sat back in his chair and changed to a more casual tone.

'I would have expected you'd have interviewed Ah Tay before now, to ask about his uncle's business dealings,' he said.

Bellamy smiled. 'We interviewed Ah Tay the very morning you carried out the necropsy, I told him you had examined the body.'

The blood rushed to Hamish's cheeks. He flicked back the hair that had fallen over his bandages and onto his face. So that's why Ah Tay was looking out for him at the market. Why didn't Ah Tay tell him he had been interviewed? Hamish collected his thoughts. He didn't want Bellamy to see that he was caught off guard.

'What about the sword?' he asked. 'Do you know who the sword belongs to?'

Bellamy spoke with authority. The sergeant appeared to enjoy being a step ahead.

'Officially, the *Jian* that was used to kill Ah Chit is owned by the secret society, the Sheathed Sword, of which both Ah Chit and Sam Hung are members. The sword was kept on the wall in the library of the house occupied by Ah Chit, a townhouse in the Terraces on George Street. The house also belongs to the Society. I believe Sam Hung is preparing to move in there now. The sword is evidence, it stays here at the depot until this case is closed.' Bellamy stared down his friend.

Hamish thought about the *Jian* he had seen covered in Ah Chit's blood almost to the hilt. His first thought was it would have required someone strong to wield the sword and thrust it so cleanly through Ah Chit's body. But then it occurred to him that was not necessarily the case – the sword was razor sharp and thin. It would have taken some strength but not an excessive amount to send the weapon through the flesh. And the route, though effective, may not have been planned.

'Who had access to the sword?' said Hamish, thinking aloud. 'Certainly, Sam Hung.'

'Yes,' said Bellamy. 'But he is not the only one. Many of the Society's members frequented the house. There is also Cy Wong, who was staying there ...'

'Who is Cy Wong?' asked Hamish, as he noted another subtle flinch from Ah Tay.

'Cy Wong is a young Chinese woman, a distant relative, I believe?' Bellamy looked enquiringly at Ah Tay. He could enquire all he liked, thought Hamish. Ah Tay was not going to speak.

Bellamy went on. 'She appears to have been brought from China on a credit ticket by the Society, sponsored by Ah Chit. Anyway, she is, or was, staying at the house. She's disappeared since the raid. My constables have not been able to find her.'

Hamish recalled seeing Daisy and Kate Walton usher the young Chinese woman from the Pearl during the raid. That must've been Cy Wong.

'Then there's the prostitute,' said Bellamy.

'What?'

'The prostitute. I'm told Ah Chit was seeing her regularly. He brought her back to the house several times. Daisy, they call her. Dizzy Daisy because she is out of it on opium most of the time. Got a daughter in the game as well, poor pet.'

Hamish's head was reeling.

'There's blood seeping through your bandage,' said the sergeant. 'You'd better have Doctor Cartwright redress it. We can't find the prostitute. Not since the raid. No one will talk.'

I know exactly where she is, thought Hamish. *Good Lord, Daisy has taken Cy Wong to the Nine Holes.* His pulse quickened a beat at the thought of the young Chinese woman he'd seen the evening before in the opium den occupied by Daisy and Kate. She had seemed pure to him, untainted, almost ethereal. Certainly, she was very young. He couldn't bear the idea that she would be introduced to the vices of Frog's Hollow, as particularly evident in the cellars of the Nine Holes.

'I think you're right,' he said suddenly. 'I need to see Rita and have this bandage changed. I'm feeling a bit unwell, to be honest.' Hamish stood quickly and tugged at his bandage.

Ah Tay took that as a cue to stand.

'Get some rest,' said Bellamy, 'and don't forget our agreement. You're to tell me where you are going at all times.' He glared at Ah Tay. For his part, Ah Tay apparently hadn't noticed.

'Certainly,' said Hamish as Ah Tay bowed to the police sergeant.

They hurried outside and boarded a cab. 'The Nine Holes,' said Hamish to the driver. 'Actually, go by way of the Lady Bowen Hospital, we need to pick someone up.'

CHAPTER SEVEN

A Chinese named Ah Hong was prosecuted in the city court yesterday by the Customs authorities on five charges of attempting to evade the customs duty, aiding in shipping dutiable goods and concealing opium which was liable to duty. On the 7th instant, the Steamer Taiwan with about 150 Chinese on board arrived from China. Their personal effects and luggage being brought ashore were placed for examination in the Customs shed. After about 50 or 60 of the Chinese had passed by with their goods, the vigilant customs officers came upon two large black trunks, the owner of which was asked to come forward. Ah Hong claimed the trunks, stating they only contained clothes. In each box, forty-five of these tins were discovered. The opium weighed in all thirty-six pounds. The opium was not entered in the ship's manifest nor were any entries passed relating to it.

The Age, Melbourne. Wednesday 22 July, 1885

Rita leapt into the cab and settled beside Ah Tay. Hamish climbed in beside her.

'I have an hour,' she said, 'before I have to get back to the hospital. What's so important?'

'A young Chinese woman. We're going to rescue her,' said Hamish.

'That's rather melodramatic,' Rita said, adjusting her hat. 'What makes you think she needs rescuing?'

'We think she's at the Nine Holes,' said Hamish.

Rita turned to Ah Tay. 'I take it this woman is connected to you?'

'Cy Wong is my cousin. My mother's sister's youngest daughter,' he said.

Rita's brow wrinkled. 'Ah Chit was your uncle, wasn't he? How is Cy Wong related to him?'

'Through marriage. Ah Chit is … was … my father's brother.'

Rita turned back to Hamish. 'How does Cy Wong come to be at the Nine Holes?'

'I saw her leaving the Pearl last night with two women we know to reside there.'

'Does Sergeant Bellamy know about your rescue mission?'

Hamish felt his neck and ears flush.

'Don't bother answering,' said Rita.

When the cab stopped, Hamish paid the driver and asked him to wait. Hamish took a deep breath before striding into the yard beside the Nine Holes. It would be the last clean air he would take in until they returned. His lungs filled with the now-familiar stench as he knocked loudly on the door. Rita was behind him looking unfazed by the smell and decay. No one answered so he knocked again, louder the second time.

After a moment the door opened and a woman with long, tangled hair stumbled out holding the door jamb to steady herself. She lit a cigarette with trembling hands and gazed at them with eyes that struggled to focus. Her faded dress was unbuttoned at the bodice, falling away to reveal a torn black camisole. Her lip was swollen and bruised.

'Good morning Daisy,' said Ah Tay, pushing past Hamish and Rita.

Hamish was unsure how to interpret what he was seeing. The woman was hardly the beautiful, if jaded, temptress of the dimly lit Pearl. She had transformed back into the frail, ageing figure of pity who had struggled to greet them at the door a day earlier. In his mind, Hamish couldn't reconcile the two identities as a single woman.

Rita also passed Hamish so she could place her arm around Daisy's shoulder. 'Let me help you,' she said.

Hamish was left standing in the doorway while Rita supported the woman as she stumbled back inside. Daisy could not have been much older than Rita, and Kate not much younger. Mother and daughter seemed so close in age as to be more likely sisters.

Hamish followed, taking a moment while his eyes became accustomed to the smoke and the lack of light. His head felt foggy. The sweet smell of the smoke mixed with the tart odour of sweat, decay and mould. He placed his hand on the bandage around his head and wondered if he was suffering the effects of the hit to his head the night before or whether he was becoming intoxicated from the fumes in the cellar.

The same Chinese man of indefinable age Hamish had seen previously, sat cross-legged on a mattress in the corner. He appeared to have not moved a muscle in the last twenty-four hours. A fog of smoke surrounded him giving him an aura of unreality. He might have been dead but for the small rising and falling of his chest. His eyes were closed.

There was a mass of green satin on another mattress. Surely that must be Kate. Long black curls rested against the satin, the only other identifier a small, white hand peeking out from the sea of simmering green fabric. Hamish could not see her face.

Sitting quietly beside her, her knees tucked up under her chin, was the slender little Chinese woman from the Pearl. Her tiny face could have been made of porcelain. Hamish was reminded of his friend Ah Tay's immovable face. She regarded them with disinterest. It felt to Hamish as though she were looking through them, not as if they were not there but as if she saw them there but they had no substance.

When Rita had assisted Daisy safely onto one of the mattresses, she turned her attention to the pile of green satin. She found the small white wrist within the folds of fabric and held it.

'Her pulse is very slow,' she said, looking up at Hamish.

Hamish gently brushed away the mane of black hair covering the woman's face and placed two fingers at a vein in her neck. He had to adjust his touch several times to register the faint flow of life through her body. He placed his face to her lips and felt only the lightest touch of air on his skin.

'Her fingertips are blue,' said Rita.

'Kate.' Hamish called loudly into her face. 'Kate.'

He looked to Ah Tay. 'Help me to lift her.'

Ah Tay tried to assist but Kate's limbs were lifeless. They lay her back on the mattress.

Daisy had moved closer to them, nervously watching as they prodded her unconscious daughter.

'What are you doing?' she cried. 'She's all right. Leave her be.'

Hamish, Ah Tay and Rita ignored her cries.

'Should we take her to hospital?' Ah Tay asked.

Hamish was about to answer when Daisy lunged at his chest.

'Leave her be,' she shouted, pushing Hamish hard. He stumbled a few paces and Daisy threw herself over her daughter and glared up at them.

'She's not going anywhere.'

'It would do no good anyway,' said Rita calmly. 'She's taken too much opium.'

'We should try to get her moving,' suggested Hamish.

'My girl's all right,' sobbed Daisy. 'She's a good girl, she is.'

Rita held Daisy firmly and maneuvered her body away from Kate. 'Come now,' she soothed, 'the poor girl can't breathe with you on top of her.'

'She's a good girl,' came through the tears but the woman allowed herself to be moved.

'We know she is.' Rita held Daisy's head to her chest and stroked her hair.

'Should we make her take water?' Ah Tay asked.

'No. No water,' cried Hamish. 'She may not be able to swallow. Here, you lift her from that side and I'll take this side. Tuck your arms under her shoulders, like this.' Hamish pushed the bandage back away from his eyes, along with his fringe, which was beginning to stick in the seeping blood, and showed Ah Tay what to do.

They lifted and Kate hung like a rag doll between them.

'It could take hours for her to come to,' Hamish said.

'It's the woman's life, we must save her,' said Ah Tay with such conviction that it startled Hamish. His friend had shown little emotion in the past days.

All this time, Cy Wong sat motionless, while her eyes followed their movements.

They moved forward slowly dragging Kate's limp body with them.

'Wake up, Kate,' Hamish repeated. 'Keep moving.'

They tripped across the mattresses clumsily as they propelled an unresponsive Kate forward.

'Outside,' said Hamish, nodding toward the door. 'Fresh air might wake her.'

Rita continued to hold Daisy and rock her while the tears flowed.

Hamish and Ah Tay stumbled into the yard with Kate. As soon as she was out of the confined space of the cellar she sucked in a large gulp of air. Encouraged, they plodded across the yard and back again, dragging Kate between them, her skirt catching in the mud and debris. Their own boots sunk deep into the mud with each step. The effort was exhausting. Hamish's shoulders ached as though a vice had been clamped down on him and was being winched tighter with every movement. He was about to declare the effort hopeless when Kate coughed, took in a loud breath of fetid air and vomited. She coughed several more times while Hamish slapped her on the back. She was stumbling but her legs were starting to take her weight. She was breathing properly at last and strength returned to her body.

Suddenly she pushed Hamish and Ah Tay away and fell onto her knees in the mud coughing and spluttering.

'Fuck off,' she cried.

Hamish and Ah Tay beamed.

'She's come round,' Hamish said.

He stretched out his hand. 'You're going to need a hand getting up.'

'Fuck off,' she said again but she took his hand and drew herself up.

Ah Tay helped support her while she made her way back into the cellar. She dropped down on a mattress, her head slumped against the wall and closed her eyes again. She was breathing normally and within minutes she was snoring.

Daisy had stopped crying and was sitting beside Rita with her hands in her lap.

'You both need to move out of here,' said Rita. 'I have a house where women come to stay when their husbands are violent. It's a short walk from South Brisbane station. You are both welcome to stay there. I have one room you could share.'

Daisy narrowed her eyes.

'It would be free until you get on your feet. You can't bring men there, though. It would be dangerous for the other women. If their husbands were to find out where they were, they wouldn't be safe. Also, I will tolerate no alcohol and no opium on the premises.'

Daisy shook her head. 'We won't give up the only life we know,' she said.

'Shouldn't Kate have the chance to make her own choice?' asked Rita.

'She can choose when she has recovered. But I can tell you now, she'll not be taken from this life.'

Rita sighed. 'At least let me help clean this place up if you are determined to stay. I can have beds put in. These mattresses need to be burned.'

Ah Tay had positioned himself beside Cy Wong on the mattress. She was still silently watching, while Ah Tay watched her. Hamish noticed the emotion in his eyes and it occurred to him for the first time that Ah Tay had strong feelings for her.

'What about you, Cy Wong? Will you go with Doctor Cartwright?' Hamish said.

'No,' came the quiet but firm reply.

Ah Tay let out an exasperated gasp.

'You cannot stay here,' he cried.

Cy Wong turned to her cousin. 'I go to Sam Hung's house.'

Ah Tay looked about to explode. 'I cannot allow it.'

It seemed apparent that the calm exterior Ah Tay presented to the world had been hiding a raging volcano within.

'Not that,' said Ah Tay, a tremor of passion and finality in his tone.

Cy Wong stood. 'It is not up to you to *allow*. I owe debt.'

She tried to move past Ah Tay toward the door but he stopped her. He held her firmly by the shoulders.

'Don't,' he said. 'You don't have to do this. What about Foong May? I can take you to her.'

'*Bu ke neng.*'

'Why is it impossible?' cried Ah Tay but she had already extracted herself from his grip and was heading out the door.

He moved to follow her but Hamish put a hand on his shoulder.

'You can't force her.'

Ah Tay threw his arms in the air.

'Go back to Foong May's house and calm yourself,' said Hamish. 'I would like you to dine with us tonight. By then you will be able to discuss the events of the past days with a clear head.'

Ah Tay faced him with an expression as dark as thunder but he quickly regained his control and strode off toward the tea house.

CHAPTER EIGHT

If the multitudinous dishes inscribed on the menu of the trial lunch with which the Chinese restauranteurs lately opened their campaign at the Health Exhibition are set before the public, it is easy to foresee that they will be at a great loss which to choose. It is right, therefore, to give a little advice. The hungry sightseer may with confidence order birds-nest soup. It is served in a tiny slop-basin and is excellent. It will have great success in London and will probably be naturalised in England from and after 1884. Let one only of the party order Shaohsing wine. It is warm, like the soup, and also served in a tiny slop-basin. But a taste of it will be enough for each of the guests. It is made from rice and its flavour is indescribable. Besides birds-nests, the Chinese eat many things which we do not. Either of the two following dishes, called respectively in Franco-Chinese jargon 'Timbal Beche-de-Mer' or 'Sharks Fin a la Bagration' will give to any curious barbarian some notion of the skilful manner in which they realise treasures of the deep which we waste.

The Beche-de-Mer is a sea-slug two-and-a-half inches long and an inch thick. It lies at the bottom of the deep seas off the Chinese coasts and looks, when dried, like a piece of India-rubber, from which protrudes a row of short spikes. It is cut up and cooked into minute pies. The taste of the sea-slug is not as bad as might be imagined, their taste being not unlike turtle. The Shark Fin, however, is for the more audacious. It is cartilaginous and eaten with rice. It is here that the chopsticks which lie beside your plate may be tried. It is hoped that a real Chinaman may be deputed to show you how to use the chopsticks.

The Capricornian, Rockhampton. Saturday 30 August, 1884

That evening as Hamish tidied his consultation room after his last patient, he took in the aroma of Wallace's lamb stew wafting in from the kitchen.

He had questioned the wisdom of installing the kitchen behind his consulting room but there had been no other option given the dimensions of the house. He was determined the space on the second floor would be a sanctuary of sorts, a place he could feel comfortable and safe, regardless of what was going on in the world. He believed he had achieved that admirably, with Wallace and Rita frequently providing him with company in his sitting room.

He would have preferred Rita join him as his wife but he accepted that would never happen. Rita shocked her parents at the age of seventeen when she announced she preferred the company of women to men. At first her mother pretended not to fully understand her meaning but it became increasingly obvious as she became older. So much so, that when she returned from her studies in London with a young woman in tow, it came as no surprise to her family. Still, her parents insisted she 'would grow out of her eccentricities' and provided assurances to their friends that she was far too committed to her work to consider marriage. He had known how the land lay since his first meeting with Rita when he was a medical student, but it didn't make him love her less or stop wondering if she might one day come to love him in the way he desired.

Hamish had to admit that he enjoyed the domestic feel created by having the kitchen behind his rooms. The aroma of baking bread was also commented upon favourably by his patients. They said it improved their appetites. They claimed to always be ready for a hearty meal after a consultation.

Hamish climbed the stairs this particular evening feeling his own hunger pangs and was disappointed to find that his guests had not arrived. Rita bounced up the stairs full of life only moments later but Ah Tay was still missing. Hamish wondered if he would come at all, then there was a knock at the door and he heard Wallace greet the Chinaman. Soon they were all seated at the dining table, Wallace with his wiry terrier at his feet, the dog apparently keen that if any morsel of food fell opportunely, he would be there to clean it up. Once they were all seated, the conversation immediately turned to the investigation.

'We know that Ah Chit was killed by a *Jian* that had been hanging in his own drawing room,' began Hamish. 'Someone with access to his home must have taken it while he was at work during the day he was murdered.

Otherwise, he would have noticed it missing and reported it.'

Ah Tay took a bread roll, broke it in half and dipped it in his stew. 'The members of the Sheathed Sword use the house as a meeting place. They come and go as they please. I believe they all have keys.'

'That makes it difficult to narrow down,' said Hamish. 'Can we obtain a list of members?'

Wallace laughed. 'It's a secret society. There won't be a list,' he said, handing a small piece of buttered bread under the table. The terrier took it gladly and licked butter from his whiskers.

'I can write down the names of those I know,' said Ah Tay.

'Does anyone other than Cy Wong live in the house with Sam Hung?' Hamish asked.

'No.'

'Where are you staying while in Brisbane?' asked Wallace.

'I'm boarding at Foong May's house,' said Ah Tay. 'There is a small accommodation behind the tea shop and a single room upstairs.'

'That reminds me,' said Hamish, 'why didn't you introduce me to Foong May when we were at the teahouse?'

'Foong May knows who you are.'

'Yes but I didn't know who she is,' protested Hamish.

'It is not important,' said Ah Tay.

Hamish wondered if his friend was ashamed of his relationship with him. Perhaps he still didn't want the Chinese community to know they were working together in the investigation. Still, their appearance together at the Pearl certainly let that cat out of the bag. Half of the Chinese community saw them there. Surely, it would be less conspicuous to introduce Hamish as an old friend, than to not mention him at all.

'Getting back to the murder,' said Wallace, 'what is our current theory in regard to motive?'

Red put his front paws on his master's lap, gently nudging his arm to remind him of his presence. Wallace slipped him a piece of lamb. The dog retreated to his spot under the table to devour it.

'There's control of the businesses,' suggested Hamish.

'And the house,' said Rita.

Hamish swallowed a mouthful of stew. 'I'm inclined to consider Sam Hung our prime suspect. I'll wager Bellamy is of the same mind.'

'Sam Hung is a dangerous man,' said Ah Tay.

'How so?' Hamish asked.

Ah Tay's waxen face darkened but he didn't speak.

'He certainly had the most to gain, I suppose,' Hamish said. 'Although if the businesses were in that much debt to the Society, it is only power he gained, not wealth.'

'Power means everything to some men,' said Ah Tay.

'If you won't say why you believe Sam Hung is dangerous, can you tell us more about Ah Chit?' asked Hamish, pouring red wine in all their glasses. 'Why did he come to Brisbane?'

'Ah Chit set up the furniture business in Little Lygon Street with money he made from the mines. He brought Chinese workers into Victoria on credit tickets. His business paid for their passage and they worked on the mines until the debt was paid. It is common.'

'Yes,' said Hamish. 'Most of the Chinese immigrants are in debt to agents.'

'It wasn't enough for my uncle. He started importing opium in the tea chests brought in by the immigrants. There were hidden compartments in the bottom of the chests.'

'But why? It isn't illegal to import opium,' said Hamish.

'Ah Chit did not want to pay the Government duties. A steamer from China arrived carrying about one hundred Chinese. When half of them had successfully progressed through customs, one of the officers discovered two large trunks with false bottoms and a large amount of opium. The opium was not entered into the ship's manifest nor were any entries passed relating to it. The man responsible for the trunks, when questioned, admitted that he was bringing the opium in for my uncle.'

'He was smuggling opium?' said Wallace. Red stood to attention at the sharp tone of his master's voice.

'Yes.'

Wallace whistled. 'Dangerous … but lucrative.'

'He also gambled. In Victoria he was not, as you say, a big fish.'

Ah Tay nodded to Hamish. 'Like your father.'

'I don't …' Hamish began.

Ah Tay put his hand up, his palm outward.

'You may not be aware, my friend. But it is so.'

Hamish flushed deeply.

'My uncle owed a lot of money, much of it to your father—' he looked at Hamish without judgement '—and other men, Chinese men, resented that he was profiting from the import of opium without paying the duties. Other furniture makers were angry that he was placing their industry at risk.'

Hamish could feel his skin burning. He tried to live his life without thinking about his father's position as a prominent SP Bookmaker in Victoria and the range of shady activities he was involved in on the side. He had no knowledge of the range of his father's business enterprises and he worked hard to keep it that way.

'Why didn't someone go to the police?' he asked.

'That's the last thing they would do surely,' said Wallace.

'Ah Chit was offered a way to save face by the members of the Sheathed Sword. Our family is respected in Southern China. Members of our family fight hard against Qing rule. This brought Ah Chit a way out of his troubles. The Sheathed Sword offered to pay out his debts and set him up in Brisbane where he could start again. They said there was less competition in Brisbane and he would soon make the money to pay back the debt.'

They were all silent for some time while they processed the information about Ah Chit.

Red had made himself comfortable on Hamish's favourite chair. There was nothing more of interest to him in the conversation, now that dinner was complete. He was not a devotee of red wine.

As intriguing as the information was, it didn't reveal much about Ah Chit's murder beyond what they already knew. Furthermore, Hamish suspected there was nothing in what they heard that Sergeant Bellamy didn't also know.

'Then there is Daisy Walton,' said Ah Tay, breaking them out of their reverie.

'What about Daisy Walton?' asked Hamish.

'She frequently spent time at the house,' said Ah Tay. 'She had access to come and go.'

Hamish screwed up his face.

'You mean, Daisy was in a relationship with your uncle?' said Rita.

'Of sorts. She frequently spent the night. He was fond of her.'

'How could he leave her and her daughter in that squalor if he was fond of her?'

Ah Tay remained impassive. 'My uncle was not sentimental and Daisy values her independence.'

'She had access to the sword,' said Rita.

Hamish wasn't ready to let go of his outrage. 'He could have at least maintained the place. He was the legal owner, even if the debt was held by the Society.'

Everyone ignored Hamish.

'Could Daisy have stabbed Ah Chit though?' asked Rita. 'You said it was a particularly clean wound. And that it was carried out in such a way as to minimise the loss of blood. More like a ceremonial-style killing, would you say?' She turned to Hamish.

'It could have been unintentional, judging the nature of the wound,' mused Hamish. 'It was certainly purposeful. It wasn't a momentary lapse into unbridled rage. The killer premeditated the act and carried it out with precision.'

'Doesn't sound like Daisy,' said Wallace.

'She is strong enough,' said Rita. 'As is her daughter.'

'Who supplies them with opium?' asked Wallace.

'They purchased the opium from my uncle until his death,' said Ah Tay. 'I assume that side of the business has also been taken on by Sam Hung.'

A thought entered Rita's mind. 'Did Ah Chit act as pimp to Daisy and Kate?'

Hamish shifted uncomfortably in his seat.

'Daisy and Kate work independently,' Ah Tay said. 'Daisy would not be owned by anyone.'

'Tell us about Cy Wong,' said Rita.

'Cy Wong's father was arrested. Effectively she was orphaned as her mother died years ago. Ah Chit brought her from China to work for him.'

'What is it that she does for your uncle?' asked Rita.

Ah Tay's face hardened.

The three of them kept staring at Ah Tay, waiting for a response.

'He expected her to work as a hostess,' he said at last. 'There are few Chinese women in Brisbane and she would attract customers to the Pearl.'

Hamish gasped. 'Did he expect her to prostitute for him?'

'Not necessarily,' said Ah Tay carefully. 'Her presence was enough.'

'She's a child.'

'She is seventeen, in her own country she would be married with several children by now.'

'She doesn't look seventeen.'

'It is true, she is small.'

Hamish grimaced. Ah Tay had missed his point.

'Pour us all another, will you?' Rita said to Hamish, holding up her glass.

'How did Cy Wong feel about the expectation he placed on her?' she asked.

'Cy Wong was sent to this colony to earn money and pave the way for family members to follow,' he said. 'She will behave honourably.'

'What does that mean?' screeched Hamish.

Rita shot him a glance that strongly suggested he calm himself.

'Is that what Cy Wong meant when she told you she would do her duty this morning?' she asked.

Ah Tay hesitated. 'I assume so.'

Wallace took a long drink from his glass and placed it on the table, empty.

'So, Cy Wong now owes her passage and keep to Sam Hung,' he said.

'Correct,' said Ah Tay.

'Not much point to her killing Ah Chit then. Her circumstances have not changed,' said Wallace.

Ah Tay's black eyes revealed his hatred for Sam Hung. But why? Was Ah Tay's cousin in worse danger with Sam Hung than she had been with Ah Chit? If so, why didn't she agree to live with Foong May?

As Wallace removed the empty plates and glasses, Ah Tay rose from the table. 'Thank you for your hospitality,' he said. 'The funeral is early tomorrow. I must assist in the preparations.'

'The funeral?' said Hamish. 'Is it Ah Chit's funeral you mean?'

'It will be a traditional Chinese funeral.'

'I would like to attend.'

Ah Tay hesitated. 'I must go now to change into appropriate clothing,' he said. 'Tonight's preparation is most important. The body must be prepared. In China the burial would take place no sooner than seven days after the death; however, it is hot here and the body will not keep that long. Tonight, we prepare the Hereditary Jar with rice and bread for my uncle's long journey. I will tie a small red bag of silver to my uncle's buttonhole in case there is anything he needs to purchase. Also, I will provide food for him to feed the dogs as he passes over the Great Dog Mountain. These are our ways. To forget one's ancestors is to be a brook without a source, a tree without roots.'

'I wouldn't dream of intruding on these ceremonies,' said Hamish. 'But surely I could attend the funeral tomorrow?'

Ah Tay hesitated again.

'You can join the mourners if you wish to be up before dawn. We meet at the temple at five o'clock.'

Hamish stood tall. 'I'll be there.'

Rita helped Wallace with the dirty dishes, while Hamish saw Ah Tay to the door.

'Off the chair,' he said to Red on his way past. Red opened an eye but stayed where he was.

There were still so many questions but his friend remained distant. The easy friendship they shared as children had not returned.

As Ah Tay bowed and stepped through the door, Hamish acted on an impulse. He placed his hand on his friend's shoulder. Ah Tay stopped but he didn't look Hamish in the eye.

'We trusted one another once, my friend,' said Hamish. 'It feels like there is a great distance between us now.'

Ah Tay placed his hand over Hamish's as it rested on his shoulder and held it there briefly. Then the moment passed and he stepped away without looking back.

'Tomorrow,' said Hamish as he watched his friend's back move into the street.

When Hamish returned upstairs, he found Rita gathering her coat and gloves from where she always left them, flung across his blue velvet armchair. How many times had he asked her to hang them on the coat rack inside the front entrance?

'I'm going to the Nine Holes in the morning,' said Rita. 'I've arranged it with Daisy. We're going to stage a clean-up.'

'I didn't know this,' said Hamish.

'Of course, you didn't. I'm just telling you now.'

'Are you sure this is consistent with the wishes of the occupants of the house?'

'What are you saying?' Rita smoothed her gloves carefully, as she did when she was biding her time.

Hamish felt like a mouse caught in the sights of a cat. 'I'm suggesting you may cross a line between welcome care and unwanted interference.'

Rita's hands became still and her eyes drifted up slowly to peer at Hamish from under long lashes. 'I will not leave those women living in that filth,' she said. 'Kate, at least, is looking forward to the assistance.'

Hamish took in a cleansing breath. There was no point fighting the inevitable. Rita would do what she had decided to do regardless of his protest or caution.

'Well then, should I assist?' he asked.

'That would be very helpful,' said Rita. 'We'll see you at nine.'

'Ah Chit's funeral is at five. So, I can be at the Nine Holes by nine,' said Hamish.

When Hamish arrived at the house where Ah Chit's body was being prepared, close by the Joss House, it was still dark and cool. The gaslights shone in the house and he could see people moving about inside. When he entered, he saw that the mourners were burning paper money and pouring ashes into an earthen basin. As dawn approached, four men lifted the coffin from the wooden bench where it sat and another man lifted the basin and threw it to the ground where it shattered. Ash and tiny fragments of paper spread across the floor.

Ah Tay was wearing a sack cloth and his head was bound with rope. It was so unfamiliar that Hamish almost didn't recognise his friend. Ah Tay took the place of the chief mourner and led the procession of men and women wailing quietly. He walked the block to the Joss House in front of the coffin holding the Heredity Jar in his arms. Hamish had seen Chinese funerals in his childhood but he had never seen his friend in this traditional Chinese light. Ah Chit had seemed as much European as he was Chinese. Hamish wondered what Ah Chit would have thought of his funeral. Perhaps his soul needed the comfort of the ancient rituals.

The procession made its way to the Temple and from there the coffin was transferred onto a European mourning coach replete with four horses with plush black plumes. The coffin was delivered to Toowong Cemetery for burial in the Chinese section. Those who had transport followed and participated in a feast held at the gravesite. Hamish scanned the mourners carefully but found no sign of Sam Hung or Cy Wong at the gravesite.

He continued watching from a respectful distance. Ah Tay thus far had carried out his duties with solemn grace. While Hamish had known his friend to traverse two cultures throughout his life, in the past twenty-four hours he had been truly Chinese. How gratifying it must be to have such an intense, deeply held knowing of one's culture. Hamish wondered how that would feel, to be part of something larger than himself.

Hamish was born in Melbourne of English parents but he felt no connection to their birthplace. His single overriding impression of England was of a country of oppressive class divisions and traditions that kept the masses poor and the mobility in power. He wanted none of the pomp and ceremony of old England. He preferred the freedom of spirit and bumptiousness of youth that characterised this new country. But he didn't feel entirely connected to Australia, not in the way Ah Tay was connected to his homeland.

Was it that the Australia of convicts and immigrants had not had time to develop deep traditions of her own? Aboriginal Australia had eternal depth – it was bound to be challenging to drown out the songs of such an ancient past. To Hamish, non-Aboriginal Australia felt like an impoverished and poorly regarded extension of Britain, where the presence of class was upheld tenuously by an inept elite, while the rest of the population laughed at them. He appreciated the joke but it troubled him that even while they laughed, the poor remained without access to the resources they needed to live long, healthy lives.

Hamish watched the funeralgoers feast on all manner of delicacies. He thought about the tightrope they walked between the traditions of the old country and the expectations of the new one, clustered together to draw on the strengths of the community, while at the same time negotiating the notions of Western industrialisation, capitalism and competition.

Chinese immigrants were workers and businesspeople. But they couldn't survive on the custom of their own countrymen alone. There were nowhere near enough Chinese people in Brisbane to ensure business success, so the businesses had to appeal to a wider proportion of the population. In order to attract the non-Chinese custom, they had to offer value that could not be found elsewhere. It was a matter of being different enough to be interesting – but not so different as to be threatening. Still, people were threatened. The newspapers were replete with references to the great yellow peril and workers were convinced the Chinese were taking jobs that white Australians could have had. The Chinese were blamed for almost everything that citizens saw as being wrong with their lot. There would always be someone else to blame for the problems inherent in one's own society.

At last Ah Tay appeared among the mourners by the graveside. Hamish couldn't see where he had come from but that wasn't unusual. He had become used to him appearing as if from nowhere. He waited until the last of the guests left the gravesite before approaching Ah Tay. The young Chinaman was kneeling by the grave, now a mound of red dirt in a sea of long, green grass. Hamish knelt beside him and remained silent.

'You may be the only other person here who knew Ah Chit as a young man,' said Ah Tay after a long while.

Hamish didn't respond.

'He was different then.'

Hamish nodded. 'I admired him.'

'As did I,' said Ah Tay, 'at first.'

They stayed there together comfortable in each other's company for the first time in many years.

'You must feel quite alone,' said Hamish.

Ah Tay gave a small nod.

'I thought I would not have to be alone again when I came here,' said Ah Tay.

'Do you mean when you came to Brisbane?'

Ah Tay stared out across the mound of dirt into an endless sky.

'Yes. I heard Cy Wong was here and thought we would marry at last.'

'I see,' said Hamish. 'Then you came for her and she didn't want to marry you.'

'She is determined to repay her debt to Sam Hung.' Ah Tay almost spat the name into the dirt.

Hamish thought carefully before he asked the next question. 'I realise she was promised to you at a young age but do you love her?'

Ah Tay looked Hamish in the eye. 'You've seen her. She is perfect.'

Hamish thought that was all he needed to hear but Ah Tay went on. 'She is also cold like the frozen river,' he said.

Hamish knitted his brow. 'You call her cold because she rejected you?'

'Cy Wong has a heart of ice.' Ah Tay suddenly stood. 'I both love her and hate her. It has nothing to do with her feelings for me. Cy Wong has no feelings for anyone.'

'Not even Sam Hung?' asked Hamish as he also stood. He knew he was on thin ice himself.

Ah Tay gave him one of his darkest stares.

'Not even him,' he said.

Hamish thought carefully again. 'Perhaps Cy Wong has her own dreams to follow.'

Ah Tay held his head high. 'To believe in one's dreams is to spend all of one's life asleep.'

Hamish liked Ah Tay's Chinese proverbs but he couldn't agree with this one. It was troubling to him that his friend did not believe in following one's dreams.

They walked back to the waiting carriage in silence. Though Hamish did not feel any closer to understanding Ah Tay's feelings for Cy Wong, he felt closer to the man himself. They had reconnected in a small way and he would do whatever it took to find out who killed Ah Chit. That should be one secret that Ah Tay should not have to worry about.

CHAPTER NINE

The party paid a visit to the houses of ill-fame in Charlotte and Albert Streets. The first place visited was a notorious house in Charlotte Street kept by a Mrs Hogan. The building is described as a long cottage with its basement several feet below the level of the street. It stands back from the street a few feet the distance of which is covered by a veranda, fixed from the footpath with close latticework. Descending a few steps, the visitors found the veranda occupied by furnishings of two bedrooms which were in the process of being repapered. The landlady, a stout, determined-looking woman, at once presented herself and appeared to be pretty familiar with the officials. She conducted the party through the front rooms and back premises with a considerable amount of civility and readily afforded all the information required. She had eight girls of the town staying with her and had accommodation for a few more. The girls paid her two pound per week each and she paid their rent on to the property owner.

It was noted that the buildings were not up to the mark from a strictly sanitary point of view. The rooms were stuffy and did not provide the requisite quantity of living space. There were outbuildings around the square-built backyard. The backyard was unpaved and had in some parts the appearance of being saturated with slops. The building at the rear was an old, dilapidated structure, rat-holed, and on each side held up by corrugated iron and wooden posts. The opinion was that the place was rotten from old age and that the rooms there were rendered unhealthy by their smallness and position. These rooms at the back were occupied but it was considered right that they should be pulled down.

The Brisbane Courier. Saturday 5 December, 1885

When Hamish arrived at the Nine Holes, Rita was already there. She was throwing a bulky mattress with hay protruding through mouldy, decaying cotton, onto a pile of similar items in a makeshift fire pit.

'Here, let me help,' Hamish said, taking one end of the mattress. Folded over on itself, it threatened to engulf her small frame. Together they managed to place the mattress on top of the others. Hamish turned around to see Kate emerge from the cellar struggling to manoeuvre another mattress of similar disrepair through the narrow doorway. He ran over to assist. They persisted until they were able to throw the mattress onto the pile. Hamish stood to check that the tower they were creating was not at risk of falling and failed to notice Daisy standing beside him, her feet apart and her hands firmly on her hips.

Hamish could see she was not pleased. He pushed the bandage up from his forehead, the damn thing was always working its way over his eyes. He yanked it off his head and threw it onto the pile of mattresses. The wound was dry, so far so good.

'This is your doing,' said Daisy.

'I'm afraid you're wrong there. I assure you, this is Rita's idea, not mine.'

Hamish watched the mattress on top of the pile slip to the left and hit the ground. He wanted to push it back onto the pile but Daisy was still glaring at him.

'You think you know better,' she said. 'You're all the same. You ought to leave well enough alone. Proper beds won't change what we are.'

The heat rose in Hamish's face. He pushed back the hair from his forehead and felt a trickle of blood drip from his wound. The sight of the blood on his fingers made him embarrassed for both himself and for Daisy.

'What you are is more than what you do,' he assured her quietly.

'And what's wrong with what I do?' cried Daisy. 'I'm good at it. It's kept Kate and me fed all these years. And we're beholden to no one.' There were tears of rage forming in the rims of her eyes.

'I'm not judging you,' said Hamish.

'You are judging us, right enough,' she scoffed.

'Surely a clean environment and comfortable beds will improve your health ...' began Hamish.

'Ha! Our health, is it? You think a clean bed will restore our health?' She shook her head slowly while still glaring at Hamish, turned and stormed back to the cellar.

Rita joined him, her hair loose from the bun at her neck and stuck to her sweaty face. She was flushed from the effort but her eyes were bright.

'She thinks we're judging her,' he said.

Rita glanced in the direction Daisy had gone. 'Hmm,' she said. 'Where's your bandage?'

Kate joined them and gazed admiringly at the pile they had made. 'Good job,' she said.

'The mountain of many mattresses is a testament to your perseverance,' said Hamish. He pushed the rogue mattress back to the top of the pile.

Rita rummaged in the pocket of her skirt and brought out matches. She held them out to Kate who happily took them and lit a tuft of straw poking out of each mattress. The straw took the flame instantly and there was soon a roaring fire in the pit. Kate smiled and Hamish saw that the flames were reflected in her dark eyes. Unlike her mother, it was clear she was thrilled to see the stinking, vermin-infested bedding burn. Kate and Rita exchanged a satisfied glance.

'Come on,' said Rita. 'We haven't much time before the wagon arrives.'

Hamish followed them into the cellar where they found Daisy leaning against a wall smoking a cigarette. Kate and Rita lifted armloads of old curtains that had been repurposed as sheets and carried them outside to dump on the fire. Daisy followed them as far as the door where she remained casually puffing on her cigarette. Rita disappeared to the laundry and returned with a bucket and scrubbing brushes. She threw one at Hamish who caught it the instant before it hit him in the face.

The three of them set about removing the inch or two of silt that was ground into the cement floor of the cellar until a squeal from Kate made them stop.

'Dog paws,' she cried, standing up.

'What?' said Hamish.

Kate was pointing at the floor. 'Dog paws.'

Hamish and Rita stretched to their feet and joined her. They stared down at the floor to see what she saw. Two perfectly formed impressions in the cement.

'Dog paws,' said Hamish.

Somehow the sign of a life now long past in the cement sent them into fits of laughter. Kate cleaned the area thoroughly to make sure she could always see the dog paws.

When they had scrubbed the entire surface, Rita fetched a clean bucket of water and threw it across the floor. She then brushed the floor with a straw broom.

They gathered themselves at the entrance and stared back at their work. The little light that entered through the single window cast diagonal shadows onto the cement.

'Thank you,' said Kate quietly. Before Hamish and Rita could respond she left them to join her mother who was now sitting on a beer barrel in the yard.

Hamish had barely caught his breath from the hour of scrubbing when he was startled by the rattle of a dray pulling up in front of the building. On the tray were four shining metal bed frames with taught springs and four plump mattresses stuffed with horsehair. There were stacks of woollen blankets, cotton sheets and pillows.

Kate ran to the dray and began gathering up pillows to her chest. 'I've never had a real pillow,' she cried.

Hamish and Rita helped the driver transport the precious cargo from the wagon into the cellar. The whole time they worked, Daisy remained on her barrel, chain smoking. She had turned away from them and was staring into space. Rita and Kate told the men where to put the beds and they set about making them. When they were done, they stood back and admired the room. It was perfectly liveable. Daisy had walked up behind them to peer in.

'That'll last 'til the first rain,' she said. 'This whole block floods every summer.' Still, she pushed past them and chose one of the beds for herself, lay down and went to sleep.

'Would you two like to join me for a cup of tea?' asked Hamish. 'I know a tea house close by.'

'You are becoming quite at home in Frog's Hollow,' said Rita. 'Let me clean up your face, first. You look like someone has knocked you on the head.'

'Someone did knock me on the head, with a chair,' he said.

'That was days ago, Hamish. You ought to stop complaining about it. And stop bleeding.'

Kate peered at the wound with a worried expression.

'Don't encourage him,' said Kate. 'He's bleeding for attention.' She wiped away the blood with a clean handkerchief. 'See, it's nothing,' she said when the wound was clean.

Kate and Rita followed Hamish the two blocks to Foong May's teahouse in Elizabeth Street.

Foong May greeted them warmly, settled them at the back table and brought them green tea in tiny cups with dragons, and delicious custard tarts.

'I'm afraid Daisy is angry with us for interfering,' said Hamish.

Kate swallowed a custard tart whole. There was a look of ecstasy on her face. 'She's had a hard life,' she said. 'My mother knows no other way than hard. To be truthful, I don't either.'

'Has your mother always worked … in her current profession?' asked Rita.

Kate laughed. 'Daisy has been a prostitute since she was old enough to know her mind. Her mother abandoned her when she was three and a neighbour took her in. The neighbour resented her. She had nothing herself, as I understand it. Daisy didn't like feeling she was a burden so she ran away when she was ten. I think she started on the game then. Certainly, soon after, soon as she realised men would pay for her services. She says it made more money than begging.'

Hamish and Rita were staring into their tea. 'Don't feel sorry for her,' Kate said. 'She hates that more than anything. She likes her work. She says she has some control when she services these middle-class men who think they are so much better than us. She feels like she has something over them and their smug wives.'

'What do you think?' asked Rita.

'I hate it, to be honest. I hate their fat, ugly bodies and the smell of the sweat and alcohol on them. I've been taught well, though. I know what to do to please them and get the most money out of them. Sometimes I empty their wallets while they're snoring if they're stupid enough to leave them where I can get them. We have access to rooms kept by Ah Chit for our work. Well, kept by Sam Hung now, I suppose.'

'If you hate it, why don't you do something else?' asked Hamish.

Kate looked at him as though he was mad. 'What else would I do, someone like me?' She laughed.

'What would you like to do?' asked Rita.

'Never really thought about it. Not worth wasting energy on, is it? I'm not going to have any other life so I might as well make the best of this one.'

'Do you stay to look after your mother?' asked Rita.

Hamish was surprised by the question.

Kate popped another custard tart into her mouth. She chewed slowly this time, giving herself time to think.

'I can't very well leave her, can I? What would she do without me?'

'You could get a job and make money to keep you both,' suggested Hamish.

Kate exhibited the same incredulous expression. 'What job would I get to make enough money to put us up in a proper house? There's nothing we could do that would make more than we make now. We do alright. We make good money. More than you'd think.'

'Why do you live in a filthy cellar at the Nine Holes then?' asked Hamish.

Kate flinched. 'It ain't dirty no more, is it?'

Rita sent Hamish a dark look.

'It's the opium,' Kate said.

Hamish and Rita stared at her.

'The money goes on the opium. For Daisy, it stops her from going mad. For me, it eases the pain a little. Dulls the senses so I don't mind so much. Whatever gets you through, as they say.' Kate drank down the last of her tea.

'I'd stop, if I could.' Kate was quieter now. 'That last overdose scared me. I reckon it's only a matter of time until I end up dead from the opium.'

The sudden change in her demeanour shocked Hamish. She slumped in her seat and appeared to age before his eyes. Her skin was drawn and sallow, without the plumpness of youth one might expect of someone her age. Her eyes were dull and lifeless. She appeared tired, not the sort of tired that might be mediated by a good night's sleep but a tiredness that penetrated through to the soul.

'I can help you,' said Rita. 'If you want. There are drugs that ease the pain of withdrawal. It's still hard but …'

'I gotta get back,' said Kate. 'She'll be waking up soon.' She stood quickly and strode through the door.

Hamish and Rita were left staring into their teacups.

'She has to want to give up that life,' said Hamish. 'It won't be easy.' He knew his friend too well. To Rita everything was possible, she had no sense that some things simply can't be shaped to her will.

'It will take more than her wanting it,' said Rita. 'She will need to give up a great deal and be able to persevere through the pain of withdrawal. Not to mention the pain of leaving her mother behind.'

'There'll be the stigma that follows her through life as well. Society is ruthless in its judgement of the Chinese opium smokers and the women they believe to have been seduced by them.'

Rita scoffed. 'The plight Daisy and Kate find themselves in has nothing at all to do with the Chinese. In fact, it has been the Chinese community that has taken them in when others would have left them on the street. The local newspapers are far too eager to blame the opium problem on the Chinese. Remember it is the British who benefit from the sale of opium.'

'I agree wholeheartedly,' said Hamish. 'The sale of opium from the crops in British India forms a considerable proportion of British revenue. Some say upwards of fifteen million pounds per annum. The Chinese are not the source of the problem, rather they are victims of British Imperialism.' Hamish sighed. 'You're going to pursue this with Kate, regardless of what I say. Aren't you?'

'That I am,' said Rita.

CHAPTER TEN

Five Chinamen appeared at the police court yesterday charged with maliciously destroying vegetables in the garden of a countryman named Ah Chong near the racecourse on Saturday night last. Ah Chong entered the witness box and was sworn through the interpreter by the blowing out of a match. He had been cautioned that if he told a lie, his soul would be blown out at the same time.

Warwick Examiner. Saturday 17 September, 1887

Wallace placed the meal of pickled beef, chutney and cheese before Hamish as well as a newspaper that was neatly folded to present a particular column. Hamish ignored the food and picked up the paper. Red jumped onto his lap and settled himself there while Hamish held the paper higher so he could rest it on the dog's warm body.

> *At the Brisbane Court House today, Sam Hung was charged with keeping a gambling house and Ah Yong with being concerned therein. Sam Hung was fined ten pound or three months incarceration and the other man was remanded. Three other Chinamen arrested on the premises were fined one shilling each.*

'Ten pounds,' cried Hamish. 'That's of no consequence to Sam Hung.'

'There was obviously no evidence to charge him with anything else,' said Wallace.

Hamish put the paper down and hooked a forkful of pickled beef. 'I wish Ah Tay would tell us why he thinks Hung is dangerous.'

'I've found out about a court case involving Foong May as well,' said Wallace.

Hamish stopped chewing to look at him.

'I was talking to the Chinese grocer who sells us our vegetables. He knows Foong May. He said she recently pressed charges of unlawful assault against four young men named Batten, Davy, Winter and Edmonds.'

'How does our grocer know so much about it?' asked Hamish, his attention slipping back to his meal.

'The grocer attended the court hearing because Foong May showed him her injuries the morning after the assault. The story told by the grocer was hilarious in a way, much of the court's time was lost in extracting the evidence, the interpreter being barely able to speak English more sufficiently than the witnesses.'

'What was the charge?' Hamish asked, popping a chunk of cheese in his mouth.

Wallace was not to be rushed when he had command of a good story. 'After the prosecutor was sworn in using the Bible,' he said, 'and the Chinese by means of blowing out a lighted match, the prosecutor gave evidence that on the night of the Joss House Opening, between the hours of ten and eleven, the young men entered Foong May's garden and pulled out a number of vegetables. It seems she keeps a garden at the back of the building which services the tea house. Mostly herbs and such but some vegetables as well ...'

'Yes, yes,' said Hamish. 'Get on with the assault.'

'Foong May says she was aroused by a noise. She went outside to investigate and yelled at the louts to "get away". But they pelted her with stones instead. The next day she showed them to the grocer. After the boys left, she found two dilapidated hats which she produced in court, adding that she had seen the boys' faces clearly in the moonlight and could name them. Constable Pennyweather said he had interviewed a young man who knew the boys and he led him to their home. They denied having anything to do with it. Each one had an alibi and witnesses to back him up. Two of the lads reckon they were at a dance competition at Mr W.D. Goodall's assembly rooms and another was supposedly at band practice with other Brigade members. The mother of the remaining lad said he was in the reading room of the library until a quarter past nine and then proceeded home and went immediately to bed. Witnesses attested that all the boys were tucked in their beds asleep by eleven.'

Hamish laughed in disbelief. 'The library? I doubt these boys know where the library is.'

Wallace lifted one thick eyebrow. 'Nonetheless, all four boys were discharged and set at liberty. The magistrate granted the sum of three pounds three shillings court costs against Foong May.'

'Foong May was charged the court costs?'

'That's right. The boys were shown to have done no wrong.'

'Pillars of the community, then,' said Hamish.

Wallace scratched his chin.

'Do you think these boys assaulted Foong May?' asked Hamish.

'Our grocer is certain of it,' said Wallace.

'That's the evening of Ah Chit's murder. If these boys were out and about in Frog's Hollow, they might have seen something.'

'Exactly,' said Wallace.

'We need to talk to these youths. Do you know where to find them?'

Wallace packed a thick slice of bread with cheese and pickles.

'Robert will know,' he said.

'Who is Robert?'

'Young Bob, they call him. His father is Old Bob – he frequents the pubs and gambling houses in Frog's Hollow. Young Bob runs papers for the Courier from six o'clock in the morning until late at night. There's nothing about Frog's Hollow Young Bob doesn't know.'

'He'll know these boys?' asked Hamish.

'Certainly. They are all in the Boys' Brigade together.'

'How do I find Young Bob, then?'

Wallace licked pickle from his fingers. 'He'll be here at the house at four.'

Hamish stared at his friend. His ginger hair seemed thinner than ever and sat in contrast to his bushy orange-grey eyebrows. The clear blue of his eyes twinkled as though mocking Hamish. The crinkles at the corners told of a lifetime of laughing. Wallace had a deep, resounding laugh that came right up from his belly. But he wasn't laughing now. Though Hamish wasn't convinced he was not mocking.

'He delivers your newspapers,' he said. 'Every afternoon at four o'clock and every morning at seven.' Wallace finished his bread and cheese in two bites and got up to clean the table. Red jumped down from Hamish's lap and followed his master in the hope there'd be scraps.

'I have patients this afternoon,' said Hamish. 'I'll be finished by four with a bit of luck. Come and get me when the boy arrives.'

Wallace nodded. 'He won't put in his friends if he thinks they are in trouble. You'll have to think of an indirect way to find out their whereabouts,' he said, tipping a plate of crusts onto the floor for the dog.

The afternoon went quickly attending to Mrs Thistlewait's cough and Mrs Carter's headaches. Mrs Carter brought her daughter with her, to have her rash examined. Hamish dispensed powders and creams and advice on healthy living. All these ailments could have been adequately dealt with by the pharmacy in Queen Street but the women had money to pay for a doctor's advice and they enjoyed the attention. Hamish felt shame in the knowledge that the people with real health problems were those that could not afford a consultation.

At precisely four o'clock Hamish was standing at his front door waiting when Young Bob arrived. He was a small boy who might've been about ten, though he was thin and pale and could easily have been younger. His coat and hat were several sizes too big for him, giving the impression he was even smaller. He wore no shoes and his fingers were covered in newspaper ink.

'Young Bob,' said Hamish as he exchanged a newspaper for a coin.

'Yes, sir,' said Young Bob.

'Have you time for a drink and a snack?' asked Hamish.

Young Bob eyed him suspiciously.

'Wallace has just now taken scones from the oven if you would care to try them.' Hamish stepped aside and gestured for the boy to enter.

Young Bob watched him closely for another moment before the temptation of hot scones overcame his suspicion of the doctor's motives and he entered.

When he was seated at the table with a mug of milk and a plate of steaming scones before him, the wiry terrier sitting pleadingly at his feet, Hamish began.

'I've heard a lot about this Boys' Brigade,' he said. 'It's a club for newspaper boys, isn't it?'

Young Bob popped a piping hot scone into his mouth whole.

'Are you a member?' Hamish persisted.

Young Bob's cheeks swelled like two balloons either side of his mouth.

'Yes,' he managed to say without letting a single crumb escape.

'Do all the paper boys belong to the club?'

'Most of them, sir,' said Bob as he took a long drink from the mug. He used his other hand to pick up a second scone so he could stuff it in his mouth immediately after swallowing, without having to wait until he put down the mug.

'What sorts of things do you do in this club?'

'Play the drums, the fife, march in parades,' said the boy.

'I'd love to see that,' said Hamish.

Young Bob looked thoughtful. 'We have a dinner on tonight at the Hall. There'll be no parade but the committee will talk about what's coming up. You might find something interesting.'

'Will all the boys be at the dinner?'

'For certain, sir. On account of the free food. Good food too, sir.' He threw a glance Wallace's way. 'Not better than your scones though.'

Wallace refilled his milk.

The boy was being careful not to say anything that might reduce his chances of further afternoon snacks at the doctor's house. Hamish exchanged a knowing wink with Wallace.

'Tonight, you say?' asked Hamish.

'Yes, sir.'

Hamish smiled. 'I think I might come along. Maybe I'll see you there.'

He put out his hand and Young Bob gave it a firm shake then nodded to Wallace and left them to finish up. He sent a message to Rita to join him at seven when they would be attending a dinner meeting of the Brisbane chapter of the Boys' Brigade.

As Hamish and Rita strolled along the riverfront, they saw a group of excited boys gathering in front of Customs House. The boys were organised into a formation and marched with much cheering to the assembly rooms referred to locally as 'the Hall', where they found rows of long tables decorated with flowers. Hamish and Rita walked alongside the procession. The boys, full of eager anticipation and chatter gradually filled the seats and before long were joined by ladies and gentlemen, including Hamish and Rita, keen to hear about the club and how they might contribute to the cause.

Hamish noted that the boys seemed more at home on the streets than they might have been in comfortable houses. They were mostly thin, with sharp faces, alert eyes and rebellious hair and they all had a shrewd expression indicative of wits sharpened by life. These boys walked the streets for fourteen hours a day and more selling papers for the various companies in town.

When everyone was seated volunteers placed before each guest a plate of roast beef and vegetables, plum pudding and other dainties. The boys were served first, then the seated ladies and gentlemen. The boys ate with enthusiasm. Even Young Bob, who was presumably full of scones, ate everything put before him. When the appetites of the young men were appeased a gentleman in a neat suit stood up to speak. He explained that the purpose of the Boys' Brigade was to bring boys engaged in the newspaper business together and provide them with a sense of camaraderie and healthy entertainment. It was not exactly a club or a night school but a place where they would find amusement, sympathy, help and instruction and the cultivation of pride.

Brigade Boys could aspire to the rank of sergeant and they wore badges so the public learned to deal with them in preference to others. He explained there was a drum and fife band, and the boys participated in weekly trips to the Victoria Baths in Roma Street. Eventually, they planned to establish a rifle brigade. When the speaker ended his speech, the boys applauded.

A gentleman seated to the right of Rita leaned over to her and declared how much he admired the concept of the Boys' Brigade and had consequently donated a monthly stipend to contribute to costs.

Rita smiled at the man, then leant toward Hamish and said quietly, 'I've seen girls on the street selling papers, I wonder if they can join this Boys' Brigade?'

'They cannot,' said the man sitting at the other side of her. He raised his eyebrows as he continued, 'in fact, the committee is seeing what can be done to prevent girls from becoming news runners at all.'

Rita's own eyebrows arched as she turned to him. 'Really, sir? Why so?'

The man scoffed. 'To a family in strained circumstances,' he said, 'and in which there are no boys, the earnings of a girl by newspaper calling may be welcome but surely the girl runs too great a risk of injury both socially and morally.'

'I'm sure there are vocations that pose a greater risk to girls than selling newspapers,' said Rita curtly.

Hamish put his head down and braced himself.

The man did not back down. 'The street is not the proper place for a girl and the practice of news running cannot fail in the majority of cases to have a coarsening effect. Either by remonstrance with the parents or by finding the girls more suitable employment, the committee may successfully deal with this matter and I hope the public will render their assistance by buying their papers from boys only. It may go against the grain for a kind-hearted person to refuse a paper from a girl but taking all the probabilities into account, it is better in the girl's interests that this be done.'

Rita was sitting upright, her back straight, her chin high and her face as dark as thunder.

'What else would you have these poverty-stricken girls do? Would you force them into prostitution?'

The man's eyes swelled to the size of saucers at the word 'prostitution' coming from a lady's lips. Young Bob appeared by Hamish's side.

'You came, sir,' he said, full of cheer.

Rita closed her mouth mid-sentence and the fellow beside her rose from his seat to seek more suitable company.

Young Bob unashamedly sat down in the vacated seat.

'Yes,' said Hamish. 'It was a wonderful dinner. I learned a great deal. Tell me about your friends.'

'That's Bluey over there, sir. He's me best mate. He's more my age. But I get on with Thomas Batten there. He looks out for us younger ones.'

Hamish locked his sights on the boy called Thomas Batten. He was one of the boys Foong May had named. He chatted to Young Bob for a short time, not taking his eyes off Thomas for a second. As the evening came to an end and people started moving away from the tables, Hamish saw Thomas and three other youths swagger toward the door. They were between the ages of fifteen and eighteen and full of confidence. Hamish nodded to Rita and they followed the boys out into the street. They caught up with them, congregated at the corner sharing out cigarettes.

'Thomas Batten, is it?' said Hamish to the oldest boy as he held out his hand.

A dark look came over Thomas's face and his eyes narrowed. 'Who wants to know?' he said, ignoring the outstretched hand.

'Doctor Hamish Hart. This is Doctor Rita Cartwright.'

'A lady doctor,' sniggered one of the other boys.

'I know,' said Rita. 'It seems unlikely, doesn't it? Still, here I am.'

Hamish was defiant. 'Doctor Cartwright graduated from the London School of Medicine for Women.'

Rita smiled at the boys. 'It's true,' she said.

The boys seemed to warm to her a little but they remained suspicious of Hamish.

'I want to ask you boys about the night my friend was killed,' he said.

'We're not involved in no killing,' said the boy who had sniggered earlier.

'I know,' said Hamish quickly. 'I was hoping you might have seen something. It was the night of Tuesday the twenty-second.'

'I was at home in bed,' said one of the other boys.

There was a flash in Thomas' eye and his bearing changed. Hamish stared hard at him and he stared back. Neither shifted for a moment, then Thomas looked away first. He flicked his half-smoked cigarette onto the road.

'We're done here, Mister,' he said. The boys all turned to continue up the street.

'Wait,' said Hamish. 'I'm not interested in making trouble for you. I only need to know if you saw anyone around the furniture warehouse in Elizabeth Street that night,' he called out.

The boys stopped and glanced at one another.

'There was someone,' said the snigger boy. 'Not that I'd swear to it in court but it were strange, like.'

'We all saw it.'

Thomas nodded.

'It was like a shadow,' the first boy said. 'It ran, graceful like, from that direction. More animal than human. All in black. Face covered and everything.'

'Gave us a start, it did,' said a second boy.

Hamish looked at Thomas. 'It's true,' he said. 'About ten o'clock.

Definitely came from Elizabeth Street.'

'Which way did the figure go?' asked Hamish.

'Can't rightly say,' said Thomas.

'It just disappeared, like,' said snigger boy.

'Just like that,' added Thomas. 'Puff.' He demonstrated with a flourish of his hands.

The boys laughed as they sauntered off along the street.

Hamish hailed a cab. 'At least we have a time,' he said as he and Rita climbed in. 'It fits with the necropsy finding.'

'I've been thinking,' said Rita, 'most of the Chinese community was at the Joss House opening that night. Why not Ah Chit and Foong May?'

'I don't know,' said Hamish. 'I'd wager the boys expected Foong May to be at the opening. They thought they'd have a free run at her garden.'

'What do you make of this shadowy figure?' asked Rita.

Hamish's brow furrowed.

'An agile person,' he said, 'in a black costume, probably a balaclava. It fits with the use of a ceremonial sword and the assassination-style killing. It seems to me the killer is either Chinese or someone who wants us to think the killer is Chinese.'

'That doesn't help at all,' said Rita.

CHAPTER ELEVEN

Queensland has a Contagious Diseases Act – a damnable piece of hypocrisy. The Contagious Diseases Act is intended to keep immaculate and in a state of pristine cleanliness the male and female population of this great proud land. So, once a week, Fanny is whitewashed by the local health officer and sent back pressed and clean to the environment of bawdyism. She is then supposed to retain the cleanliness until the following week. A big order surely in our alien-cursed communities. If any traces of a virulent disease make themselves manifest during that interval, after a cursory examination, the woman may be sent to the Lock Hospital where she reposes in graceful retirement until she is once again discharged with a clean ticket. If Fanny be good looking, she may hoodwink the doctor and escape inspection. When her term of incarceration is ended, after she has been pronounced free of disease, she may retire to her old haunts and her old life or go into domestic service. If Fanny escapes the eye of the health officer, there remains yet another alternative open to her. She may tally with a Celestial and help spread all the foul diseases in the calendar.

Truth. Sunday 30 April, 1889

Hamish woke the next morning to the sound of bacon sizzling. He dressed for church and joined Wallace in the dining room to find Red already crunching bacon rind, pleased with himself as he licked the grease clinging to his whiskers.

Wallace piled crispy bacon and poached eggs on Hamish's plate and placed a basket of freshly baked bread in front of him on the table. How Hamish enjoyed Sunday mornings. He enjoyed the leisurely breakfast before church. And he enjoyed the comradery of the churchyard before and after the service. The church service itself was irrelevant to him. He had his own relationship with God and his own way of communicating with him or her. He had no difficulty imagining God as a woman once Rita suggested the possibility to him. He understood the Bible as a set of stories providing humanity, or a portion of it, with lessons to live by. The Bible referred to a loving Father but Hamish could see no reason why the lessons wouldn't hold just as well if the benevolence were to spring from a maternal figure instead. Hamish believed in the teachings of Jesus. He believed in 'do unto others,' and 'love they neighbour,' but he found the dark images of the Old Testament more threatening than soothing and his own Minister's concentration on them more than was usual or necessary for a Presbyterian congregation. But he didn't find it difficult to ignore the sermon for the most part. He enjoyed being part of the church community and it was his habit to chat with his neighbours in the churchyard long after the service was complete.

Wallace and Rita did not attend church. Hamish knew that Wallace was unable to reconcile his life on the sea and the cruelties and prejudices he had experienced with the teachings of Christianity. Perhaps more importantly, Wallace always said that the relationship with a sea captain that had shaped his boyhood both intellectually and emotionally was not something he would ever be ashamed of. He was proud of the man he had become and would not have the church require shame of him. He assured Hamish that religion had nothing to offer him.

Rita, on the other hand, viewed the church as an institution built on hypocrisy and was vocal on the topic at every opportunity. She had been raised Catholic and it shocked her parents when, as an adolescent, she refused point-blank to attend church any longer. In the context of a long string of other deviances attributable to her youth, her parents considered this a minor example in comparison. Like every other way in which she rebelled, they told themselves she would grow out of it.

Hamish walked down Wickham Terrace and along Ann Street looking forward to catching up with Bellamy before the service. He wanted to tell him what the boys said about the shadowy figure. When he was in sight of the small stone church, he began scanning the congregation members milling about in front of the building. He saw Agatha Bellamy almost at once in conversation with two mature women who were both his patients.

He slipped between several women's voluminous bustles to reach her.

'Good day to you, Doctor,' said one of the women.

Hamish smiled at each of them warmly.

'It's lovely to see you, Hamish,' said Agatha who was used to addressing him by his given name.

'Exquisite morning for a walk, Doctor,' said the third woman.

'Yes,' agreed Hamish quickly, then put his head down so that his long fringe fell over his face. He was hoping to speak with Bellamy prior to the service.

'Is Bellamy here?' he asked Agatha from under his fringe.

Agatha pursed her lips. 'The sergeant has decided to spend the morning at the police depot, rather than in praise of the Lord,' she said, ensuring that everyone present could hear.

The women joined in a chorus of disapproval.

'He's not expected at church this morning at all?' asked Hamish.

'No. He is working. On the Lord's Day, if you please.'

Hamish was silent. It had not occurred to him Bellamy would not be there. He quickly excused himself from Agatha and her friends and made his way through the congregation to a chorus of calls from his friends and patients. 'Good day to you, Doctor,' 'What is the hurry?' 'You're going the wrong way, Doctor. Look, the Reverend has opened the doors.'

Hamish excused himself again and again as he went. When he was free of the churchyard, he almost ran up the hill to the police depot.

Sergeant Bellamy was in a fierce exchange with Pennyweather when Hamish entered the office.

'Bring me tea,' he barked when he saw Hamish. 'You'll have to make it two cups by the look of things.'

'Difficult morning?' asked Hamish.

'Come through if you must,' said Bellamy, ignoring the question.

Hamish followed the sergeant into the office and cleared folders from the chair so he had somewhere to sit.

'I'm getting nowhere on this case,' said Bellamy. 'I doubt we'll ever know who killed the Chinaman.'

'Ah Chit,' said Hamish.

Bellamy ignored the interjection.

'I wouldn't be surprised if the Chinese community got rid of him themselves. No one will ever talk, of course. Why are you here? Have you found something?'

Constable Pennyweather entered with a tray, a teapot and two mugs. He placed it on a stack of folders on the desk and retreated as quickly as he could, with a slight nod to Hamish on his way.

'Why are you not at church?' asked Hamish.

'Why aren't you?' replied Bellamy.

'I intended to go. When I arrived, Agatha said you were here. She's not impressed, as it happens.'

'I can't concentrate while this case is ongoing,' said Bellamy. 'I've half a mind to close it down. Unsolved.'

Hamish caught the sergeant's eye.

'What is it? What have you?' said Bellamy.

'All I've learned is that the four boys allegedly involved in the assault against Foong May, who incidentally were not snug in their beds on the night in question after all, saw a shadowy figure in black running from Elizabeth Street at ten o'clock. They won't attest to it in court, for obvious reasons,' said Hamish.

'Huh,' said Bellamy. 'That gives us a probable time at least. Did they see anything that could identify the figure?'

'Nothing,' replied Hamish. 'Said it was more animal-like than human.'

'What the hell does that mean?'

Hamish poured the tea when it seemed evident that Bellamy was not going to do it.

'Cream?'

The sergeant shook his head and took up the mug.

'What about you, you must have something?' said Hamish.

'Pennyweather was called out to a disturbance at the Nine Holes last night.'

Hamish sat forward in his chair.

'Constable on the beat sent for Pennyweather when he heard a report of women screaming. When Pennyweather met him at the Nine Holes, they went in and found Daisy and Kate going at one another. They were both out of their minds with opium and clawing at one another like tigers.'

'What was it about?' asked Hamish.

'Who knows? They're trouble, those two.'

'I like them,' said Hamish.

'You what?'

'I like them. Daisy is a strong woman. She's a survivor. Kate's just living the only life she knows.'

'Good Lord, you are a bleeding heart. Scratchley always says so.'

Bellamy drank his tea in one long draught.

'What's Ah Tay up to?' he asked.

Hamish sipped his tea slowly. 'I didn't see him yesterday.'

'The truth is,' said Bellamy, 'if something doesn't come up soon, this murder will go unsolved. I have no leads. No one in the Chinese community is talking, except to confirm that Sam Hung was at the Pearl all night. All I have is the sword, which every Chinamen in Brisbane had access to.'

'Most of the Chinese community were at the Joss House opening that night,' said Hamish.

'There's no way to tell who was and who wasn't is there?'

'Have you talked to Cy Wong?' asked Hamish.

'Yes. I talked. She sat there still as a cat staring at me. I brought in an interpreter but there was no response. Nothing.'

Something stuck in Hamish's mind. The sergeant had described Daisy and Kate as tigers and Cy Wong as a cat. Were these women animal-like?

'I wonder if Rita could get her to talk,' Hamish said out loud.

'The only consolation in this is that the Chinese community have not bristled in the way Scratchley feared. They've closed ranks. That's what leads me to think it was one of their own. Perhaps it would be best to leave the matter at that.'

Hamish's mind had wandered. He was recalling the boy he had admired so completely, the boy who walked with his uncle from Adelaide to Ballarat. Ah Tay had been a hero to Hamish at seven years old, unsure of himself and living in a transient camp of adults obsessed with gold. Ah Chit was the only relative the boy from Southern China had in the new world. If Hamish could help Ah Tay by finding out who killed his uncle, he would not hesitate to do so. The next thing to do was to meet with Ah Tay, then he would collect Rita and return to the Nine Holes.

'Thanks for the tea,' he said. 'I'll let you know if something turns up.'

'Remember our agreement. Tell me where you are going. If the Chinese want this kept to themselves, they won't take kindly to an outsider poking his nose around.'

'I'm going to Foong May's Tea House to find Ah Tay,' Hamish said.

He was halfway through the door when he turned back to the sergeant. 'What were you arguing with Pennyweather about?' he asked.

Bellamy rolled his eyes. He picked up a decorative gold pin and waved it at Hamish. 'One of the women dropped this last night,' he said. 'Pennyweather picked it up and brought it back to the station. Then he lost it this morning. Said he'd put it in the drawer but it was amongst that mess on his desk, the electrical bits and bobs he's always fiddling with. I told him to clean the mess up. An ordered desk leads to an ordered mind.'

Hamish glanced at the sea of papers on the sergeant's own desk as he walked back and took the pin. It was a dragon, a solid gold dragon on a long sharp stick, the kind women wore in their hair or their hats.

'Where would Daisy get something like this?' he asked.

'I imagine Ah Tay gave it to her,' said Bellamy. 'Or one of her other Chinese clients.'

KATE

Kate skirted Ah Chit's house and peered in through the window beside the back entrance. The gas light shone but she couldn't see anyone so she tapped lightly on the glass. Nothing. She knew Sam Hung was at the Pearl because she'd checked on her way past. Cy Wong usually left to go home before him. She must be here. Kate tapped again, more loudly. She thought she saw a shadow pass across the window, then the view inside was clear again. There was silence. Had she seen a shadow?

'Cy Wong,' she called in an exaggerated whisper.

She heard the smallest sound of movement from inside. Then the door opened a crack. Kate couldn't see the person who had opened it but she seized the opportunity to step inside. The door shut behind her and an arm caught her around the shoulders tucking her into a space beneath the staircase. Her pulse racing and her breathing heavy, she found herself face to face with Cy Wong.

'What are you doing?' she said in a strangled whisper. 'It's only me.'

Cy Wong was so close she could feel her heartbeat.

'What do you want?' said Cy Wong.

'I've had an argument with Daisy,' Kate said. 'Can I stay here tonight? I don't feel like smoking opium but if I stay with her, I will.'

Cy Wong visibly relaxed. 'Come,' she said, checking the door once more to be certain it was closed and no one would see them.

She led Kate up the polished wooden staircase and into an exotically furnished room. There was a couch with several layers of silk draped over it against one wall and a low square platform of bricks against the other. It had a thick mattress and appeared to serve as a bed. There were also two embroidered chairs in the room. Kate sat in one of them.

Cy Wong went to a small table that had a teapot and several cups. She poured green tea into two of them and passed one to Kate. 'I was having tea myself,' she said.

Kate held the cup in two hands and sipped slowly while she began to feel herself relax.

Cy Wong sat in the other chair and watched her.

'Will you listen to a story about my home?' Cy Wong said.

Kate nodded.

'My family was wealthy once,' she began. 'That has not been the case for a long time. My grandfather smoked opium. He gambled and gradually there was less and less money. When my grandfather died, what was left was divided between my father and his two brothers, and my grandfather's youngest brother. It wasn't much and these brothers had been raised to be proud. My father was at least a good cook. He made steaming millet cakes and carried them through the streets in a basket. His older brother Ah Chit hated that he peddled millet cakes. But it fed us. What Ah Chit disliked the most was that his older brother, the number one son, received the greatest share of my grandfather's money. Ah Chit resented this.'

Kate listened as she sipped the soothing tea.

'Look at my feet,' said Cy Wong, holding them up. 'See how large they are?'

Kate looked.

'At the age of three, my mother's feet were wrapped tightly with a long, narrow cloth bandage, forcing her toes under the soles so only the big toe stuck out. The bandage was tightened daily for years, squeezing the toes inward and arresting the foot's growth,' said Cy Wong, still admiring her big feet.

Kate screwed up her face and unconsciously wriggled her toes.

'I didn't have my feet bound as a child because I was stubborn, and my father took my side. Ah Chit insisted my mother bind them, telling her no one would marry me and they would be stuck feeding me forever. My mother tried. She bound my feet in warm bandages every day but I struggled and tore at them. The pain was unbearable. She tried again and again but I screamed and tore off the bandages every time. When they tied my hands up so I couldn't grab the bandages, I refused to eat for three days. My mother beat me. Still, I refused. Finally, my father intervened. He said if she loves her toes free so much, she can have them free. My mother cried for a week because the other women said she was neglectful. She died not long after that and I have always felt guilty, as though I killed her with my stubbornness. They say if a wild goose lands in your court, the family will have good fortune. But if a tame goose flies away to follow a flock of wild geese, the fortunes of your family will disintegrate. Not long before my mother died one of our geese flew off. My father said it was this that caused my mother's death, not my stubbornness.'

'I'm sure your mother died because she had smallpox or some other disease,' said Kate.

'But why did she get the disease?' asked Cy Wong.

Kate swallowed the last of her tea.

'The point is that I now understand that my mother loved me in the only way she could.'

Kate's eyes opened wider. 'Are you saying that Daisy put me on the game at twelve because she loves me?'

'How else was she to feed you?' Cy Wong continued. 'My grandfather's younger brother shared my grandfather's love of opium. He smoked until all the money was gone, then he sold his wife's silver hairpins, the only possessions she had, and continued to smoke. Then he sold their daughter and bought opium.'

'He sold his own daughter?'

'His wife was heartbroken. He took the child to the market and sold her.'

Kate felt sick but in her line of work she had come across European girls as young as six who had been sold by their desperate parents. It wasn't a singularly Chinese custom.

'I'm an adult now and I'm sick of it,' said Kate. 'I can't stand the belching red-faced men and I don't want to be a slave to the opium.'

'As an adult, you must choose your own path,' said Cy Wong.

Kate scoffed. 'Do women ever have the right to choose their own path?'

'I believe so.' Cy Wong admired her bare feet, stretching her toes.

'What will you do?'

'I owe Sam Hung for my passage out of China and for my keep,' she said. 'I will repay the debt. I also have a debt to repay in my own country. I will work for Sam Hung until this commitment has been met. Then I will be free to make a life of my own.'

'How will you live?'

'I will start a business, I think. This colony is not like my home. So much more can be done here. The Society will help me, just as they helped Foong May set up her business. I will make money to bring my father to Brisbane.'

'I have no idea what I would do if I left my life,' said Kate. 'There's going to be a time when Daisy can't work anymore. I'll have to take care of her as well as myself.'

They heard the front door open and close.

'We must sleep now,' whispered Cy Wong. She extinguished the light and motioned for Kate to join her on the brick bed. 'Quiet. He must not know you are here.'

Kate slept soundly for about two hours until the first rays of light filtered through the lace curtains. She climbed off the bunk without disturbing Cy Wong and tip-toed down the stairs. She left through the back door without making a sound.

HAMISH

Daisy opened the door at the back of the cellar and blinked as the light poured in. 'You again,' she said as she stepped aside.

Hamish and Rita entered, noting the clean made beds and the folded clothes in a trunk at the end of each. There was a slight mustiness but no truly offensive odour as before.

'I came to return this,' said Hamish as he handed Daisy the pin.

Daisy's eyes widened. 'Where'd you get it?' she demanded.

'Sergeant Bellamy. His constable picked it up last night. You must have dropped it.'

Daisy snatched the pin. 'Interfering sod,' she said. 'What goes on between a mother and daughter is no business of the police.'

'I was wondering about the pin,' said Hamish. 'Was it a gift from Ah Chit?'

Daisy's eyes narrowed. 'A gift from Cy Wong, as it happens,' she said.

'Someone alerted the police – about the argument,' said Rita. 'They have to investigate.'

'Ungrateful little bitch.' Daisy glared back toward her daughter. 'Thinks she's too good for the likes of her own mother. The woman who gave birth to her no less. Tore me whole body apart, giving birth to her. Wants to make something of herself, she does. Ha! What's she good for, you reckon?'

Kate's shoulders were slumped; her head was down and her hands were still in her lap. Her eyes were red and swollen. She clearly hadn't slept much.

'She's been out all night,' said Daisy. 'Not a thought for the worry she might cause her mother.'

'I came home to change my clothes,' said Kate. She wore a clean gown and her hair was tied back into a neat bun at her neck. Daisy was also dressed in what appeared to be her best day gown, at least it was her cleanest.

'Are you on your way out?' asked Rita.

'It's Monday, ain't it?' said Daisy.

'What happens Monday?' asked Hamish.

Rita signalled to him to be quiet.

Daisy laughed and pushed past him on her way out the door. Kate followed her and Hamish and Rita were left standing in the cellar alone. Hamish noted that the Chinese opium smoker was absent, at least. They followed the mother and daughter to the road where a cab was pulling to a halt, with four women inside, laughing and hollering.

One of the women called out the window, 'Get in then. It's time to be cleaned and pressed, haha!'

Daisy and Kate climbed into the cab and it rattled off, with a great deal of merriment, whooping and calling floating back as they went.

'What's that all about? Where are they going?' asked Hamish.

Rita sighed. 'The Lock Hospital,' she said.

The colour drained from Hamish's face. He should have known. The Lock Hospital was a twenty-two-bed ward at the Royal Brisbane. Its purpose was to service the prostitutes of Brisbane who, under an Act of Parliament were required to show up for a mandatory examination for venereal disease every Monday. Any woman behaving in a way that aroused suspicion could be referred by the police to a magistrate who could order that she be held at the Lock Hospital for examination and if necessary, treatment. Known prostitutes had to visit for check-ups weekly. A woman could be held in the hospital for up to three months.

'At least their health is monitored,' said Hamish, only half-convinced.

Rita shot him a look of disdain.

'What's the point of treating venereal disease in the women without treating the men?' she said. 'They send them back into the same infectious pool they came from.'

Hamish brushed back his hair with both hands. 'You're right,' he said. 'Wholly ineffective as a public health measure. More a moral indictment.'

'Exactly,' said Rita.

CHAPTER TWELVE

What brings you here, John Chinaman?
Why come to New South Wales?
Why do you sail when breezes fan
the north side of your sails?

Our native country scarce can hold
the increases of the year;
so we, allured by love of gold,
will try our fortunes here.

What do you bring, John Chinaman?
As offering of your heart?
To us who feed, protect your class
and let you rich depart?

We bring you smallpox for our land,
nay do not raise your ire,
we opium bring – a noble brand
and to your wealth aspire.

Published in the Punch, Sydney. July 1881

Hamish watched the trap carrying the women to the Lock Ward until it was out of sight, then began the long walk back through town and up the hill toward his home. His mind was reeling with pictures of Cy Wong working at the Pearl and what that might entail. Ah Tay was clearly desperate to remove her from her financial bond to Sam Hung and

Hamish couldn't blame him for that. As he reached the corner of Queen Street, Ah Tay materialised alongside him. It startled Hamish every time his friend appeared, emerging as he did out of nowhere.

The day was warm and Hamish faced a hot climb up Wickham Terrace, so he was happy to have the company, if his friend would walk with him. Hamish had a lot of questions but he was content to hold them back and enjoy the easy companionship for the moment.

'Apart from the terrible loss of your uncle, how do you find Brisbane?' Hamish asked his friend.

Ah Tay glanced around as though he was only seeing the place now. 'It's a small town,' he said. 'Rough. Uncivilised.'

'Small, as you say. But growing rapidly,' said Hamish, nodding toward the blocks of building works they were passing. 'They say the township will double in size over the next two years.'

'There is certainly plenty of work happening,' agreed Ah Tay. 'I fear the authorities are under the spell of a golden millet dream.'

Hamish watched his friend closely. 'What does that mean?' he asked.

Ah Tay glanced upward toward the sky. Hamish followed his glance and squinted in the glare. It was a colourless sky.

'A man takes a brief nap, while his host is cooking a bowl of millet. He dreams he is married to a beautiful wife and is immensely rich. When he wakes up, the millet is cooked but he finds he is still poor.'

Hamish was deep in thought analysing his friend's comments when he heard a *woosh* behind his ear and caught a glimpse of Ah Tay ducking and grabbing his head with both hands. A brick fell to the ground behind him and smashed into small pieces. Looking up at the building site they had just passed, Hamish saw two youths glaring at them, one still holding a brick, rolling it from one hand to the other, seeming to indicate he was willing to throw it if he deemed it necessary. Hamish turned his attention to Ah Tay who had kneeled on the ground to steady himself. A nasty cut was evident where the brick had hit Ah Tay's head and it was bleeding. Hamish took out his handkerchief and held it to the wound but the handkerchief was soon saturated.

'Go home, John Chinaman!' cried one of the lads. 'No one wants the likes of you here.'

Hamish kept one hand on the wound while he turned to shout at the larrikins. 'I'll be talking to your master.'

The boys laughed. 'He'll tell the Chink to get off as well,' called back the one with the brick.

An older man appeared behind the boys and placed a large hand on each of their shoulders. 'Come on, boys,' he said. 'Back to yer work.'

The boys turned around slowly.

'Nothin' to see here,' he called to Hamish. 'These boys are good workers. Been under my supervision all morning and I'll swear to it in court, if I have to. You and the Ching better move on, ain't no stragglers allowed on the work site.'

Hamish felt the rage rise in his chest but his training forced him to tend to the wounded party before he would allow himself the luxury of feeling affronted.

He supported Ah Tay to stand. 'That wound will require sutures,' he said. 'It's worse than the knock on the head I received at the Pearl. Can you make it up to the house? I can stitch the wound and dress it in my consultation room.'

Ah Tay nodded, then stumbled as he took his first step. Hamish peered around helplessly for a cab but there wasn't one in the vicinity. Passers-by kept their heads down to indicate they did not wish to become involved.

Hamish placed his shoulder under Ah Tay's arm and supported him as he walked. In that way they managed to stumble up the hill toward Hamish's house. Wallace met them a hundred yards on and slipped his arm under Ah Tay's shoulder, easing the weight on Hamish. 'I saw you coming from the kitchen window,' he said. 'What happened?'

'They threw bricks at him. For being Chinese.'

Wallace groaned. Together, they could provide more balanced support for the remaining few yards, which was just as well because Ah Tay was unconscious by the time they lowered him onto the couch in Hamish's consulting room. Wallace fetched boiled water from the kitchen while Hamish prepared his instruments. He gave Ah Tay a mouthful of laudanum before cleaning, stitching and bandaging the wound. It was less serious than Hamish suspected once the blood was washed away. Still, it required three stitches. Ah Tay drifted in and out of consciousness while Hamish worked, more in response to the laudanum than to the injury. Wallace sat alongside the Chinaman in case he or Hamish needed anything.

'I'm sorry for the ignorance of these people,' said Wallace when Ah Tay's eyes were open.

'Don't be sorry,' said Ah Tay. 'My people believe Europeans have more hair than monkeys, large ears and noses like anteaters and smell more awful than dead bodies.'

Hamish and Wallace laughed.

'You should go to the hospital for observation,' said Hamish.

'Don't be ridiculous,' said Ah Tay emphatically.

'Stay here, then. I'll observe you. You are likely concussed.'

'I'm not … what you suggest. It's nothing. I'm returning to the teahouse.'

'You shall travel by cab in that case,' said Hamish. He stepped out and saw that there were plenty of cabs waiting along Wickham Terrace. There were many professional rooms on the hill apart from his own and the occupants and their clients were frequently in need of transport. Hamish assisted Ah Tay to a cab and made his friend promise to lie down when he reached the teahouse. He warned Ah Tay he may suffer dizziness over the coming hours.

When Ah Tay was safely dispatched, Hamish was free to allow the rage to take hold. He couldn't abide the hatred that had grown against the Chinese. He couldn't remember such hatred on the minefields as a child. Or had he simply been unaware of it? He knew the European miners would not allow Ah Tay to sell his vegetables within the European camp but it didn't matter because their wives went to the Chinese sector to buy the vegetables. Hamish's own father spoke highly of Ah Chit and the Chinese workers. It occurred to Hamish that his father was an opportunist. If he saw an opportunity to exploit the Chinese, he would take it. Was Ah Chit helping his father to exploit his own people? Hamish felt a sudden rush of blood to his face that made him suspect he may be right. He shook off the troubling realisation and reminded himself that despite the complicated relationship between his father and Ah Chit, his own relationship with Ah Tay, as a child, was pure. They were friends. Hamish was a lonely boy in a world of adults intent on finding gold and Ah Tay was his friend. His resolve to find out who killed Ah Chit was solidified. He would do this one thing to repay the friendship that had meant so much to him as a child.

KATE

Sweat gathered on Kate's brow. The air was always heavy with moisture in January, even when the sun was shining. The sky, which should have been a dazzling blue at this time of year, was white. Not actually white, more devoid of colour. It hung close around her shoulders. She tucked a curl of moist hair behind her ear. What was taking the others so long? If only the carriage would return, she could sit inside it.

'Good morning,' came a cheerful voice from the road. Rita was stepping out of a handsome carriage. She instructed the driver to wait and headed toward Kate.

'Good morning,' said Kate. 'I'm waiting for Daisy and the others.'

'Oh, I see,' said Rita. 'I'm here to collect pharmacy supplies. They are always delivering them to the Royal Brisbane Hospital instead of the Lady Bowen.'

Kate smiled.

'It's awfully hot standing here,' said Rita. 'Why don't you walk with me? It will only take a minute.'

Kate nodded and stepped into the building with the doctor, finding it several degrees cooler within the brick walls. Rita collected her package and led Kate into a sitting room at the front of the building.

'We'll see your mother when she comes out from here,' she said, pointing to a large sash window.

Kate sank into the leather chair and breathed in the comforting smell of leather with a hint of the inescapable odour of carbolic from the hospital ward.

'What is it you dream about for yourself?' asked Rita.

Kate opened her eyes, realising only at that moment they had been closed.

'I dream of living in a house with chairs such as these,' she said, patting the leather arms.

Rita laughed.

'What are you doing inside your home with comfortable leather chairs?' asked Rita.

'I write,' she said. 'I sit at my oak desk and write my thoughts, my stories, the stories of others.'

Kate saw that Rita was surprised by her answer.

'My stepfather taught me to read and write,' she said. 'Daisy was with him for twelve years, from when she was with child. He agreed to take care of both of us. He was the kindest man I've known. He bought books and taught me to read and write in the evenings after work. He was so tired but though his hands would tremble from the effort, he held them around mine, a pencil placed between my thumb and forefinger, and taught me to write letters. He read to me while Daisy slept. She said he was wasting his time. But he always smiled at me and said that learning was never wasted. He passed away when I was twelve. I haven't felt safe since. Daisy returned to the game and soon I was working as well. Young, pretty, I was able to command a decent price and Daisy saw the opportunity.'

'What work did your stepfather do?' asked Rita.

'He worked on the railroad. His father was a convict but he worked on the railroad as well, a ticket of leave man. It was a difficult life, my stepfather was away a lot but he always came back with a purse full of coins for Daisy and time for me.'

'Has Daisy ever spoken of your real father?'

'She said he was a trick, a customer. She said she was young and didn't know how to protect herself. I don't care who he was. I had a father growing up. He was more father to me than Daisy was a mother.'

Rita sighed.

'I've wanted to get away for a while,' said Kate. 'I tried once. A customer offered to set me up in a place of my own. I suppose that's not getting away, is it? Anyway, Ah Chit had me beaten. I was a mess, black and blue with the bruises. The man was scared away and I never saw him again. Daisy says Ah Chit did a lot for us but I hated him. Ah Chit treated everyone as a means of making money. He exploited everyone, even his peers in the Sheathed Sword.'

Rita raised an eyebrow. 'The Sheathed Sword? How did he exploit them?'

Kate went on as if she hadn't heard.

'Ah Chit was a thug, a bully. I hate bullies. You know, we were attacked on the way to the Nine Holes on the night of the raid. They went for Daisy. Bullies always go for the most vulnerable in the group. They didn't have time to collect their senses when I belted one of them. I jumped on the back of the one holding Daisy but I'd have been in trouble if Cy Wong had not been there. There was three of them, you see. Cy Wong sped in like a whirling dervish and put an end to them. The men skulked off toward the river.' Kate let out a low sound, not quite a laugh.

'Tell me more about Ah Chit and the Sheathed Sword,' asked Rita.

At that moment, Kate noticed movement through the window. The carriage had returned for the working women and the first of them was climbing in. Daisy was looking up and down the street, presumably for Kate.

'I have to go. We're going to the Shamrock Hotel. Will we see you there?'

'Of course,' replied Rita. 'I'll drop this off at the Lady Bowen and meet you there.'

CHAPTER THIRTEEN

There is no doubt that there is a most serious outbreak of smallpox in Sydney and although the authorities have shown promptitude and sound judgement in the measures they have taken to prevent the spread of the disease, it is too much to hope that their efforts will prove to be entirely successful, as the infected persons before being quarantined had mixed very freely with other people. Then it must be bourne in mind that the malady did not appear only in one house or in one street or neighbourhood but broke out in various parts of the city and suburbs almost simultaneously. Where the infection originally came from has yet to be discovered but it spread rapidly and soon made itself felt in localities widely separated.

On the 26 November, the first case was reported, the patient being a man who was at once removed to the hospital ship Faraway. Within two or three days from his removal, he developed true variola in a rather severe form, so his wife and children and a servant girl were all removed to quarantine. Last Friday, a lad, eighteen years of age, was found to be suffering from smallpox and on the same day two more cases were discovered, both children. Within the next 48 hours, eleven more cases were reported and in connection therewith 57 persons were quarantined in their houses. It is hardly likely that the sanitary authorities have yet succeeded in quarantining all the infected persons and for some time to come they will keep the most careful watch for fresh appearances of the disorders. The public have yet to receive a full history of this outbreak of one of the most loathsome and fatal maladies known to humanity; to learn when and where it made its first appearance. It may be taken for granted the plague was brought in from some vessel probably from a Chinese port.

The Telegraph, Adelaide. Wednesday 3 December, 1884

Infectious laughter emanated from the closed-in veranda as Hamish approached the Shamrock Hotel. He found himself smiling as he peered through the close latticework at the cheerful group inside. There were seven of them, including Rita. He recognised Daisy first then saw Kate beside her on the bench facing the door. Another bench stretched along the table on the opposite side with four more women crushed together, their skirts creased at their laps. They raised their glasses to a toast but Hamish could not hear the words. He braced himself to be the only male among a group of women, yet again.

Rita noticed him immediately as he stepped onto the veranda.

'Over here,' she called, as if they weren't already making enough noise to draw attention to themselves.

He wriggled onto the bench while Daisy, Kate and Rita slid further along to make room for him.

'A pot, please,' Hamish told the boy collecting the glasses.

The women all shouted for another and Hamish wondered how long they had been at the hotel and whether they'd had enough already. The hotel was crowded both inside and on the closed-in veranda where he sat with the working women. He noticed the men inside casting knowing glances their way. They poked one another with their elbows, made lewd gestures and laughed so hard, a couple almost fell from their stools. Hamish felt his head swimming from the smell of hops, yeast and cigarette smoke. Why did people enjoy these places? As he watched his companions, it was clear they were having a good time. Their faces were flushed and their eyes as bright as the sound of their voices.

'Where've you been, then?' asked Daisy as Hamish took his first mouthful of the frothy brew deposited on the table in front of him.

'We thought you'd be here at three with our girl.' She winked at Rita.

'I've been at the police depot,' said Hamish.

'Have you found out who killed Ah Chit?'

The women stopped chattering to listen.

'No,' he said.

'Wish I knew who killed my Chinaman,' said Daisy. 'I'd have a go at him meself. Not the same doing business with that Sam What's-'is-name.'

'Shut up, Mother,' said Kate. 'Ah Chit wasn't "your Chinaman". He was taking advantage of both of us. I'm getting out now he's gone.' She lifted her glass.

'Don't start that bullshit again,' snapped Daisy. 'We had that out the other night. Y'er going nowhere, my girl. Don't know y'er place, that's y'er trouble.'

Kate's face deepened in colour. Her lips were pressed into a tight line. The rage inside her was building and the pressure would soon have to be released. The thought of what form that release might take made Hamish uneasy.

The other women remained quiet for a moment. Hamish assumed they were waiting to see if Kate would respond. He sensed they also anticipated an explosion if the tension were further stretched. Then one of the younger women spoke. 'We're not going to argue, are we? Not after the poking and prodding and cleansing we've had today? Who'd want to leave the game?'

She laughed and the others joined in. Except for Kate. Kate didn't laugh. She stared into her drink then put the glass down without taking any.

Daisy shoved her playfully with her shoulder. 'Go on, drink up,' she said. 'We're working tonight. It'll take the edge off.'

The women laughed again.

Hamish noticed that Rita was watching Kate closely. He could see Kate was troubled but none of the other women seemed willing to confront the tension head-on. They continued to enjoy the beer and the cheerful teasing, even while Kate drew further and further into herself. Rita glanced at him from over her glass and he lowered one brow and shifted his eyes from Rita to Kate and back again with a slight nod of his head. He wanted her to bring the conversation back to Kate's resolution to leave her current work. Rita used her eyes to tell him that she would not do so. It was as good as a resounding 'no', even though she didn't utter a sound. Hamish received the message and kept quiet.

The topic of conversation soon turned to a raucous stream of imaginings regarding the male doctor who had examined the women earlier. They speculated on the size and efficacy of his sex organs, making Rita screw up her face in disgust. Hamish went a deep shade of fuchsia. He was fearful the topic would shift to his own attributes and was greatly relieved when Daisy sculled the last of her beer and announced they had to go. She and Kate shuffled along the bench and stood with the rest of the party following almost immediately. The women scattered in various directions with friendly slaps on the behind and waved kisses.

'Shall we walk?' asked Rita, her skin glowing from the beer and the laughter.

'Certainly,' said Hamish. 'It is a delightful evening for a walk.'

They enjoyed the space of the street for a few minutes after the claustrophobic sensation of the crowded hotel. Walking away from the heavy scent of spices that emanated from the open doors of the big warehouses and from the creaking hulls of the ships docked at the wharf with their cargo of wool departing for the looms of West Riding, they continued toward Queen Street. Behind them, heavy drays churned up the road from the dock. As they turned from Edward into Queen Street they met with a throng of shoppers and businessmen completing their day's business and rushing home for supper. The sidewalk was almost impassable at this hour, on this main thoroughfare of Brisbane. It was a single surging mass of jostling human beings, numb to the scene around them, simply moving with the crowd because resistance would be futile anyway. The population was growing too quickly, the sidewalks were too narrow and the carriages on the road too many.

'Kate did not look happy this evening,' said Hamish as they pushed their way into the crowd heading toward Wickham Terrace. Once they were in the stream of movement, they simply had to keep pace.

Rita's brow furrowed. 'No. She has had an argument with Daisy, it seems.'

'I believe the argument between Daisy and Kate came about because Kate has aspirations beyond her current occupation.'

'She does,' said Rita. 'Kate writes. She would like to write for the popular magazines.'

Rita slipped her arm through Hamish's and he held her tight so she didn't become separated from him in the jostling crowd. 'She's very clever, given her limited education. A long-term beau of Daisy's taught her to read and write when she was young. He died when she was twelve, apparently. It seems that it was after his death that Daisy put her to work. According to Kate, Daisy is no longer able to attract as many clients or as great a fee as she used to and they need the income Kate brings in to survive. This is especially so since they no longer enjoy the patronage of Ah Chit. Kate told me that Ah Chit had her beaten when she tried to leave her mother a year ago. He said he would find her wherever she went. Kate said she hated Ah Chit.' Rita tugged Hamish gently and led him across the street and to the left. They broke away from the throng and found themselves heading up the hill.

'I find I'm liking him less with every passing day myself,' said Hamish. 'As a child I admired Ah Chit but everything I'm hearing about him now seems to relate to an entirely different person.' Hamish stopped himself from expressing his next thoughts aloud. Could Ah Chit have changed so much? Or was his childhood memory really that skewed?

The first sting of a headache pierced Hamish behind the eyes. Every time he thought the clouds around this case were clearing, his vision became foggier. Still, he couldn't be sure the pain in his head was not brought on by the beer and the effort of carrying out a conversation while manoeuvring through the crowd.

'There's one more thing I have to tell you,' said Rita. It was quieter now they had left the main thoroughfare. But the hill was steep and Hamish felt his breathing become heavy. 'Cy Wong and Kate have become friends.'

'That's an odd combination,' said Hamish, gasping a little from exertion.

'Not really. They are close in age and both are headstrong. Kate told me she admires Cy Wong's strength. They were attacked the night of the raid, on the way home. Kate fought back but she said they would have been overwhelmed if Cy Wong hadn't stepped in.'

Hamish stopped in his tracks. 'Kate can fight?'

'Takes pride in it,' said Rita.

Hamish tilted his head to one side. 'Do you mean she threw her arms about to protect herself or do you mean she fought, properly fought?'

Rita scratched at her temple. 'Kate said that she threw herself onto the attacker's back to pull him away from her mother. She said she knew how to fight to protect herself and her mother. She seemed confident they would have been triumphant if they hadn't been outnumbered. Once Cy Wong stepped in, the fight was put to a rapid end. Cy Wong is apparently, exceptionally agile and strong, though she's small.'

They walked the rest of the way home in silence while Hamish thought about Kate and Cy Wong, both practised in physical combat and both with reason to hate Ah Chit.

Half an hour later, Hamish and Rita were seated at the kitchen bench watching Wallace knead dough. His big hands moved quickly and expertly. The terrier sat on a seat by the bench watching him closely, alert in case some dough magically came his way.

'I'm at my wit's end,' said Hamish. 'I am no closer to knowing who killed Ah Chit.'

'Go back to the beginning,' said Wallace. 'Tell me about each of the people surrounding Ah Chit before his death.'

'There are the employees at the factory,' began Hamish. 'However, they say they were treated well by him. No one there seems to have any reason to wish him dead.'

'Sam Hung profits by his death,' said Rita. 'And we now know he was unaccounted for at the time of the killing.'

'Sometimes the simplest explanation is the correct one,' said Wallace, pounding the dough.

Hamish brushed away a cloud of flour that rose in front of his face.

'There are plenty of people who had reason to wish him dead,' said Hamish. 'Foong May hated him. Although I doubt she'd have the strength to kill him herself.'

'The next step is to either build a case around Sam Hung as the killer or eliminate him,' said Wallace, passing a small blob of dough to the terrier. 'Find out where he was that night at ten o'clock.'

'Bellamy says he questioned him. He insists he was at the Pearl. Others maintain he was at the Pearl the whole evening.'

'If he wasn't there, someone will have seen him elsewhere,' said Wallace.

Hamish remembered the boys on the street selling papers. They said they saw a figure in black but no one asked them about Sam Hung. Even if the boys who raided Foong May's garden didn't see him, some of the others might have.

'Come on,' said Hamish, suddenly jumping to his feet. 'We're going to find the newspaper boys. If Sam Hung was out there, one of them will have seen him.' The terrier didn't shift his brown eyes from the dough now being thrown into ceramic bowls to rise.

Rita also eyed the fresh dough longingly.

'You can enjoy Wallace's fresh bread later,' said Hamish.

Rita grabbed her hat and gloves and followed him. 'We just climbed this wretched hill,' she said. 'Can't this wait until tomorrow?'

'No, it can't,' said Hamish. It was his turn to tug at her arm. 'No one has asked the boys if they saw Sam Hung in town that night.'

They walked back down to Queen Street first. It was quieter now that the crowd of shoppers and workers were snugly in their homes awaiting the evening meal. The night crowd were not yet out.

Queen Street was where most of the boys would be at this time of the evening, hoping to catch the workers on their way home. They would scatter throughout the remaining streets and Frog's Hollow later in the night when the revellers were leaving the pubs and gambling dens.

Hamish spotted Batten and Davy first. The boys greeted them enthusiastically and Hamish handed over a coin for a newspaper. 'Do you boys know a man by the name of Sam Hung?' he asked. The boys shook their heads.

'He's a Chinaman, is he, sir?' asked Thomas Batten.

'Yes,' said Hamish. He described Sam Hung as best he could.

'They all look the same to us, sir,' said James Davy, shaking his head.

'I need to know where he was the night of the incident at the tea house,' Hamish explained. The boys showed enough respect to blush.

'Young Bob might have seen him, sir. He knows just about everything that goes on in town.'

'Do you know where he is?'

Thomas screwed up his face. 'Wait a minute, weren't most of the Chinese at the Joss House that night?'

'That's why I thought someone might have noticed if he was in town,' replied Hamish.

'Hey!' James called out to a small boy at the next corner. He strode up to them.

Looking Hamish up and down, he said, 'He ain't a cop, is he?'

'Nah,' said Thomas. 'He's a doctor. He's looking for Young Bob.'

'Why? Is he sick?'

'No,' said Hamish. 'He's not sick. I'm wondering if any of you boys saw a Chinaman in town on the night of the Joss House Opening, around ten o'clock.'

'I didn't see one of 'em. I saw five of 'em. They went into that Chinaman's house. All secretive they were, kept the lights out until they was all in. Then I saw a candle in one of the rooms.'

'Which house?' asked Hamish.

'That one where the Chinaman lived. The one that was murdered. Chinese coming and going all the time at that place but that night they were definitely sneaking about, like I told yer.'

'Thank you,' said Hamish.

'Buy a paper, sir?' The boy held out his hand.

'I just bought one,' said Hamish, showing him the paper.

'That's the Courier,' said the boy. 'I got the Telegraph for yer.'

Rita gave him a coin and tucked the Telegraph under her arm.

'Do you think Sam Hung was one of the men who met at Ah Chit's house that night?' she asked.

'I don't know,' said Hamish. 'What I do know is that, if Ah Chit hadn't been killed, he would've been on his way home from the warehouse. Either they expected him to join them or they knew he would be dead already.'

The boy was on his way back to his corner when Hamish called out to him. 'Do you know where we can find Young Bob?'

He turned and pointed toward George Street. Hamish and Rita walked along Queen Street and turned right into George where they saw Young Bob in front of the Dunmore Arms Hotel on the opposite corner. He seemed pleased to see them and ready for a chat. He told them about band practice and his new drum. They all had new instruments funded by an anonymous benefactor. Hamish turned to Rita and read her smile.

'Do you know the Chinaman, Sam Hung?' asked Hamish.

'I know him. He runs the Pearl now Ah Chit is dead. Pa prefers him.'

Hamish blinked. He was expecting the boy to say he didn't know the man.

'Did you happen to see him about town the night Ah Chit died?' Hamish asked.

The boy didn't hesitate. 'He went to that meeting at Ah Chit's house. There were five of them – arrived together, left together. I tried to sell them papers but they was in too much of a hurry. Looked like they didn't want to be seen.'

'You're sure Sam Hung was one of them?' urged Hamish.

'Course I am, I told yer, didn't I?'

'Do you know what time they arrived and left?'

'I reckon it was just after nine they arrived.' He rubbed his chin. 'And about eleven when they left. They headed back to the Pearl.'

'Thank you,' said Hamish, handing the boy a coin.

'Which paper do you want?'

'None,' said Hamish. 'The coin is for the information. You have been very helpful.'

Hamish and Rita made their way back up the hill toward Wickham Terrace. This time Hamish was energised. He didn't notice the climb and his breathing came easily however there was a rise in his blood from the excitement.

'Sam Hung could not have killed Ah Chit after all,' said Hamish.

'That doesn't mean he wasn't behind the killing,' said Rita. 'All those men could have had something to do with it. They could have hired someone.'

'The patrons at the Pearl said that Daisy and Kate were there until midnight when they left for the "rooms" with their clients. They also say Cy Wong was present all night, until four o'clock in the morning when the place closed. Apparently, she usually leaves before Sam Hung but this night she locked up after the last of the patrons left,' said Hamish.

'Maybe you should suggest to Bellamy that he interview the patrons again. They all said Sam Hung was there all night but if a specific timeframe is mentioned, they may reconsider,' said Rita.

KATE

It was early in the morning for Kate to be up and about. She stood on the balcony of the Lady Bowen Lying-In Hospital waiting. Young women in starched uniforms hurried by. The balcony provided a shortcut between the wards. One of the girls, no older than Kate, agreed to inform Doctor Cartwright of her presence. Kate squeezed her hands together while she worried about how the doctor would greet her. She wondered if she would think she was wasting her time. Maybe she was. Maybe it was rude to turn up unannounced at her workplace but she didn't know what else to do.

She had considered doing nothing but that didn't seem viable. If she was wrong, it would be a small case of embarrassment. If she was right and she did nothing, she would be negligent.

As soon as Doctor Rita Cartwright stepped onto the veranda and Kate saw her beaming face, she knew she had done the right thing. The doctor put out a hand and greeted Kate warmly. 'I'm so glad to see you,' she said. 'Come. Sit down in the shade.' Rita led Kate to a table and chairs that were under the shade of the roof but still on the veranda. 'There's a cool breeze here,' she said. 'It is where I sit for my morning break.'

Kate folded her skirt beneath her as she sat.

'What can I do for you?' asked Rita.

Kate wrung her hands on her lap.

'I'm not sure,' she began. 'You see, I've only seen it once before and I might be wrong … I was very young …'

'Seen what?' asked Rita.

'The marks,' Kate said. She was struggling to find the words to describe what she wanted to report. 'There is a boy living in Albert Street,' she began again. 'Down by the river, near the wharf. Actually, the house is more on a lane that comes off Alice Street. He's about ten, I think. He plays with the other children. I often see him and I give him a sweet if I have one. Sometimes the punters give me sweets,' Kate explained.

'Lucky you,' said Rita.

Kate was too busy running her story over in her head to acknowledge the comment. 'I haven't seen him for a couple of days and one of the other boys said he was poorly. Then, this morning he was out playing again, so I greeted him. That's when I noticed. He had red marks on his forehead and some of them had erupted into pustules. Not many, mind, two or three but it reminded me of something I've seen before. In Sydney, when I was very young.'

Rita's face became anxious.

'It might not be anything to worry about,' said Rita carefully. 'But, on the other hand, it might be very serious.'

Kate nodded.

'Did you speak to the boy's mother?'

'No. I didn't think she would appreciate hearing from me that her son might be infectious,' said Kate.

'Quite right,' said Rita. 'You've done exactly the right thing. Wait here, while I fetch my hat, then you can take me to the boy. We should pick up Doctor Hart on the way. He is more familiar with infectious diseases than am I.'

Within minutes they were in a cab and on the way to pick up Hamish. Rita went into the house and emerged with the doctor a moment later. The cab hurried toward the wharf. When they reached the end of Albert Street, where the corner of Queen's Park meets the road, they rattled to a halt.

'There are the boys,' said Kate. 'They're playing with stones in the gateway to the park.'

The boys looked up startled at being approached by three adults, only one of which they had ever seen before.

'Don't be afraid,' said Kate. 'I've brought these two doctors to meet you.'

The boys stood up slowly and angled away from her. The boy with the spots on his forehead brushed down his shorts with grimy hands and kept his head down.

'Good morning,' said Hamish cheerfully. 'Looks like a marvellous game you've invented.'

Kate could see the boys were unsure and likely to scarper at any moment. 'It's alright,' she said. 'I brought these two to meet you.'

'I'm Doctor Hamish Hart,' said Hamish, 'and this is Doctor Rita Cartwright.' Hamish directed himself to the boy with the spots on his skin. 'Kate tells us you have been poorly of late.'

'I'm good now,' said the boy.

'May I see your forehead?' asked Hamish, bending down to the boy's height. He used his handkerchief to brush away the boy's ginger hair. When he stood up again, his face was full of concern. 'This is smallpox,' he said. 'Without a doubt.'

'This boy must go into quarantine,' said Rita, 'as well as the other boys. Do you know where they live?' she asked Kate.

'I know where this boy lives.'

'Give us directions,' said Hamish. 'Rita and I will go there to speak with this boy's mother. You take the other boys home and tell their mothers to keep them indoors. Tell them someone from the Board of Health will visit soon.'

Kate gathered the boys together and asked if she could see their homes. 'It's a game,' she said. 'Who has the house with the biggest tree in front?' The boys glanced at one another.

'I do,' cried one of them. 'No. There's a Moreton Bay Fig in front of mine. No tree is taller than that,' said another. 'That's not in front of your house, it's all the way across the street. That doesn't count.'

The boys squabbled as they led Kate on to prove their various claims.

CHAPTER FOURTEEN

Put broadly, its [the Opium Bill] object is to stop the sale and use of opium otherwise than as a drug for medicinal purposes. This is a step that will commend itself to all save the poor besotted victims of its use and the few persons who profit from its sale.

The term opium is to include opium, laudanum and any preparation of either. The Act will place the sale of this drug and its compounds into the hands of persons registered under the Pharmacy Act of 1884, and of such other persons as answer the conditions set forth in the Act.

Every person must be licensed and must give pledge where it is proposed to be sold, and that he will only sell it for medicinal purposes. Possessing opium otherwise than as permitted by this Act will be contrary to law and will subject the holder to liability to be fined twenty-five pounds.

No apology can be permitted for doing things that are wrong in themselves, as is the selling of opium to be used as it is now by many Chinamen and others, and no sympathy will be felt for those who, in spite of the prohibitions of the law, persist in doing wrong.

The Telegraph, Brisbane. 10 August, 1886

Hamish and Rita picked their way through the front yard of a two-storey weatherboard house off a small lane that emerged from Alice Street. The houses in the area seemed to have been built in an earlier time before order was imposed on the street. A number of men and women were gathered on the balcony calling out to passers-by. They saw Hamish and Rita approach and went quiet.

'Is one of these people your mother?' asked Rita.

The boy shook his head. 'These are the boarders. Ma does the laundry and the cleaning and that. She'll be round the back.'

'How many people live here?' asked Hamish.

'Thirteen,' said the boy, 'including me and Ma.'

They stepped over a drain filled with stagnant water, rubbish and a decaying rat, and made their way to the back of the house. The small backyard had an outhouse in one corner and a pile of kerosene tins stacked in front of an old tumbledown shed in the other. There was a tub of dirty clothes in the shed and the water closet's stench filled the yard. Hamish braced himself against the stench. Behind a makeshift fence, another house backed onto the property. The door was open and a man was sitting in the doorway binding his foot. Behind him, inside the house, Hamish saw piled up dirty cups, plates and empty beer bottles. The wail of a baby floated across the yard from within the house.

'What're yer lookin' at?' said the man.

'We're looking for this boy's mother,' called Hamish.

'She ain't here.' The man struggled to his feet and slammed the door shut. The door hung on an angle from a single hinge and afforded him little privacy. Hamish was still staring into the house through the skewed door when a small woman stepped out from within the shed.

'I'm his mother,' she said. 'What's he done?'

Rita stepped forward and offered her hand to the woman. 'Nothing,' she said. 'We're here because your son is unwell. We're doctors.'

The woman looked from one to the other. 'He ain't sick,' she said, grabbing the boy by the shoulder and drawing him to her. 'And we can't afford no doctor.' She turned to step back into the shed and dragged the boy with her.

'Wait,' said Hamish.

She hesitated.

'The boy has smallpox,' he said.

The woman snapped her hands from the child as if he were a hot stove. 'He hasn't. It's a mild dose of chickenpox is all.'

'No,' said Hamish. 'It's smallpox, I'm afraid. I'm going to have to notify the Board of Health and your house will be quarantined. Everyone must stay inside.'

The woman's face paled.

'You can't order decent folks about and lock them in their houses.'

'I can't,' said Hamish. 'But the government can.'

'I'll sue the government,' she said, her voice getting louder. 'It's nothing but chickenpox. I'll sue. All the boys suffer chickenpox when they're young. It's best to have it young.'

'I'm sorry,' said Hamish.

'Get off my property,' yelled the woman. Her son skirted around her legs and stood behind her as she ran toward Hamish and Rita with her fists raised.

Hamish raised both hands, palms outward. 'Calm down. We'll leave you. The police will be back though.'

She rushed toward them but Hamish and Rita had already turned to leave. She stopped short.

When Hamish returned later in the morning, the Board of Health had been informed and the house was in quarantine. Hamish nodded to the constable standing in front of the house and stared up at the yellow placard with black lettering that read: *this house is infected with smallpox.* A shiver ran down his spine. He avoided a pile of decomposing potato peelings and cabbage leaves to get to the back of the building where there was an identical yellow sign and another policeman.

'Have you news about the status of the people in the house?' Hamish asked the constable.

The policeman nodded. 'Seven of the boarders have never been vaccinated against smallpox,' he said. 'And the remainder were vaccinated as infants and not since.'

'I will need to vaccinate them all,' said Hamish. 'I don't expect it to be an easy task.'

'It won't at that,' agreed the constable.

After two hours spent persuading and reassuring, Hamish left the house with his task accomplished. He was relieved to have had access to the animal vaccine, as he would never have been able to convince them it was safe otherwise. The newspapers were full of stories about the risks of transmitting syphilis through arm-to-arm vaccinations, even though it would be an exceptionally inexperienced or inept doctor who would mistake a syphilis infection for a smallpox one. Nonetheless, the vaccine he was using came from calves and was perfectly safe, as he told the boarders.

As he walked up Albert Street, past the Nine Holes, Hamish wondered if Daisy and Kate were vaccinated against smallpox. As the place was quiet, he imagined they were sleeping. Kate had been out early to report her suspicions to Rita. She would need to sleep until late afternoon when she'd begin to prepare for the evening's work. He made a mental note to return later and offer the vaccine.

Hamish caught a glimpse of Young Bob dashing across Elizabeth Street. 'Hoy!' called out Hamish.

Young Bob stopped at the call. 'Morning Doctor,' he said as Hamish approached.

'One of the boys who lives on Alice Street has smallpox,' said Hamish. 'I've just attended him.'

'Gorblimey,' said Young Bob.

'Have you been vaccinated?' asked Hamish.

'When I was a baby.' Young Bob pulled his shoulder around to show Hamish the scar.

'Good lad,' said Hamish. 'But it's best to have another vaccination at your age. Can you stop at my rooms for a moment this afternoon when you drop the papers off?'

Young Bob hesitated.

'It's perfectly safe,' said Hamish.

'It's not that,' said Young Bob. 'I have no money to pay.'

'Don't worry about that. In fact, bring the other boys with you, as many as you can convince to come. I'll wager many of them have never been vaccinated.'

'I'll do me best,' said Young Bob.

Hamish spent the rest of the morning sourcing sufficient vaccine to immunise all the boys in the Boys' Brigade, which wasn't a simple task because the calf-lymph vaccine was not easy to come by. He called in all favours owed him by other physicians and advised the Central Health Board members to do the same. He was genuinely afraid that the handful of cases identified that day could result in a spreading epidemic. Queensland had largely avoided the disease, while southern colonies were perpetually plagued with new and serious outbreaks. He didn't want this to be the beginning of a catastrophic outbreak in Brisbane.

Half a dozen boys came along with Young Bob at four o'clock and they thanked Hamish for seeing them for no payment. Hamish advised them to steer clear of the wharf end of Albert Street for a while because he couldn't be sure how many children were infected. It could be fourteen days before they would know. Hamish didn't allow his voice to reveal the inner panic that was rising. He was fearful an outbreak may be imminent. Someone infected the boy he had seen this morning and that person was moving freely about in the community. The only thing that could be done was to vaccinate.

Hamish received a telegram after the last of the boys had left. The telegram notified him that the Health Authorities had taken control of the situation and were visiting the houses in the area. Two additional cases had been identified, another in the same household as the boy and one in an adjacent property. They were not calling it an outbreak, as yet. The whole block had been quarantined and they hoped to have contained the spread. They thanked Hamish for his quick action. Hamish felt his ears heat up as it was Kate who noticed the first case and alerted Rita. Still, he was relieved the Health Department had taken action and his Boys' Brigade lads had been vaccinated.

KATE

Kate sat on the edge of the bed and spat blood into a chipped ceramic bowl. She felt the puffiness growing around her lips on the left side. One tooth was loose and she fussed around it with her tongue. She needed to save that tooth, it was near the front and her looks would suffer if she lost it, so she forced herself to leave it alone. There was no clean water in the room but she desperately wanted to wash the taste of blood from her mouth. The one consolation was the thick wad of notes she gripped tight in her palm. And the cry of pain she heard as she kicked the man who'd hit her, hard in his privates before she pushed him out the door, trousers still around his ankles. She promised herself this would be the last time. That's why she took the money from his coat. He didn't know she'd taken it when he hit her. That would be a surprise for him later. She needed the money to set herself up somehow, somewhere new maybe. She would not allow herself to think of Daisy.

Kate gathered her wrap, smoothed down her dress and fixed her hair.

Without water she couldn't do much about her swollen bloodied face but she would get away from this room. That fat pig of a man would be back once he realised she'd robbed him. He might go to the police but it would be difficult for him to point his finger at her for the robbery without admitting to being a customer. The police knew her as a prostitute, not a thief.

When she'd sufficiently restored herself, Kate stepped into the laneway that led back toward the Nine Holes. She let the thickness of the night wrap around her. Where the dark might be frightening to some women, Kate found it comforting. Her favourite hours were those between midnight and dawn. She relished the ninety or so minutes of peace that were sandwiched between the numbness of her work and the delirium of her opium habit. For about ninety minutes in each twenty-four hours, she almost felt safe, she could almost imagine not smoking the opium, not pleasing the red-faced belching hogs that were her customers. But once she reached the Nine Holes, the familiar odour would fill her lungs and her whole body would ache for the freedom of the pipe. Not this time, she decided. Not anymore. It wouldn't be long before the fat pig came looking for her anyway. She had to be somewhere he couldn't find her.

Kate entered the cellar and saw Daisy sprawled across her new bed, face-down on the pillow. There was a damp patch where she had drooled. Daisy's peaceful face sent a wave of emotion through Kate. It might have been pity, it might have been love, she wasn't sure. Perhaps it was a combination of both. She wrapped her few dresses and underclothes in one of the clean sheets Rita supplied and left. The first rays of light were piercing the clouds now and the sky was more grey than black behind them. There was a small breeze lightly touching the skin on her arms and goose bumps appeared, not from the cold but from anticipation.

Kate walked along the river with her few possessions tucked under her arm, listening as the water lapped quietly at the bank. The river was as dark as ink and Kate imagined herself slipping silently into its depths and ceasing to exist. As she turned onto Victoria Bridge a breeze blew the clouds further east and a sliver of moonlight rippled and danced across the surface of the water. The cool breeze brought new energy to her soul. It wouldn't be much further once she stepped off the bridge. She hadn't seen another person on her journey and she was glad of it; she hoped she would continue to be alone as she travelled the last mile to her destination.

Kate trembled as she strode up the staircase at the front of the weatherboard house with the plaque saying 'Thalia'. This had to be the right house. She almost turned back, the yearning to lose herself in the familiar was almost too much to overcome but she willed herself forward. She tapped lightly at the door and was surprised when a middle-aged woman in her nightgown answered almost at once. Kate didn't know what to say but it didn't matter because the woman stepped aside and motioned for her to enter. No questions were asked as she took her things and indicated for Kate to follow her into a well-appointed bedroom at the front of the house. She put her fingers to her lips to let Kate know she did not want her to speak. There were others in the house, mothers and children, Kate expected, who did not need to be disturbed. Kate smiled while the woman held both her hands in hers and squeezed. Then the woman left, closing the door behind her.

Kate curled up on the bed, fully clothed and cried herself to sleep. The tension of six years on the game was released. Anxiety about the future had not yet set in.

At nine o'clock Kate heard a light tapping on her bedroom door. She'd been woken from a deep sleep and felt slightly nauseous. She was initially surprised to find herself in the bright airy room with the window overlooking a wide veranda. Then she felt a throb in the side of her face and the sting in her lip and she remembered the violence of the evening before and her decision. She panicked. In the light of day, the decision seemed too drastic. Why had she acted so rashly? Why had she not slept off the pain like she always did? The damage to her face would take but a few days to heal. She feared the damage to her soul would never heal. She had to regain her dignity, her sense of her own worth. She mustered all the determination she could and opened the door.

'Good morning,' said Rita, handing her a basket of steaming currant buns. 'I picked these up from the doctor's. It'll amuse you to know they were to be the doctor's breakfast but Wallace gave them to us.' She chuckled.

Kate took the basket and sat back on the bed.

Rita examined Kate's lip gently. 'I have some ointment for that.'

Kate took a bun from the basket and nibbled at it from the other side of her mouth. Rita sat on the bed and ate also. Neither woman spoke until the basket was empty.

'There is always a kettle on the boil in the kitchen,' said Rita. 'Make tea whenever you like.'

Kate smiled.

'I have to go to work. If you need anything let Mrs Townsend know. You are welcome to stay as long as you like.'

Kate put her hand under her pillow and pulled out a leatherbound journal about the size of her palm. The cover was well worn and the edges of the pages were uneven. She handed it to Rita without saying a word.

Rita accepted the book. 'Do you want me to read it?' she asked. 'Or do you want me to keep it safe for you?'

'Read it,' said Kate quietly.

Rita nodded. 'I'll return this evening to see how you are settling in,' she said. 'The evening meal is at seven. You will meet the other guests then if you haven't done so already. I will join you.'

CHAPTER FIFTEEN

A Chinese Secret Society. A recent Consular report from China describes the origin and working of a notorious secret society called the Kalao Hui, which for many years past has given much trouble and which quite recently caused much commotion in Nankin and its neighbourhood. This Kolao Hui is described as a society somewhat resembling the Socialists of Europe and much dreaded by the people of China. It originated during the Taiping rebellion among the soldiers in Human for the purposes of affording aid to the wounded soldiers and the families of men killed in service. The Human men serve all over China and their mutual aid society spread by their assistance over the whole country. The aims of the society developed with its growth and a sentiment of equality of worldly possessions and position became prevalent among its members.

The Braidwood Dispatch and Mining Journal, NSW. Wednesday 24 April, 1889

Hamish opened his eyes and breathed in the aroma of fresh currant buns. He washed and dressed quickly, eager to enjoy breakfast and head over to the police depot. He finally felt as though he had some useful information to share with Bellamy, which may lead them to the killer.

He sat at the kitchen table and Red sat himself at his feet. This was his position every morning during breakfast. He would sit patiently, staring up at Hamish with large brown eyes and wait for the treats to come.

'Good morning, Red,' said Hamish, patting back the long hair above the terrier's eyes. 'Currant buns for breakfast this morning I'd say, judging from the aroma coming from the oven. Our favourite, my friend.'

Wallace came in with a tray of buttered toast and local honey. 'Sorry, no currant buns. I gave them to Rita to take to Kate.'

'Excuse me?' said Hamish.

Red glared at him. The hair behind his eyes stood upright from his head then curled forward across his brow.

'Rita called in on her way to the house at Milton. Kate turned up in a state in the early hours of this morning. It seems she has made her decision to leave. I felt so excited for Kate on her momentous decision, I handed over your breakfast.'

Hamish forgot all about the buns. 'I'm happy for Kate,' he said. 'It will be a difficult road ahead. I hope she is ready to travel it.'

Red had not forgotten about the aromatic promise of currant buns. When Hamish handed him a corner of toast, he sniffed it disdainfully and wandered off.

'A poor substitute indeed,' said Hamish. 'I don't blame you.'

After breakfast, Hamish put on his hat and coat and caught a cab to Petrie Terrace.

Bellamy was sitting behind a mountain of paperwork as always when Hamish joined him in his office. There were several empty coffee mugs among the papers.

'Good morning to you,' said Hamish. 'You appear to be struggling with this administrative work.'

Bellamy looked up at him from beneath lazy eyelids. It often seemed he hadn't slept enough.

'What with the general policing, the water police and the native police to report on, I'm forever writing bloody reports,' said Bellamy.

Hamish felt the smallest tinge of concern for his friend's health.

'Sit down, if you can find somewhere to sit,' said the sergeant.

Hamish moved a stack of papers from one of the chairs in the room.

'Have you information to share?'

Hamish told Sergeant Bellamy about his informants within the Boys' Brigade.

'I suggest you ask the two men who were arrested at the Pearl where Sam Hung was at precisely ten o'clock on the night Ah Chit was killed. While you are at it, you might also enquire further into the whereabouts of Kate and Cy Wong at ten o'clock on the night of the murder,' he added.

Bellamy tapped his pencil against his chin. 'Do you know something about Sam Hung's whereabouts?' he asked. 'Sam Hung is our prime suspect.'

'One of the boys says he saw Sam Hung at Ah Chit's house at ten o'clock,' said Hamish. 'They say five men went into the house.'

'And Sam Hung was one of them?'

Hamish nodded. 'The boy is certain of it.'

Bellamy continued tapping his pencil. 'Why did the patrons say he was at the Pearl?'

'Perhaps they assumed he was there the whole evening,' suggested Hamish.

'You are correct. We need to talk to them again,' said Bellamy. 'Pennyweather,' he shouted.

The constable appeared at the door.

'Fetch the interpreter and bring back the two workers who were detained during the raid at the gambling house,' he ordered.

Pennyweather scuttled off with his instructions and Hamish and Bellamy settled in to wait.

When everyone was in place, Hamish and Bellamy sat on one side of the desk while the interpreter sat to one side and the two men to be interviewed sat opposite. They had shaved heads except for their long black pigtails.

'We want to ask you again about the night Ah Chit was killed,' explained Sergeant Bellamy. The interpreter repeated what Hamish hoped was an accurate translation. The men both looked at the interpreter with blank faces. Hamish found the men difficult to read, just as he did Cy Wong and his friend.

'Was Sam Hung at the Pearl the whole time, on the evening of Ah Chit's death?'

The two men looked at one another.

'Perhaps we should speak to them separately,' suggested Hamish.

'You must tell the truth,' prompted Bellamy. 'It will not go well for you if you do not.'

'We already have witnesses who say that Sam Hung was seen entering Ah Chit's House that evening.'

One of the men leant forward toward Bellamy and spoke in Chinese. Bellamy's attention shifted to the translator.

'He was not at the Pearl between nine o'clock and eleven o'clock,' said the translator.

'Who was not at the Pearl?' asked Bellamy.

The interpreter confirmed with the man that he was referring to Sam Hung.

The second Chinese man looked terrified.

'Is that your recollection also?' said Bellamy.

The man nodded.

'Why did you say that Sam Hung was at the gambling house all evening?' Bellamy said.

The men looked at their hands and mumbled.

Bellamy looked to the interpreter who appeared confused himself.

'They thought he was at the gambling house all evening. Now, they think they may have been mistaken. Apparently, he was not seen by them specifically between the hours of nine and eleven.'

Bellamy groaned. 'Lord, give me patience,' he said. Then he started again with his next question.

'The two women, Daisy and Kate Walton, were they at the Pearl at ten o'clock that evening?'

Both men nodded emphatically.

'What time did they leave?' asked Hamish.

The two men spoke simultaneously in Chinese.

'They say midnight,' said the interpreter.

'Are they certain of the time?' prompted Bellamy.

They both nodded.

'What about Cy Wong? Where was she at ten o'clock?'

The interpreter repeated the question. One of the men answered immediately, the other faltered.

'Well?' said Bellamy.

The interpreter said something in Chinese and the men responded.

Hamish and Bellamy leant forward in their seats.

'They have agreed that Cy Wong was at the Pearl all night. But before ten o'clock she took the evening's takings to the safe room. She was gone for no longer than thirty minutes.'

'Why didn't they tell us this before?'

'No one asked about Cy Wong's whereabouts at ten o'clock,' repeated the interpreter.

When they were alone again, Bellamy leant back in his chair, the two front legs tipped up off the floor and his head rested against the wall. 'Do you think Cy Wong had time to make her way to the factory, kill Ah Chit and return in half an hour?'

'It's possible,' said Hamish. 'I'd still like to know what those five men were up to at Ah Chit's house.'

'I'll bring Sam Hung back in. Why would he lie to us when he has an alibi for the time of the murder?' said Bellamy, losing his patience. 'Pennyweather,' he shouted.

The constable appeared at the door, with electrical wires hanging around his neck and a flat iron in one hand.

'What the devil are you doing?' said Bellamy.

'It's a flat iron, sir. There is a bed heated by electricity that warms the surface of the iron ...'

Bellamy shook his head and interrupted before the lad could dive into a lengthy explanation. 'Put the contraption down, Constable, and bring Sam Hung in for me. You might need to take a couple of constables with you – he may not want to come.'

Pennyweather's face paled visibly before he left the office.

Half an hour later Sam Hung was sitting before the sergeant and Hamish. Hamish was shocked that he seemed calm and unbothered about being brought in for questioning. Pennyweather looked relieved.

'You have previously told us you were at the Pearl all night on the evening of Ah Chit's death,' began Bellamy.

Sam Hung neither confirmed nor denied the statement.

'Yet, you were seen entering Ah Chit's house that same evening with four other men.'

Again, Sam Hung seemed content to allow the sergeant to tell his story uninterrupted.

'My question to you is this: where were you at ten o'clock on the night of the twenty-second of January?'

'I was at the Pearl for most of the evening,' said Sam Hung, 'however I did attend a meeting at the Mansions that night. It lasted for no more than an hour but that hour may have included the time you suggest.'

'Why didn't you mention it when we last spoke?'

Sam Hung chose not to respond.

'What were the names of the men at the meeting? asked Bellamy.

Sam Hung named the men one at a time. They all had Chinese names that Hamish didn't recognise. Sam Hung added an occupation to each of the names. There was a merchant, a laundry owner, a man who imported textiles and a herbalist. There was nothing obviously significant about these men.

'What was the meeting about?'

'It was a meeting of the Sheathed Sword,' said Sam Hung. 'It is a benevolent society supporting the Chinese community.'

'I am aware of the Sheathed Sword,' said Bellamy. 'Was not Ah Chit a member?'

'He was.'

'Why was he not at the meeting?'

'He was not a member of this particular committee.'

'What committee is that?'

Sam Hung appeared to weigh up the consequences of several answers.

The sergeant placed his palms flat on the desk and leaned toward Sam Hung. 'You see, I think it is an amazing coincidence that right at the time Ah Chit was killed, you and four other men were holed up together in his house having a meeting. It means you can speak for one another's whereabouts. I find that most convenient. Almost too convenient. In addition, you chose not to inform us of this alibi when initially questioned. This also raises my suspicions.'

Sam Hung continued to stare at the sergeant without speaking. Several seconds passed while Bellamy stared back.

At last, the sergeant sat back in his chair and tapped a pencil on the desk. 'Is there anything you want to tell us about the death of Ah Chit?'

Sam Hung said nothing. He looked comfortable with the silence.

Bellamy threw the pencil onto the desk. 'Alright, you can go.'

Sam Hung bowed deeply to each of them and left the office.

'He's behind this,' Bellamy said. 'You mark my words.'

Hamish wasn't sure. 'He might be. Those at the meeting may all be behind the killing. We may never know.'

Bellamy retrieved his pencil. 'You're right,' he said, pointing the writing end toward Hamish, 'we may never know.' He returned to his ledgers.

It was a pleasant day so Hamish decided to walk home and give himself time to think. He couldn't help thinking that while the proposal that the

Sheathed Sword members plotted and commissioned the killing of Ah Chit for some unknown internal grievance seemed the most likely scenario, it didn't quite ring true. Why kill him? His livelihood was entirely funded by the Society, why not simply cut him off?

Hamish was no more than one hundred yards from his house when he felt a shudder through his spine as two men grabbed him from behind. One man hooked his arm around his neck, while the other pulled both his arms behind his back and held him. Hamish experienced a sharp pain in his back as they threw him against the cold cement render of the old windmill. The two men continued to restrain him while Sam Hung strode into his sight from behind, carrying a sword similar to the one that had killed Ah Chit. He jabbed it point-first into Hamish's chest, delivering a terrifying pressure to his skin. Hamish was forced against the wall, one man applying his weight against his shoulder, the other holding his hand across his throat, with Sam Hung leering over the sword at his breast. The reservoir containing Brisbane's water supply was directly behind them and Hamish could hear the slap of the water against the bricks.

Sam Hung continued to press the point of the sword through his shirt and onto his skin. He leant in close to Hamish so that he could feel the heat of his breath on his face. 'The death of Ah Chit is not your concern. Leave us to carry out our own justice.'

Hamish flinched as he increased the pressure on the sword but he couldn't speak because the other man was leaning against his throat.

'Tell your sergeant this death is an internal matter,' said Sam Hung. 'Or you will not live past this day.'

Hamish could see into his dark eyes and saw that they reflected only resolve. Hamish didn't doubt Sam Hung's ability to kill him. The fact that he hadn't already done so meant that he needed him to influence Bellamy into dropping the investigation. Without Hamish's persistence, Bellamy would have been prepared to leave the case unsolved. Inspector Scratchley lost interest when he realised the Chinese community were not going to push for a resolution. It seemed that everyone would have been happy to let sleeping dogs lie. The Europeans didn't really care if the Chinese community killed one another off in petty squabbles about internal power. But Hamish needed to know. He believed that his friend Ah Tay needed to know.

Sam Hung nodded to the man to ease the pressure on Hamish's throat.

'Bellamy won't cease the investigation on my say so,' gasped Hamish, relieved to breathe at last but not convinced he could speak for long.

The men resumed the pressure on his throat and Sam Hung lifted the point of the sword to place it under Hamish's chin.

'He will,' he said. 'Tell him it is Chinese business, and it is done.' Sam Hung placed sufficient pressure on the sword so that its point pierced the skin under Hamish's chin. He nodded to the two men who released Hamish. Hamish continued to lean against the windmill trying to regain his composure. He patted down his shirt and adjusted his coat. He looked to the left and right and out onto the street. There was no one to be seen; the Chinese assailants had disappeared as quickly as they had appeared.

CHAPTER SIXTEEN

A singular instance of a premature disagreement occurring between a newly married couple was exemplified in the police court yesterday. A young man of delicate appearance was charged by the police with threatening the life of his wife, a rather prepossessing young woman, who upon making her appearance in the witness box, discarded her husband's appeal to withdraw the charge. In her evidence, she said that she married the accused in November last year. But after repeated threats from him and his ultimate action of locking her in a room and threatening to smash her head in with a large jug, she left him and took a situation. While thus engaged earning her living, her husband annoyed her by coming around to her mistress's house and on Thursday last she found him in her room, having gained entrance through the window. On account of his wild and threatening demeanour, on that occasion she swore an information against him and had him arrested. The police found him in a house in South Yarra. The occupant of the house gave witness that he was violent and behaved like a madman when following his wife and had threatened to do for his wife many times.

The accused said he was exceedingly sorry for what had occurred, he had never treated his wife with violence and being a 'thoughtless giddy girl', he was afraid of the future that awaited her. The bench bound him over to keep the peace for six months on his own recognisance of twenty-five pound.

The Age, Melbourne. Tuesday, 13 July, 1886

Hamish leant back against the windmill and concentrated on his breathing. He took deep breaths, feeling the air fill his lungs and calm his nerves. He could see his front door from where he stood. With one long intake of breath, his resolution returned and he strode onto the street making his way the short distance to his house. As he approached the door he heard Red inside barking as if he knew there was a threat close by. Hamish opened the door and leapt inside, snapping the door shut behind him. Red jumped up at him, pawing at the bottom of his coat.

'It's alright, lad,' he said, placing his hand on the dog's bobbing head. He felt tremendously relieved to be in his house and began to feel his heart rate return to normal.

Still, his head was swimming with questions. Why did the Sheathed Sword want to stop the investigation? Sam Hung could not have murdered Ah Chit himself as he was at the meeting at Ah Chit's house. Ah Chit's death was certainly convenient as it cleared the way for him to take Ah Chit's place as headman. But if the Society preferred that Sam Hung be headman, they could have simply replaced Ah Chit. Hamish was certain there was something missing, something the Sheathed Sword did not want known.

Wallace came into the entry hall to see what all the fuss was about. 'Sit, Red,' he called. Red sat. 'What's happened? You look flustered,' said Wallace.

'I'm fine,' said Hamish, hanging his coat and brushing down his trousers. 'I have been warned by Sam Hung to stay out of the investigation into Ah Chit's death and to tell Bellamy to stay out of it as well.'

'Surely, they don't think the police can let a murder go unpunished?' said Wallace.

'That is exactly what they expect. They believe it is the business of the Chinese community and the law should stay out of it. Certainly, I should stay out of it.'

Wallace rubbed the flour on his hands onto his pants. 'Of course, the police must continue the investigation but you should take heed of the warning. There is no reason for you to put yourself in any more danger.'

Hamish set his jaw and pressed his lips together. 'I will find out what happened to Ah Chit,' he said, 'for Ah Tay's sake.'

Wallace shrugged his shoulders in resignation and returned to the kitchen while Hamish prepared himself for his patient who was due in less than fifteen minutes. By the time Mrs Carmody arrived, he had regained his composure and most of his colour. Mrs Carmody suffered from a patch of dry, itchy skin that spread from her hand to her elbow on her left arm. She told Hamish she found it unattractive and infuriating. Hamish advised against the use of carbolic soaps on the area and gave her a bottle of the new experimental paw paw ointment being trialled by another Brisbane doctor, Thomas Pennington Lucas. Mrs Carmody was excited to be invited to participate in a medical trial. She left clutching the ointment to her chest and promised to return in a week with a journal reporting daily on the results.

Once Mrs Carmody had gone, Hamish retired to his room. He was going to have to decide what to tell Bellamy but he knew Sam Hung would be having him watched closely. He thought about talking to Ah Tay first. Perhaps he could make sense of Sam Hung's motives. But no, Ah Tay was behaving strangely himself. There were so many secrets. The only solution was to bring them all to the surface. But that could wait until tomorrow. He suddenly felt all the energy drain from his body. The shock of the assault was catching up on him. He'd held himself together for the consultation because he couldn't afford to send away a paying customer. He had few enough patients as it was and building his practice required positive testimony from important citizens like Mrs Carmody. Hamish lay down on his bed intending to rest his eyes for just a moment. He fell fast asleep and only woke when Wallace brought him toast and tea in the late afternoon.

KATE

Kate stayed in her room until mid-morning. She wasn't ready to risk meeting up with the other occupants of the house yet. She could hear the cheerful calls of the small children and she caught a glimpse of a young woman in a tattered shawl and bonnet on the veranda through her bedroom window. She wondered about the women in the house and the stories they must hold. The woman in the bonnet looked barely twenty years old. Surely, the children she heard running up and down the hall did not belong to her. Then again, her own mother was only sixteen years of age when she was born.

The women staying as guests in this house had found a way to leave behind violent men. But what would they do now? They could enjoy Rita's hospitality while they recovered their strength but it was not a long-term solution. It struck Kate that she was luckier than these women on many counts. Firstly, she was not burdened by children to feed and secondly, she was used to being independent.

She could take care of herself. She had seen the worst of the streets and the wharf, and nothing could shock her. She had woken once to find her body partly submerged in the muddy south bank of the Brisbane River. Her gown was tangled in the mangroves and soldier crabs were nipping hungrily at her toes. A punter had beaten her and dumped her onto the bank, doubtless expecting her body to drift away with the rising tide. But she didn't wash away. She lifted herself out of the mud and picked her way back up to the road. She walked back to the Nine Holes ignoring the jeers and taunts of the workers going about their early morning tasks.

The young woman in the bonnet, she felt certain, would not be able to withstand either the beating or the humiliation of the walk home caked in mud from the river.

Kate heard the clock in the sitting room opposite chime eleven times. With a sense of deep reluctance, she forced her body to rise from the bed for the second time that morning and search for a day dress among the few possessions she dumped on the floor the previous evening. After the effort of dressing herself and smoothing her hair, she slumped back down on the bed. What would she say to these wives and mothers? She was what she was and while she was not ashamed, she was acutely aware of the shame others may feel in her presence. A pang of anxiety gripped her in the stomach. She was beginning to feel the disorientation that came with not having taken opium for over twenty-four hours. She swallowed heavily and forced her mind past the building nausea.

Kate stared through her window onto the street, realising that as her bedroom was located adjacent to the veranda, she could easily leave through the front door without being seen. Fresh air was what she needed. She listened for movement in the hallway and waited until all was still. Then she crept into the hallway, took the few steps to the door and slipped out, closing the door quietly behind her. She hurried down the staircase and continued to the corner before stopping. She was safely away from the house and any risk of being confronted by the guests or the caretaker who had greeted her the evening before. But what to do next?

Faced with the option of turning inland or walking toward Western Creek, Kate chose the creek which flowed into the Brisbane River at the Reach. She was always drawn to water. Kate followed the bank of the creek enjoying the white petals peeking up from the clover and the powdery yellow butterflies that danced among them. It was full summer and the brilliant yellow light of the tropical sun infused everything with a shimmering glow. She was sweating under her heavy skirt but she didn't mind. It was a long time since she had enjoyed the countryside away from the stink of the city streets. She refused to acknowledge the swaying sensation in her head.

Kate kept to the left side of the creek until she noticed a wooden bridge. It was comprised of little more than a few planks held together with rusty bolts but it looked sturdy enough to be safe. She crossed the creek and surveyed the view, delighted to see a quaint house with three gables and a pretty garden. The house overlooked paddocks spanning from the Western Creek down to the river and along the riverfront for acres. Kate dreamed about life in such a house. She caught herself wondering what the people who owned such a property looked like, what they did to earn their living. She tried to imagine herself in such a house but the image wouldn't come. It was too far distant from her experience to imagine. She hadn't ever set foot in such a house. The closest she'd come was Thalia, the modest house kept by Rita for women to escape their husbands. And she'd only seen one room and the hallway, even there.

Leaving the gabled house, Kate walked back along the creek, away from the river, passing some small stores until she reached the Railway Station. There was a humble station house and a platform with seating. Her head was swimming from the withdrawal. She slumped onto the bench seat, resting there for a few moments before a train rattled in. People stepped onto the platform and she wondered about their lives too. Were any of these people the residents of the gabled house? Kate was taking in the sight of the passengers as a group, not really focused on any particular individuals, when one of them appeared to be cutting across the general direction of the others to come toward her. Too late she realised it was Daisy. She stood to move away but she knew Daisy had seen her and to run would be futile. Where would she go? She couldn't return to Rita's house because Daisy would follow and its location would be revealed. So she braced herself.

'Well, my darling,' said Daisy, affecting a cultured voice. 'Fancy running into you here. This is most unexpected.'

Kate looked her mother in the eye. 'Don't lie, Mother,' she said. 'You came here looking for me. How did you know where to get off the train?'

Daisy sat down on the seat beside Kate, primly arranging her skirts around her. 'That woman doctor mentioned the house being near the South Brisbane Station but I didn't expect the search to be quite so easy. I'm surprised you're here waiting for me.'

'I'm not waiting for you. I just happened to stop here to rest.'

'Deary,' said Daisy, leaning in close to her daughter. 'You realise it or yer don't but yer were here waiting for me. Why else would yer choose to rest 'ere? The one place I would 'ave to pass should I come for yer. Now, my deary, we can take tea in one of them miserable-looking stores in the street there and then catch the next train home. You've already missed one night's takings we can't afford to miss another. The punters'll be asking for yer.'

Kate stared ahead at the trees lining the other side of the railway line. 'I'm not coming with you,' she said. 'I am building a new life of my own.'

Daisy's voice became lower and developed an edge. 'You'll come with me, alright.'

'How do you propose to force me, Mother? Your Chinese bully is dead.'

'Sam Hung will seek yer out. He'll be no less displeased with yer fancy ideas than Ah Chit was, bless 'is soul.'

'Then I'll take my chances with Sam Hung,' said Kate, standing. 'Goodbye, Mother.'

Kate started to walk away, anxiously trying to decide in which direction to go so she did not lead her mother to Rita's house when Daisy lunged after her and grabbed her skirt. Kate turned and reefed the fabric from her mother's grip but Daisy lunged again and pushed hard. Kate managed to regain her balance but she had stumbled a few steps closer to the edge of the platform.

Daisy grabbed her around the shoulders and Kate took hold of her mother's arms. They were caught in this embrace with each trying to overcome the other, all the while not noticing how perilously close they were to the platform's edge.

Kate heard a freight train approaching and suddenly registered the danger. She stopped resisting Daisy's grip and instead tried to steer her away from the tracks but the momentum was against them and Daisy was falling backward over the platform's edge. At the same time, the station master rushed across the platform and grabbed both women in his arms. He pulled them to safety a moment before the train rumbled past.

The women fell in a heap on top of one another against the bench seat. Kate's hair had fallen from her bun and much of it was stuck to her sweating cheeks. Her mother's face was red with rage and she knew her own would be the same.

'What is this?' cried the station master. 'You ladies could have been killed.'

Daisy stood up first and brushed down her gown. She pinned her hair up and smiled charmingly at the station master. 'Thanks for the assistance, sir,' she said in her sweetest voice. 'I'll be taking advantage of yer quality rail service to make my way to Roma Street.'

Kate also stood and brushed her hair back from her face. 'I'm heading this way,' she said, pointing to the street. 'We'll cause you no more concern.' She glared at her mother as she walked away.

Daisy made a move as if she would follow but the station master was standing in front of her. She sat back down on the bench. Kate took a quick glance back to see to her relief that the station master was seated beside her mother, where it looked like he intended to stay until he saw her safely onto the next train.

Kate walked back to Rita's house agitated but confident that her mother would not follow. She had time to wash and change before dinner. She didn't want Rita to know about the meeting with her mother. She was dreading the taste of food in her mouth.

CHAPTER SEVENTEEN

Comfortable Suicide. The smart Chinaman who wants to be gathered to Confucius without any foolishness usually has some knowledge of chemistry and rams his opium pill home with a drink of vinegar. Vinegar dissolves the drug, forming an active tincture, in medical parlance and it sets to work in more of a hurry than the lazy drug exhibits when it is not driven by other agents.

The Mainland Mercury. Thursday, 14 October, 1886

Hamish woke the next morning with a sense of purpose. He would go to Bellamy and tell him about Sam Hung's threat. He was fully dressed and on his way to the door when Wallace met him with a steaming hot cup of coffee.

'No breakfast this morning?' he asked.

Hamish hesitated for a moment as the coffee aroma filled his head. 'No,' he said, drawing himself away. 'I need to see Bellamy, warn him about Sam Hung.'

'You're the one being threatened,' said Wallace. 'He might follow you.'

'If he does he will see me going into the Petrie Terrace police depot.'

Hamish grabbed his coat from the hallstand by the door and stepped out into the morning. There was a cab waiting for a fare almost directly in front of his house. The horse snorted when he climbed in, it seemed eager to move on. Hamish told the driver his destination and the cab lurched forward. He went over the details in his mind on the way. He would tell the sergeant exactly what happened and what Sam Hung said to him. He would leave out nothing. In his mind, Bellamy was outraged by the news. He declared he would send a delegation to bring Sam Hung in immediately. Hamish felt the anticipation building. This was going to be a big day. Perhaps it would be the end of his quest to find out who killed Ah Chit.

When Hamish arrived at the depot, he strode directly into Bellamy's office ready to tell his story. The sergeant was huddled over a tower of journals on his desk. 'It never ends,' he said. 'It's that bloody Commissioner, Scratchley. He wants to know everything that goes on, in minute detail.'

Hamish's attention was caught by a large mechanical device on one end of the desk. 'When did this arrive?' He was sweeping his fingers across the keys, gently tugging at the inky ribbon, eyeing the machine from every angle.

'It came months ago – I put it in the storeroom. Pennyweather dragged it out this morning. He claims it will reduce my reporting time by a mile if I learn to use it.'

'It will,' said Hamish.

'Pennyweather can have the damn thing. He can translate my handwritten reports onto it.'

'Won't that increase the time spent report writing?'

Bellamy stopped writing and looked up at Hamish. 'Was there a point to your visit?' he said.

'Yes, there is.' Hamish pulled himself away from the typewriter and went through the description he had rehearsed of the events of the previous day.

Bellamy listened intently, then to Hamish's surprise, he said, 'Perhaps Sam Hung is correct. Maybe we should leave this one alone.'

Hamish couldn't believe his ears. 'A man has been murdered. You are duty-bound to apprehend the murderer and charge him. Or her.'

Bellamy rocked back in his chair. 'If it's in-house though … why stir up a hornet's nest?'

Hamish was pacing. Both hands holding back his hair.

'He will kill you,' said Bellamy. 'He will follow through on his threat.'

'If we let this go, it means mob rule.'

Bellamy laughed. 'What do you think we have in Brisbane now? Do you think Pennyweather and I control the factions in this town? What we have, at best, is an uneasy equilibrium among con artists and swindlers. The toffs of Brisbane are as corrupt as the residents of Frog's Hollow. They just have access to the institutions of the State. But that's precarious.

How long do you think it would take to get reinforcements if that seething mass down there in Frog's Hollow were to rise against us?'

Hamish stopped pacing.

'What the devil are you talking about? What seething mass? There's no seething mass. There are citizens who deserve justice. You need to find out who killed Ah Chit and charge them.'

Bellamy sighed and righted his chair.

At that moment, Young Bob crashed into the office. Pennyweather caught him by the shoulders and was about to march him out when Hamish spoke.

'Wait,' he said. 'What is it, Robert?'

Young Bob shook free of Pennyweather's grasp.

'It's Cy Wong. She's running down Elizabeth Street like she's on fire, sir. She's knocking down everything in her path. I think she's in trouble.'

Hamish and Bellamy exchanged glances then ran into the street where the police cab was waiting.

'Drive down Roma Street then onto George,' Bellamy instructed the driver. 'She'll be heading toward the Terraces. Hurry!'

They lurched forward and raced along Petrie Terrace, turned into Roma Street and veered into George Street in record time. As they travelled along George, they noticed a group of spectators gathered on the corner of Elizabeth Street. They pulled up alongside and saw a constable detaining a young woman as lively as an eel. Some of the spectators were shouting at her. When Bellamy stepped out of the cab, they turned their attention to him.

'My stock is ruined,' said one man with a German accent. 'Who will pay for the damage?'

'She should be in an asylum,' called out a woman. 'It's the smallpox. They're all riddled with it.'

The constable was struggling to maintain his grip on Cy Wong when Bellamy pushed his way through the spectators to assist him. Hamish was right behind. Between them they took hold of Cy Wong, clutching a blanket around her shoulders, and escorted her to the carriage. The constable remained at her back to prevent any attempt at escape. Hamish and Bellamy thrust her into the cab and stepped up behind her, quickly closing the door against the crowd, some of whom were banging on the window to find out how they would be compensated for Cy Wong's mad destructive dash along the busy street.

The cab rattled back to the depot with its passengers staring out the windows to avoid looking at one another. Cy Wong's face was unreadable as always, as she sat in determined silence, clutching the blanket at her neck. Pennyweather met them at the front of the depot and assisted them to bring Cy Wong in and seat her in Bellamy's office. She was no longer resisting.

When Bellamy and Hamish were also seated in the office, Bellamy said, 'Now, tell us what you were doing racing up Elizabeth Street like a startled deer?'

Cy Wong looked sulky. 'Ah Tay kidnapped me,' she said. 'He threw this blanket around me and forced me into his carriage. I escaped when the carriage stopped outside Foong May's teahouse.'

Hamish's mouth dropped open.

'Why would Ah Tay kidnap you?' he said.

Cy Wong didn't look at him and she said nothing.

Bellamy and Hamish exchanged glances before Bellamy called for Pennyweather.

'Bring in Ah Tay,' he said when the constable appeared in the doorway.

'Now, please inform us as to why you believe Ah Tay kidnapped you,' said Bellamy, employing his most patient manner.

Cy Wong stared directly ahead, her face a stony mask.

'Is there anything else you would care to tell us?' asked Bellamy.

Cy Wong remained silent.

'Come on,' Bellamy said to Hamish. 'Nothing we can do until we get Ah Tay in here. Perhaps he'll shed some light on this.'

Hamish and Bellamy left Cy Wong to her silence and visited the kitchen. 'Do you have any ideas?' Bellamy asked Hamish while he boiled a kettle on the open stove.

Hamish shook his head. 'Ah Tay seems to think Sam Hung is dangerous,' he said. 'I can verify that, after his threat to me.'

By the time they finished their tea, they heard Pennyweather return with Ah Tay. When they came back to Bellamy's office, Cy Wong was sitting in one corner still wrapped in the blanket and Ah Tay was in another corner, sitting stiff and upright in his chair. Neither of them looked at Hamish and Bellamy.

'Cy Wong attests you tried to kidnap her,' said Bellamy.

He didn't respond.

'Do you deny the charge?'

Still Ah Tay said nothing.

Bellamy let out an impatient snort. He turned to Hamish. 'He's your friend. See if you can sort out this bloody mess. I'll leave the three of you alone if you think it will help.'

Hamish didn't think it would but Bellamy left the room.

Ah Tay and Cy Wong continued to stare straight ahead and say nothing.

Hamish brushed his fringe back with both his hands. 'Why?' he asked.

Ah Tay sat erect with his head held high. 'He who thinks too much about every step he takes will always stay on one leg.'

Hamish sighed. 'Be that as it may,' he said, 'some thought is required.'

He moved his chair closer to Ah Tay and spoke quietly. 'My friend, I cannot help you if you will not tell me what is going on.'

'It troubles me that you call me friend – a man should choose a friend who is better than himself.'

Hamish softened but he chose not to question him about the proverb.

'I understand you believe Cy Wong to be in danger from Sam Hung,' he said and waited for a response, a flicker of recognition but there was none. He glanced over at Cy Wong. There was no change in her expression either.

'Whatever your fears, it appears that Cy Wong does not wish to be saved.'

Still, no response from either of them. Hamish stood up and paced from one side of the room to the other.

'Cy Wong, do you plan to press charges against Ah Tay?'

Cy Wong turned to Hamish for the first time. She shook her head.

Hamish rolled his eyes and glanced back at his friend. 'I suppose the Sheathed Sword will be prepared to pay for the damages?'

Hamish stuck his head out of the door and called for Bellamy.

'They're not talking,' Hamish told him. 'But Cy Wong did say she does not plan to press charges.'

Bellamy huffed. 'I'm tempted to charge him regardless.'

'Is that possible?'

Bellamy grumbled something unintelligible. 'Bloody Chinese and their secrets. They're infuriating.'

'I don't believe the Chinese have a monopoly on secrets, as a race,' Hamish pointed out.

'I'll tell you one thing, Doctor.' Bellamy pointed at Hamish's chest. 'This is all tied up with the murder, you mark my words.'

Hamish suspected he was right but he said nothing.

'You are both free to go,' Bellamy told Ah Tay and Cy Wong, 'but stay away from one another or I'll lock you both up.'

Cy Wong stood first. She folded the blanket carefully and handed it to Ah Tay who accepted it with a polite nod. He then left the building. Cy Wong followed.

'What was that about?' asked Bellamy.

Hamish dropped his bottom lip on one side. 'I suppose it was his blanket,' he said.

Hamish spent twenty minutes with Bellamy, convincing him that they would get to the bottom of this case and that it was worth the effort in doing so. Then he left for Foong May's where he found Ah Tay waiting at the door of the tea house. They shook hands and moved back inside to settle at the table at the back of the room. It was a brighter day than it had been on his previous visits and Hamish was able to see the room clearly. Chinese watercolours on bamboo hung from the ceiling and at the back of the room was a small altar similar to the one at the Joss House. Incense burned in front of a carved wooden statue, filling Hamish's head with an exotic fragrance that calmed him. Foong May appeared automatically with tea and the tiny custard tarts Hamish favoured. She poured their tea silently while Ah Tay waited. When she had left them, Ah Tay spoke.

'I do not wish to discuss the incident with Cy Wong.'

He spoke with such resolve, Hamish decided to leave his questions on that matter to one side temporarily. Instead, he relayed his interview with the four boys and described the shadowy figure they witnessed.

'It is no surprise the boys were not at home that night as they claimed in court,' said Ah Tay. 'However, it is useful that they were not. If they saw the shadowy figure in the vicinity of the warehouse at ten o'clock, we have a more precise time for the killing. Did they notice anything about the figure that would identify the individual?'

'No, they were vague in the description.'

Ah Tay glanced past Hamish. 'Nonetheless, we can further investigate Sam Hung.'

Hamish put his head to the side. 'The patrons at the Pearl now agree that Sam Hung was not at the Pearl at ten o'clock. He was at a meeting with four other men at Ah Chit's house.'

Ah Tay looked earnest. He leaned forward across the table and said, 'We must get Cy Wong away from Sam Hung. She must come here to Foong May.'

Hamish blinked. 'I thought we were talking about the whereabouts of Sam Hung. We agreed we weren't going to talk about Cy Wong.'

No response.

'Cy Wong doesn't want to come.'

Ah Tay stared beyond him to the street.

'Are you listening to me?' asked Hamish.

'We must convince her to come.'

Hamish sighed. His frustration was palpable.

'Even if you had been successful in forcibly removing her from Sam Hung's house and bringing her here, how would you have stopped her from running away? You would have had to keep her under lock and key.'

Ah Tay stared at the ceiling.

'It would be easier to help you if you could tell me why you think she is in danger,' said Hamish.

At that point, Foong May appeared from the back room. 'Cy Wong must come here,' she said in the deepest voice Hamish had heard from a small woman. It was the first time he'd heard her speak English.

'I'm trying to understand why,' said Hamish.

'Cy Wong must do as her Elders direct,' said Ah Tay.

'I thought Cy Wong was Ah Chit's niece,' said Hamish. 'That would place him in control of her decisions, wouldn't it?'

'Ah Chit is my sister's husband,' said Foong May.

Hamish tried to understand how that gave her the right to control the girl's decisions while Foong May pulled up a seat and joined them. She called out loudly in Chinese and a boy of about twelve came running with a fresh pot and another cup with Chinese characters in blue. Foong May poured her tea.

Ah Tay tried to help her with the teapot but she flicked his hand away.

'My sister married first son,' she said. 'Ah Chit second son. Cy Wong daughter of third son. Ah Chit ambitious and jealous. He happy when first son die.'

Hamish looked to Ah Tay who had his head down.

'Third son is involved in politics in China. He help fight against Qing rule. Very dangerous. When he arrested, Cy Wong has no one. Ah Chit have her sent here. Very few young Chinese women in colony. Now Cy Wong owned by Sheathed Sword. Sam Hung will not protect her. She must come here. I will protect her.'

'Protect her from what, exactly?'

'European men are willing to pay a small fortune to bed a beautiful young Chinese woman,' said Ah Tay.

A veil lifted for Hamish and something he suspected became certain. 'You're in love with Cy Wong.'

Ah Tay's face remained unchanged. 'She is my cousin,' he said quietly.

'That has nothing to do with it.'

Hamish felt his perspective shifting. Had Ah Tay come to Brisbane to help his uncle? Or had he come to save Cy Wong?

Foong May slammed her fist on the table, causing both men to jump.

'Cy Wong must do her duty. She was promised to Ah Tay as an infant. She was brought here to marry Ah Tay. When Ah Chit saw how beautiful she had grown, he wanted to keep her to make money for him.'

Hamish groaned. 'But Cy Wong clearly does not want to marry you,' he said to Ah Tay.

Ah Tay was unmoved.

'Want is not important. She must,' said Foong May.

Hamish shook his head. 'It doesn't work that way here. A woman can make her own choices …' He hesitated. '… to the extent that circumstances allow. Cy Wong has another option and she has chosen it.'

Ah Tay softened a little.

'Cy Wong was always headstrong,' he said. 'At the age of three she refused to have her feet bound. Her father allowed her to be stubborn.

Her mother was angered but had to obey. She complained that no husband would ever accept Cy Wong. She was promised to me and I will accept her.'

'I take it Cy Wong's mother has passed?' said Hamish.

'Cy Wong's mother died when she was five. Her father is an unconventional man. He resents the growth of opium dens in his province and blames the Qing dynasty for selling out China to the British forces. He resents the privileges of the British in our country and the poverty of our own people. He also believes in equality for men and women. He allowed Cy Wong to learn to read and write.'

'I think I would get along with this younger brother of Ah Chit,' said Hamish.

Ah Tay ignored the interruption and continued.

'When Cy Wong was thirteen, she was to be sent here to marry but she refused and continued to refuse every year. Her father did not pursue the match because everyone said she would not make a good wife. She is too headstrong. It was his fault this was so. Anyway, her education lessens her value. Confucius was clear that only an ignorant woman is virtuous. Cy Wong has never been able to keep her intelligence secret. She is proud. When her father was arrested for his own outspokenness, Ah Chit offered to bring her to Brisbane. Having seen what happened to her father, she became eager to escape China.'

'If Cy Wong is educated and headstrong, why are you so determined she requires saving?'

Ah Tay's gaze remained firmly fixed on an imaginary point to the left of Hamish's face.

'It seems to me you are describing a woman fully capable of making her own decisions and with managing the consequences.'

Ah Tay's gaze remained steady.

'Sam Hung is not a threat to Cy Wong, is he?' said Hamish quietly.

Ah Tay released a short sharp gasp of air and finally looked at Hamish. 'I don't know,' he said. 'I do know that whatever threat he holds, Cy Wong is able to manage him. He will come out the worse for the fight.'

Hamish shook his head and flicked back his fringe. 'Tell me what you and Foong May want from the girl.'

Ah Tay swallowed. 'Cy Wong holds a secret,' he said in little more than a whisper.

'What secret?'

Ah Tay shifted uncomfortably in his chair. 'Foong May believes Cy Wong saw my father killed.'

'You told me once your father was in a drowning accident,' said Hamish.

'That is what I believed. But Foong May is certain it was not an accident. She says Ah Chit killed my father because he was jealous. Ah Chit was second son. She says he killed my father so he would be first son.'

'Your family were poor in China, what difference would it have made?'

'First son has a lot of power over others. Foong May says Ah Chit fled China because people knew he had killed his brother.'

'I don't understand what this has to do with Cy Wong.'

'My father and Ah Chit often went fishing in the river near our village. Cy Wong always wanted to go with them. She would sit on the riverbank watching. On the day of my father's death, Ah Chit returned to the village upset, saying that my father had leant too far over the side of the small boat and fallen into the river. He said he tried to pull him back but he was dragged under and caught in reeds. Cy Wong was on the bank when it happened. She would have seen the whole incident.'

'Did people ask her at the time?'

'Yes. But she didn't speak. She has never spoken of the incident. I did not question Ah Chit's account until I heard from Foong May. She blames Ah Chit for the death of her sister, who died of a broken heart after her husband was killed.'

Hamish's face softened. 'People don't die from broken hearts.'

'My mother did,' said Ah Tay with certainty. 'Besides that, I truly wish to marry Cy Wong.'

'You want her to tell you what she saw when your father died ... and you want her to marry you ... these are the reasons for attempting to kidnap her?' said Hamish.

'Yes,' said Foong May and Ah Tay simultaneously.

Hamish glanced from one of them to the other. 'You have to know that kidnapping someone is not likely to result in them feeling warm toward either proposition'

Foong May placed her tiny hands on the table palm down, the tension clear in her knuckles as she pressed.

'Cy Wong knows what she must do.'

Hamish swallowed the last of his tea. The conversation was travelling in circles and he could see no benefit would come from pursuing it with them. He bid them farewell and stepped out into the dull street. Everything seemed grey in contrast to the vibrant colours inside the teahouse. A light rain was falling so he flicked the collar of his coat up around his ears and walked on. There were a few shoppers huddled beneath the eaves of the larger stores, sheltering from the rain but for the most part, the streets were clear. Hamish shook himself and tried to clear the tangle of whispers in his mind. Why did it seem so crowded in his thoughts when the streets were empty? He enjoyed the light touch of the rain on his face. He tried to concentrate on the tingle of each drop separately. He needed to focus. He needed to find clarity. Hamish crossed the street in front of a carriage and a splash of muddy water flicked up at his legs. He shook himself and strode on.

This gets more confusing with every hour, he thought. He couldn't decide whether Ah Chit's murder was the result of an internal argument within the secret society, or something more personal.

CHAPTER EIGHTEEN

It would be difficult nowadays to mention any sphere of labour into which women do not enter – even in laborious and toilsome work they try to take a share. I have read with great interest the census returns reporting the remunerative employments entered into and creditably performed by what is known as the gentler sex. It is admitted they make efficient clerks, bookkeepers, postmistresses. The telegraph department in some countries encourage busy female manipulators. Then there is now introduction in the form of a machine called a typewriter, by which women of intelligence make a very fair income.

Today doctoresses and dispensers, lecturesses and preachers are deemed desirable, more or less so. Photography is another field for them, especially the branches of tinting and retouching of negatives, which requires delicate handling.

Literature is also a pecuniary prize suitable for ladies of education, many of whom win fame and profitable distinction. Women work in artistic pursuits in glass, painting, decorative art, tapestry, wood engraving and mural mosaic work. Women are in printing establishments as compositors and proof-readers. Even shorthand reporting has been systematically undertaken by ladies.

So, after all, the term working woman is not a misnomer, however novel it might sound. The subject has undergone such eager discussion of late that it may be excusable to think at times the working woman has just arrived on our planet! Women, as a rule, are thorough; in whatever their hand findeth to do, they do with all their might. Considering the great interest taken in the increased sphere of usefulness of women – it is surprising that so little is done respecting the overworked, for all enthusiasts the world has known, there are none more eager than women workers. Of course, I refer to the energetic ones, for there are, we know, drones in every hive.

The Telegraph, Brisbane. Monday 22 March, 1886

Hamish arrived home to find Rita settled in his favourite blue armchair with the terrier reclining on her lap. She kicked her feet cheerfully over the edge of the chair when she saw Hamish arrive.

'Keep your boots off the furnishings,' he said, wondering what kind of lady threw her legs about like that. At the same time, he tried to keep himself from sneaking glances at her ankles.

Rita was waving a small leather journal about as she spoke.

'You have to read this,' she said. 'It will break your heart. She writes beautifully.'

Hamish glanced at the book. 'Who does?' he asked.

'Particularly as she could not have had much access to books, she's quite extraordinary. Apparently, her stepfather taught her to read and write.'

'If you are referring to Kate Walton, I know,' said Hamish. 'You have already told me.'

Rita went on unperturbed. 'The colour of the sea reflects my mood,' she reads. 'It's a melancholy day ...'

'Does she write about anything that will help us find Ah Chit's killer?'

'She writes that she told Cy Wong she was leaving her mother and her lifestyle. She says Cy Wong gave her that pin you are always talking about.'

Hamish was suddenly all ears.

'Cy Wong gave the pin to Kate?' he said.

'She says Cy Wong assured her it would bring strength and resolve to the person who wears it. I think she meant it to give her the confidence to follow her own path – leave her mother and prostitution behind.'

'Daisy said Cy Wong gave it to her,' said Hamish.

'That will be so you would hand it over to her. She's probably sold it for cash to purchase opium.'

'I'm sorry I didn't give it to Kate, now. It must have been a blow to Kate to see her mother take it. If she believed the pin would give her the strength to leave, it would have been devastating to lose it.'

Rita continued to flick through the soiled pages of the journal.

'My first impression of Kate was of a distinctly practical mind but reading this now I see she has a poetic side.'

'Why do you think she wanted you to read it?' asked Hamish.

'I'm going to ask her at dinner,' she said.

Hamish furrowed his brow. 'I thought you would dine with us tonight.'

Rita drew her legs in front of her and placed them on the floor.

'I'm sorry,' she said. 'I promised Kate I would dine with her and the other guests at Thalia. These first few nights will be hard for Kate. I wouldn't put it past Daisy to come looking for her.'

'Or Sam Hung,' said Hamish.

'Or Ah Tay,' said Rita.

Rita circled around him to reach the staircase.

'I was hoping to go through the evidence tonight while Bellamy is here,' Hamish said, swinging around to follow her.

Rita grabbed her coat and gloves from behind him where they were slung over the banister at the top of the stairs. 'Dear me,' she said. 'I suppose I will have to return after dinner if I hope not to be completely excluded.'

She grinned at Hamish.

'Suit yourself,' he said, while internally he felt his heart rate increase.

KATE

At six o'clock there was a tap at her door. Kate had seen Rita arriving through her window. Kate had washed and dressed in her cleanest gown in an attempt to fortify herself against meeting the other guests.

She opened the door and Rita took her hand gently. They walked together down the hall to the dining room where there were four other women already seated at the cedar table. The table was set simply with a white damask tablecloth, a simple white dinner set adorned with a single blue line around the edges and bone-handled silver cutlery. Nothing looked expensive but it was clean and in excellent condition.

'Ladies, might I introduce Kate Watson,' said Rita. 'Kate will be staying with us.'

Rita went on to introduce each of the ladies at the table by name but Kate wasn't able to listen. She forced herself to smile but she felt the skin burn around her eyes where the bruising from her last beating was reaching its peak. She felt that all eyes were on her bruises. She panicked. It suddenly occurred to her that these women may feel sorry for her. These soft women who knew nothing of the streets and could not look after themselves, might judge her. She, who had survived on her wits, the dark, murky depths of the colony's undercurrent, might be evaluated and found wanting by women who couldn't even manage their own husbands. Kate wanted to flee. She wanted to run all the way back to Frog's Hollow and the world she knew. But she didn't run. She stood fixed to the floor, her hands clenched to steady the tremble, forcing herself to focus on her breathing. Forcing herself to hold back the nausea.

By the time she felt the redness fading from her cheeks, Kate noticed that the women had picked up their spoons and were already tucking into their soup, no longer paying any attention to her. The judgement she imagined existed only in her mind. Rita smiled and pulled out a chair for Kate, gesturing for her to sit. She sat down and took up a spoon.

The women kept their eyes down, all their attention absorbed in the simple act of appreciating the delectable warm broth. When the bowls were empty, one of the women, a sturdy girl with tight ginger curls, stood up and took them to the kitchen. She returned accompanied by the cook – a large, Dutch woman with ruddy cheeks – carrying dishes of steaming vegetables and a tray of piping hot roast beef. Kate had not seen such a meal in years. Not since her stepfather used to take them to the pub for Sunday lunch.

'How is everyone?' asked Rita as they sliced the juicy cut of beef.

Kate noticed tension ripple through the group as they all remained silent for a moment. Furtive glances passed between them.

'Mary is going home tomorrow,' said the cook at last, with an edge to her voice that Kate could not miss.

'Is this true?' asked Rita.

The other women pretended to be interested in what was on their plates.

Mary reddened. Her freckled neck took on a mottled pink glow. 'Yes,' she said. 'The children and I are returning to our family home. I have packed our things and we will leave early in the morning. Richard is meeting us at the station at Roma Street.' She hesitated. 'To ensure the location of this house is not compromised.'

Kate watched Rita chew a mouthful of meat and potato slowly before she spoke. 'Are you sure this is what you want?'

'Yes ma'am,' said Mary. 'He's learned his lesson now. He won't hit us again. He promised.'

The other women at the table exchanged glances but they kept their eyes down, looking at their plates.

'Poppycock,' said the cook.

Everyone looked up from the table. Kate wondered if they were shocked by the use of the term or the fact that the cook had stated, albeit in colourful language, what they were all thinking.

Rita was watching Mary closely. 'If you are sure, Mary, we all wish you well.'

Mary smiled. Kate had no doubt the young woman was relieved to have the difficult task of telling her benefactor she was returning home behind her.

Kate sipped soup from her spoon slowly. Of course, Mary's husband would hit her again. Could it be possible the woman believed what she was saying? But Kate couldn't judge her for going back. What was the alternative? What would she, Kate, do with her own life, if she didn't go back? She cast her eye over the linen tablecloth, the matching dinner set and the silver cutlery. These things were not for the likes of her or Mary, for that matter. Mary would return to the man who beat her and prostitute herself for the roof over her head and that of her children and the small amount of respectability that comes from being a married woman. Kate imagined herself returning to life as a different kind of prostitute. *A more honest one in many ways,* she thought.

But still, there was something about respectability she craved. Not the kind of respectability that came from marriage. More a type of respect for her accomplishments, for her as a human being. Kate took in a deep breath and let it out slowly. A future radically different to her past seemed impossible to contemplate. How could anyone expect to change their own destiny? Mary was destined to live out her life in servitude to this brute who beat her and her children, and Kate was tied as securely to her own destiny. In that moment it seemed that Daisy was right after all; there was no escaping one's life. Kate was aware of Rita watching her as she finished her meal in silence.

When Kate returned to her room, Rita followed her. 'Can I come in for a moment?' she asked.

Kate nodded as she sat on the bed. She couldn't deny Rita entry to the rooms in her own house. Rita sat beside her. 'I've been reading your journal,' she began.

Kate bit her lip on the inside of her cheek.

'You have an exceptional talent.'

Kate swallowed. She was not used to praise.

'I was wondering if you are intending to do something with your writing – to make a living, I mean?'

'How would that work?' mumbled Kate, the concept so far from her experience she could not imagine it.

'There are a number of ways you can earn a living from writing,' said Rita. 'You could write stories and have them published, perhaps in the magazines. Or you could write a column for the newspaper.'

'Do they have women reporters?' asked Kate.

'Of course,' said Rita. 'Not many but some.'

Kate had enjoyed reading the newspaper any time she came across a discarded one. She could imagine herself writing for a newspaper. But she imagined reporters had a lot of knowledge, a grand education and an understanding of world politics.

'I don't know enough,' she said.

'You know more than most about many things,' said Rita. 'Like how it is to be a woman and poor in the colony. Your perspective would be enlightening to readers, I would think.'

The idea that her perspective would be of interest to anyone was a surprise but it sparked anticipation, a small light in Kate's soul.

'And you identified the symptoms of smallpox on that child before anyone – that shows exceptional perception. You knew the danger immediately and took appropriate steps. You could write a piece for the newspapers that would inform readers about prevention – clear up confusion. There are many parents who still believe the vaccination is dangerous to their children, for example.'

'What do I know of such things?' asked Kate.

'Journalists are not experts on the topics they write about,' said Rita. 'They interview people who know and communicate the information to readers. Hamish is passionate about the benefits of vaccination. I'm sure he would be happy to talk to you. You won't be able to stop him once you initiate the conversation.'

Kate's eyes widened to the size of saucers but she couldn't think of a thing to say. A story was already forming in her mind but somehow the reality of a piece written by her hand ever going to print was too remote to seriously contemplate.

'Think about it,' said Rita. 'There is no hurry to do anything. You are safe here until you decide on your future.'

Rita left Kate sitting on the bed trying to wrap her mind around a life she had never thought possible. Would someone running a newspaper take her seriously? Who would ever give her the chance to publish such a story? She changed into her bedclothes, telling herself to remove such fantasies from her thoughts. She was a survivor – her sole job was to survive her withdrawal from opium dependence and from the 'game'. Survival had to be her goal, not a fancy job writing for a newspaper. Such fantasies would drain her energy and lead to disappointment and failure. She should think about a job in a laundry. Plenty of single women were employed at the laundry owned by Sam Hung. Maybe he would give her a position. But she had angered Sam Hung by running away from the job she already had working for him. He was not likely to be well disposed toward providing her with an alternative opportunity. Surely, there were other laundries in the town. Or she could be a cleaner, perhaps not in a nice house like the one with the three gables, a wealthy family would not have someone with her past in their employ but perhaps at a boarding house …

While these scenarios flicked through Kate's mind, at another level some part of her consciousness was simultaneously outlining the story she would write about the families involved in the smallpox lockdown.

CHAPTER NINETEEN

The water police consist of an inspector, a coxswain, a carpenter and five constables, one of whom acts as cook; there are no other water police in any part of the colony. The water police are stationed on board the hulk 'PROSERPINE' at the mouth of the river. The expense of keeping up the hulk includes the keeping up of the water police. There is a sub-inspector at £200 per year, a coxswain at £120 per year, a carpenter at £120 per year and five boatmen at £96 each. The carpenter, coxswain and boatmen receive each £15 a year in lieu of rations, night allowances and good conduct money, and they all receive two suits of uniform a year, the other expense is for what paints are required.

The vessel is painted once a year. Twenty pounds a year should pay for keeping the hulk in serviceable condition. Including water police duties, the force have charge of the dredging plant lying at the mouth of the river off Fisherman's Island. It takes up much of their time.

There are twenty-seven vessels, consisting of two dredges, the 'FITZROY' and 'LYTTON'; one steam tug, the 'BRISBANE'; and twenty-three punts. The decks of the dredges and the tug have to be washed down every day and the machinery on board the dredges has to be turned once a week. There are also repairs constantly required. It fills up their time between their other duties. The sub-inspector is a health officer and boards vessels in his capacity as such and assists the tide surveyor in his duty by lending him men in bad weather to go to vessels in the bay.'

Question asked by Chairman of Committee: 'What is the duty of the water police when they are strictly at work?'

Answer: 'Keeping order amongst the shipping in the bay, they act as customs house officers and search vessels going up and down the river.

An Outline of the History of the Queensland Police Force 1860–1949 [by Commander Norman S. Pixley, M.B.E., V.R.D., R.A.N.R.] (Read at a meeting of the Historical Society of Queensland, Inc. on 27 July, 1950.)

Hamish, Bellamy and Wallace sat down to a piping hot bowl of Wallace's potato and leek soup. The aroma had been filling the kitchen and wafting up to the sitting room for an hour while they waited for Sergeant Bellamy to join them. Hamish was nursing hunger pains and silently cursing the sergeant. They were finally about to tuck in when Rita ran up the staircase making enough noise to wake the dead. Red was seated at his master's feet waiting patiently for scraps. When Rita burst into the room, he gave a startled bark.

'Sorry, I'm late,' said Rita, breathless. She glanced around the table. 'Oh, you haven't eaten yet?'

'No,' said Hamish. 'Bellamy had business to attend at the station. He has not long since arrived. Sit down with us. Will you have a taste of Wallace's soup?'

'Don't mind if I do,' said Rita, settling herself into an empty chair at the table. Wallace had already left for the kitchen to fetch another bowl and spoon. Red trotted after him in case he dropped anything. Soon everyone was settled again and Hamish smiled at Rita, who was enjoying her second meal of the evening.

For a few moments, Hamish thought of nothing but the warm, salty sensation lighting up his tastebuds. The wait made him appreciate the sensation more and now that he was eating, he was grateful for it. He was disappointed when Bellamy spoke and brought him back to thoughts of the investigation, even though the express purpose of the meal was for the four of them to discuss the case.

'This case becomes more complicated by the minute,' said Bellamy. 'Do you think it amounts to nothing more than a family feud? I must confess I have no clear picture of how the familial relationships work.'

Hamish put his spoon down reluctantly to explain Ah Tay's family structure once again. He felt as though he had done so too many times in recent days.

'Cy Wong is Ah Tay's cousin,' said Hamish. 'Her father and Ah Tay's father were brothers. Ah Chit was also a brother. Ah Chit brought Cy Wong to Brisbane when her father was jailed. She was promised as a wife to Ah Tay but Ah Chit decided to keep her to work at the Pearl. Ah Tay remains intent on saving her but she doesn't appear to want to be saved.'

'How does Foong May fit in?' asked Bellamy.

'Ah Tay's mother and Foong May are sisters. Ah Tay's mother passed away when he was a child,' said Hamish.

'So, Foong May is Ah Tay's maternal aunt.'

'Quite so.'

Rita sipped her soup thoughtfully. 'That means Cy Wong is not directly related to Foong May. She is only distantly related through marriage.'

'Indeed.'

Bellamy put down his spoon. 'What does any of it have to do with the murder of Ah Chit?' He pursed his lips. 'Sam Hung is not another family member, is he?'

Hamish shook his head. 'No. His only connection is that he and Ah Chit were both members of the Sheathed Sword.'

'It seems to me there are two possible motives behind the killing,' said Wallace. 'One is connected to the Chinese Secret Society and the other is more personal in nature and related to family tensions.'

'You always bring clarity,' Rita said, beaming. 'Wallace is correct. We should analyse each possibility separately.'

Hamish began. 'On the Sheathed Sword side, we have Sam Hung. He may have resented Ah Tay coming to Brisbane and usurping his power in the community.'

'He couldn't have carried out the murder though, because we know he was at the meeting at the house,' pointed out Rita.

'He could have arranged it,' said Bellamy. 'It's the simplest explanation and still the one I favour.'

'They could have all been in on it,' said Wallace. The others made noises of agreement. 'We need to ask ourselves why Ah Chit was not invited to the meeting. The participants have all provided one another with a tidy alibi.'

'That's true,' said Rita.

'So, why wouldn't Ah Chit be at the meeting?' asked Hamish.

'Because they were isolating him, so he could be murdered while they all had an alibi,' said Bellamy, tearing a chunk of bread and dunking it in his soup.

'Or because they were planning some activity within the Secret Society that they didn't want him to take part in,' suggested Rita.

'That's possible. Such as?' asked Hamish.

'I don't know. He was a relative newcomer to Brisbane, wasn't he? He was placed here by Society leaders from Victoria, he wouldn't necessarily have the loyalty of the local Chinese community.'

'I don't know that we're any closer to narrowing down what happened,' said Bellamy.

'Let's turn to the family relationships,' suggested Rita. 'What have we there?'

'Ah Chit does not seem to have been well regarded by any of his family,' said Bellamy.

'I've only known Ah Tay to be respectful toward his uncle,' said Hamish. 'When we were children, we both admired him. I know my father regarded him highly.'

Wallace lifted a single brow.

'I suppose that doesn't come as much of a recommendation of his character.' Hamish checked himself.

'Ah Tay says he came to Brisbane to help his uncle who he believed to be in financial trouble,' said Bellamy. 'But we now know Cy Wong was promised to him, then kept by Ah Chit. Could they have fallen out over the girl?'

'What about Cy Wong?' said Rita. 'We know she can fight. Did she want to free herself of Ah Chit?'

'She remains indebted to Sam Hung. I'm not sure she is any better off,' said Hamish.

'Perhaps Sam Hung is the lesser of two evils.'

'Foong May is the one I can't work out,' said Hamish. 'She's a strange old woman. Why does she want Cy Wong to marry Ah Tay so badly?'

'Don't all Chinese old women expect their sons and nephews to marry?' said Bellamy.

'Not only Chinese old women,' corrected Hamish, thinking of his own mother's obsession over his marital status.

'If Cy Wong was promised to Ah Tay, she must marry him, from the old lady's perspective.'

'She could also be genuinely concerned about Cy Wong's future,' said Hamish. She leads a very unconventional life for a young woman, Chinese or European. If she doesn't marry Ah Tay, she may have no option to marry at all.'

'Perhaps she doesn't want to marry,' suggested Rita with an edge to her voice.

Wallace cackled. 'You may well be right.'

Hamish was thoughtful. 'Cy Wong is definitely driven. I'd like to know what drives her, exactly.'

He swallowed a full glass of red wine. 'Did I tell you that Cy Wong may have witnessed the death of Ah Tay's father?' he said, feeling warm inside and slightly cheerful.

'No!' cried Rita. 'That could have a bearing on the case.'

'Sorry, so much has happened all at once. Apparently, Ah Chit and Ah Tay's father went to the river, fishing, and only Ah Chit came home. Cy Wong was on the riverbank at the time and would have seen what happened. Ah Chit said it was an accident and Cy Wong has never said any different. But Foong May is suspicious.'

'Did Ah Tay know about this before he came to Brisbane?' asked Rita.

'He says not. He says Foong May told him recently. He has been trying to make Cy Wong tell him what she saw ever since but she refuses to talk about it.'

They all stared at their glasses.

Bellamy was the first to break the silence. 'I think Sam Hung is the killer. At the very least he is the one pulling the strings. I have sufficient cause to search his house, Ah Chit's house. I believe that's the next prudent step. We searched the warehouse where he was killed and found nothing. Perhaps we will find something at Harris Terraces to help in this investigation. While we're at it, we also need to find out what that meeting was about. We'll make it first thing in the morning. We'll catch Sam Hung off guard.'

Hamish didn't think Sam Hung would have anything incriminating in the house. What could they find? The murder weapon was already at the station. But he agreed to meet Sergeant Bellamy at the Mansions at eight o'clock the next morning.

Rita and Wallace collected the empty bowls and glasses and took them downstairs to the kitchen. When they were out of earshot, Bellamy looked at Hamish with intensity. 'There is no reason for you to come tomorrow, you know. Sam Hung is a dangerous man.'

'So, everyone keeps telling me,' he said. 'Including him.'

'You'll stay away then?'

'No.'

Sergeant Bellamy shrugged his shoulders and stood up to leave. Hamish followed him down the stairs and watched him put on his coat. It never ceased to amaze him that Bellamy wore a woollen coat outdoors, even in the tropical climate of Brisbane. 'Have a good night's sleep then,' Bellamy said, 'and have your wits about you in the morning. You'll need them.'

Hamish stood at the door, watching until his carriage was out of view.

'He's right,' said a voice behind him. Hamish turned to see Wallace and Rita standing together like soldiers of doom.

'You should stay out of it,' said Rita. 'Whatever happens, Bellamy will share the truth with you. You will know who is responsible for the death of Ah Tay's uncle without putting yourself in danger.'

Hamish rolled his eyes. 'Good night, Rita,' he said, taking her light coat from the rack and handing it to her. He enjoyed the gesture. It was one of the only times since he'd been in his house that she'd hung her coat on the rack. Rita took the coat and placed a gentle kiss on his cheek. It felt like a butterfly had landed there. Then she was gone. Hamish turned to Wallace who shook his head and disappeared down the hall to his room behind the kitchen. Hamish assumed he knew him too well to pursue a pointless objection.

CHAPTER TWENTY

No one has ever been so cultivated as the Chinese woman. She is represented as silly, unable, on account of the malformation of her feet to walk, and passing her whole life locked up in a kind of seraglio. This is quite wrong. She is able to walk as well as you or me. She goes out shopping and making visits unveiled and takes her afternoon drive in her open Palanquin. Her occupation consists of education of her children, the care of the household, dominoes, embroideries and tending flowers.

We [Europeans] disapprove of excessive instruction as far as our women are concerned. Their education must be entirely distinct from that of the men. The latter are brought up to take and receive instruction intended to fit them for government or merchant service, whereas the woman must apply herself to learn all that is necessary for housekeeping and raising a family. We do not insult our women by imagining they are incapable of scientific instruction but we consider it would be taking them off their proper track in life and would unfit them for the place they hold in the family.

[The Chinese woman] has no need to learn to perfect herself. She is born perfect and no science in the world will ever teach her the grace and gentleness which are the two chief ornaments of the domestic hearth. From the day of her marriage, the wife becomes her husband's equal, can sign all documents in the name of the family, can sell and buy property, give her children in marriage and, with one exception, has the same civil rights as her husband.

Women, however, cannot inherit money, hence that curse of western civilisation, the marriage for money never occurs in China. Old bachelors and elderly spinsters are almost unknown in China. Marriage takes place at a very early age – boys of sixteen marry girls of fourteen. This has nothing to do with precocity. It is rather due to the determination of the parents that their children should be settled early in life and should devote all their strength and resources of their youth to the family, rather than lead a wild and immoral life away from the home.

The Telegraph, Brisbane. Saturday 1 January, 1887

Hamish and Bellamy stood back while Constable Pennyweather banged on the door of the townhouse in the Mansions' block. It was a terrace in the better end of George Street toward Queen's Park. The door was solid but Hamish judged the lock system to be breakable if it came down to it. The sun was warm, even at that early hour. Hamish peered through the window framed by lace curtains to the left of the door. A vine profuse with jasmine wound its way down from the first-floor balcony and threatened to cover the window. Hamish pushed the plant aside. The fragrance was overpowering in the morning's heat but there was no movement in the reception room.

'Try around the back,' said Bellamy. Pennyweather scooted off to the back of the building. The sergeant tugged the vine out of the way and peered through the same window beside the door. Still, nothing moved inside.

Hamish shrugged.

'There's a window open at the back, sir,' said Pennyweather, returning. 'Back door is locked.'

'Go through the window,' said Bellamy.

Pennyweather hesitated.

'Get on with it, lad,' barked Bellamy. 'Come through and open this door for us.'

Pennyweather did as he was told.

A few minutes later they heard the rattle of the front door lock from inside. Pennyweather opened the door and Hamish, Bellamy and two constables traipsed in.

'Check upstairs,' Bellamy said to the two constables. 'You check the buildings in the yard,' he said to Pennyweather. 'We'll look in here.'

'What are we looking for, sir?'

'I'll tell you when we find it,' said Bellamy.

The constables shared a confused glance before moving away.

'I don't think he's home, at least,' whispered Hamish.

'Hmm. He could be lying low,' suggested the sergeant.

Hamish and Bellamy surveyed the room. It was furnished with a mixture of European grand style flocked wallpaper, velvet swag curtains, and oriental rattan furniture, antique Chinese vases and bronze statues. On the beam above the fireplace was a framed photograph. Hamish moved in front of it to have a closer look. There were five oriental men staring at the camera. They all had European haircuts and suits. Each one was wearing a gold pin on his lapel. The same style of pin that Hamish had returned to Daisy.

'Look here,' he called to Bellamy.

Bellamy stared over his shoulder at the picture.

'That could be the five men who met here the night Ah Chit was killed,' he said.

'That one is Sam Hung.' He pointed to the tallest man.

'Here.' Hamish put his finger on the photo. 'The pin.'

Bellamy leaned in further. 'They all have one. Must be a symbol of membership. The Sheathed Sword maybe?'

'How do you think Cy Wong was in possession of one?' asked Hamish.

'She could have stolen it,' suggested Bellamy.

'Ah Chit would have had one. He was a member of the Sheathed Sword.'

Bellamy was manipulating the ornate plaster frame to remove the photo. 'We'll take the photo to the station.'

One of the constables searching upstairs called from the top of the staircase.

'I think you should see this, sir.'

Bellamy and Hamish joined him and followed into what appeared to be the main bedroom. Behind an elaborately carved wooden altar with little jars of incense at each end was an iron door flush against the wall. Bellamy was examining the intricate locking system when they heard a commotion downstairs.

They ran to the top of the staircase in time to see Sam Hung dragging Constable Pennyweather by the collar through the front entrance. He had a look of thunder on his face and a short sword in his right hand. The two constables behind Bellamy stood poised to strike. He flashed them a warning to stand back.

'I found this man on my property, then come into my house to find you everywhere like ants,' he said.

'We are searching the house as part of our investigation into the murder of the previous tenant,' said Bellamy. 'I advise you to let go of my constable and put down your weapon.'

Sam Hung stood his ground and pulled Pennyweather closer to him.

'What is in the safe in this room?' Bellamy pointed into the bedroom.

Sam Hung's face paled but his expression did not change.

'We'll use explosives to open it if we have to,' said Bellamy.

Sam Hung let the sword drop and released his grip on Pennyweather, who straightened himself up and tried to restore his dignity. Sam Hung climbed the stairs and went into the bedroom, taking a large iron key from his coat pocket. He used it to open the iron door revealing a small cabinet built into the recess of the wall. Hamish's eyes grew large as he stared into the recess. Gold bars were packed tightly from top to bottom and it looked as though the safe was at least five bars deep.

Bellamy glared at Sam Hung, waiting for an explanation. There was none forthcoming.

'I think you had better accompany us back to the station,' he said. 'Pennyweather, secure the safe and bring the key with you. We'll send guards back for the gold.'

Hamish and Bellamy waited in the interview room while two constables brought in Sam Hung, his face set in a sneer. The Chinese man's eyes drifted toward Hamish, caught his glance and hovered. He recognised a deep disdain. He knew this man believed him to be insignificant, at best an irritant to his plans and he was no more afraid of the sergeant's questions than he would be of flies at a picnic. Whatever he wanted to achieve was already done. There was nothing they could do to change the course of events. But did he order the killing of Ah Chit as part of his plan? Hamish remained unconvinced, though he couldn't have said why.

'I think you need to tell us what's going on,' said Bellamy.

Sam Hung simply stared at him. When a few minutes passed without an answer, Bellamy decided he needed to be more specific. 'What is the hoard of gold for?' he said.

'Benevolent projects,' said Sam Hung.

'In my experience, cash is turned into gold, either for storage or transport,' said Bellamy. 'I know the Sheathed Sword has a legitimate bank account where takings from the various … activities … are deposited and benevolent funds are issued. So, I'll ask again. Why is there a hoard of gold in your bedroom wall?'

Hamish imagined Sam Hung was thinking through his options.

'The Sheathed Sword also sends funds to China,' he said.

'That's a large sum of money for poor relatives in China,' said Bellamy. 'That amount of gold would buy several villages.'

Sam Hung offered no response.

'Sam Hung,' said Bellamy, standing. 'You are charged with the murder of Ah Chit and the possession of money gained through illegal means. No doubt the government will have questions about your intentions regarding duties and taxes as well. Constable Pennyweather, escort our friend to a cell.'

Hamish stood up also. 'What? We know he was at a meeting at the time of the murder. It will be easily verified by the four other men.'

Bellamy was unperturbed.

'Sam Hung gained Ah Chit's business, his position of power in the Society and a fortune of gold that was stored at his residence. He murdered Ah Chit. He may have paid one of his men to thrust the sword but he murdered him nonetheless.'

'You have no evidence to charge him. How will you convince judge and jury?'

Sam Hung remained seated, watching them.

Bellamy laughed. 'A jury will convict him in a heartbeat. A Celestial who runs a gambling house, prostitution and opium dens? They already believe the Chinese to be a race of devils intent on corrupting and exploiting good Christians.'

'Is that what you believe?' whispered Hamish as Sam Hung was taken away.

When the prisoner was out of earshot, Bellamy looked at Hamish.

'No,' he said. 'But Sam Hung knows I am right. He'll hang unless he tells us what the gold is for. I guarantee you, when this much money sits alongside a murder, the two will be connected. I'm going to find the connection.'

ATE

Kate rose early. Rita had given her drops to help her sleep. She would use them sparingly to avoid replacing one addiction with another. The drug eased her tremors and sent her into a deep sleep almost immediately. She woke feeling surprisingly refreshed. Where the morphine had created a maddening fog in her brain, the chloral hydrate seemed to bring clarity. Her only fear was that the drug would take hold of her and keep her captive, just as the opium had. She would guard against it. She would measure the drops meticulously according to Doctor Cartwright's instructions and she would reduce her intake gradually until she no longer needed the assistance to sleep. In the meantime, she accepted the help gladly – the evening sweats, the terrible nausea and the piercing headaches were too much to ignore. She could not have persevered without the drops.

This morning she felt more alive than she had in a long while. Kate thought about checking on Daisy at the Nine Holes but a wave of anxiety descended on her and she knew it was too soon. She had to help herself before she could be any help to Daisy, emotionally or in any other way.

Her mind travelled to her memories of Cy Wong. She recalled the peace she felt the evening she spent with her after the fight with Daisy. There was an inner strength about Cy Wong that she craved. Her mind was made up. She would visit Cy Wong at the Terraces, arriving as a respectable young lady calling upon a friend. The new identity she was creating needed to be tried on and adjusted to fit. Kate stood before the looking glass and brushed her long black hair. It was already beginning to shine as it had when she was younger. Her dark eyes were also regaining their sparkle and her pale skin was clear and fresh. She put on her best gown, an olive-green ribbed silk, striped with velvet ribbon and brocade on the front bodice. Over it she placed a cashmere jacket shot with bronze and red. She secured her new hat, purchased with the money she stole from her last customer, a black straw hat with olive velvet puffing, a cluster of roses intermingled with lily of the valley and gilded wild oats resting on a soft background of black lace. Even without the looking glass, she would have known she looked splendid. And respectable.

Kate walked across the Victoria Bridge with a spring in her step. It felt like a lifetime ago she had passed this way, desperate and miserable. How much difference a few short days could make.

The walk along George Street was pleasant as she noticed ladies glancing her way with curiosity and gentlemen with admiration. She had felt invisible during the daylight hours in her previous life. She was a creature of the night. This morning she could appreciate how the light of the sun sparkled on the river, how the colours of the ladies' dresses shimmered in the daylight and how endless the blue sky seemed. Everything she saw seemed larger than life on that walk.

When she reached the Terraces, Kate tapped on the front door like the Lady she was. The door swung open at her touch, so she pushed gently and peered inside. She couldn't see anyone but she went in anyway, curious as to why the door had been left unlocked. She checked each room downstairs carefully finding no one there.

As she was leaving the dining room, she heard a scraping sound overhead. A lifetime on the streets had taught her not to lose the advantage by signalling her presence before she knew what she was walking into, so she climbed the stairs cautiously.

From the top of the staircase, she detected movement in the front room. Stepping into the doorway she caught sight of Cy Wong lifting gold bars out of a depression in the wall and packing them into a tea chest on the floor. There were several tea chests in the room, each with a single layer of gold bars. There were more empty tea chests waiting.

Cy Wong looked flushed and anxious as she worked quickly to transition the gold from wall to floor.

'What is this?'

Cy Wong looked up, startled. It appeared to take a moment for her to register that it was Kate standing there in her finery. Cy Wong was wearing the same loose-fitting pants and tunic she always wore. But Kate had never seen her so flustered.

'Help me,' she said at last.

Kate stepped over some boxes with gold at the bottom and stood by Cy Wong.

'Those panels,' she said, pointing to a collection of wooden structures leaning against the wall. 'Take one and place it in each chest, on top of the gold.'

Kate did as she was instructed, being careful to fit each panel so that no glint of the secret beneath was visible.

'Where is it going?' she said.

'China.'

Kate noticed the girl seemed breathless and thought it more likely from anxiety than physical effort. Kate had seen her tackle two grown men with barely a change in her pulse.

She asked no more questions until every tea chest had its gold safely tucked under a false bottom, with the lid loosely secured.

'Other items will be placed in the chests,' said Cy Wong. 'Leave the nails loose so the lids can be easily opened.'

They heard horses stop outside and checked through the window to find they pulled an open dray. Within seconds four Chinese men had rushed upstairs and begun transferring the crates onto the dray for transport.

'Come on, hurry,' said Cy Wong to Kate. 'We have to get out of here.'

Kate followed Cy Wong downstairs and onto the street. 'Where are we going?'

Cy Wong took her hand and led her into Queen Street where they could become lost in the crowd.

The women looked back to see that the men had completed their recovery of the gold and the dray was rattling its way to the wharf by the time they reached the corner.

'In here,' said Kate as they passed a coffee house with fat sugary delights in the window. Dressed as a Lady, she knew she would blend into the usual morning clientele enjoying the sweets and conversation with friends.

She motioned for Cy Wong to take a seat in a booth built into the wall and she sat elegantly opposite.

A waitress appeared almost immediately with a look of disapproval.

She glared pointedly at Kate. 'How may I serve you, ma'am?

'Two for tea and cream.' Kate spoke in a beautifully articulated English accent.

The waitress glanced suspiciously at Cy Wong.

'Is there a problem?'

The waitress blinked. 'No, ma'am,' she said and scurried off to place their order.

'They'll never look for you in here,' said Kate.

Cy Wong glanced around at Brisbane's finest society ladies with their rustling silk bustles and monumental hats.

'Do you want to tell me what this is about?'

Cy Wong spoke in a whisper. 'The gold is to buy my father's way out of prison. Some will bribe the authorities the rest will go to purchase weapons for the resistance.'

'Resistance to what?'

'Quiet,' hissed Cy Wong.

'There is trouble in my country. The Qing rulers favour the British and the opium trade. My people become poorer and poorer until they are starving.'

Kate knew nothing of political struggle in foreign lands but she understood poverty. And she understood the oppressive force of the British upper classes. Even if she aspired to middle-class respectability herself.

'Where did the gold come from? Is it stolen?'

She fully acknowledged to herself she was in no position to pass judgement if it was.

'No,' cried Cy Wong. 'The gold is profit from the businesses.'

'Why do you have to smuggle it, then?' asked Kate.

'The government duties,' said Cy Wong. 'The British authorities would take half. They don't mind us profiting from illegal activities, as long as the government shares in the profit. Now that the police have discovered the gold, they will confiscate it all. That's why we had to move it quickly.'

The waitress returned with the tea and cream. She placed a cup before Cy Wong while continuing to glare her disapproval. How it must sting her to have to serve the Chinese girl, thought Kate. They sipped their tea and Kate focused her mind back on the gold.

'Does Sergeant Bellamy know about the gold?'

'Yes. He found it this morning when they searched the house. He is sending people back to pick it up.'

Kate suddenly felt nervous. The police were probably at the house right now. They would be infuriated to find the gold missing. No wonder Cy Wong needed to hide. Kate knew they were safe in the fashionable café for now. The police would be looking for Cy Wong in more likely places. They would certainly check the Nine Holes. Thank God Daisy didn't know anything.

But they couldn't stay in the café indefinitely.

'Where will you go?' Kate asked Cy Wong.

'I am good at disappearing,' she said. 'If we stay here for an hour or so, it will give the police time to search the immediate area. Then I will disappear.'

Kate signalled for the waitress to return. She prayed a thank you to her stepfather for those Saturday morning teas at the local coffee house. It meant she knew how to blend comfortably into this environment.

CHAPTER TWENTY-ONE

'Sam Hung will be living like an Emperor in his cell,' complained Bellamy. 'The Chinese brought him in a three-course meal this morning. They even brought him silk cushions for Christ's sake.'

'Has he said anything about the gold yet?'

'No. We've interviewed the other four men in the photograph and they confirm he was with them throughout the meeting, and not out of their sight until four in the morning. They claim they don't know anything about the gold.'

'Have you asked how Cy Wong came to be in possession of the gold pin?'

'They say it is because she is an elite member of the Sheathed Sword.'

Hamish felt the blood rush to his face. Why had he assumed she came by the pin through a man? Why had he not realised she earned it in her own right?

'Her father is a rebellion leader in China,' he said. 'That's why he was arrested.'

They were interrupted by Pennyweather who appeared in the doorway.

'Ah Tay is missing, sir,' he said. 'Foong May is in the foyer.'

Sergeant Bellamy leant forward over his desk to peer out the door. Hamish looked in the same direction. He caught a flash of black silk then heard what he imagined to be a string of Chinese expletives in a deep Oriental voice. Behind the expletives came a diminutive woman dressed in what looked like embroidered black silk pyjamas. Her hair was tied back tightly in a pigtail. The grey halo of hair around her face was the only real witness to her age.

'Do we need an interpreter?' Bellamy asked Pennyweather.

'I speak English,' said the woman. Hamish supposed she said it loudly to convince them of the truth of it.

'Sit down, Foong May,' said Hamish.

'How may we be of service?' asked Bellamy in his police voice.

Hamish cringed.

'Ah Tay gone,' she said.

'Ah Tay is missing?' asked Hamish.

'Kidnapped. Murdered.'

'Why do you think he has been murdered?' he asked, the anxiety rising.

'He no come home. Two days now. And I get this.' She thrust a crumpled piece of paper at them.

Hamish read it then passed it to Bellamy.

Return to Victoria or face death.

'When did you receive this?' asked Bellamy.

'Yesterday,' said Foong May.

'Why did you leave it until now to tell us?'

'I didn't show Ah Tay yet. I waited but he no come.'

'How did you receive the note?' asked Hamish.

'It left … *chuang*.'

'On his bed, inside your home?'

'*Shi de*.'

'English, please,' said Bellamy.

'Yes,' said Foong May.

Bellamy sighed. Hamish pulled back his fringe with both hands.

'Sam Hung wanted to kill Ah Tay,' said Foong May.

'Sam Hung is in a cell,' said Bellamy.

'No difference. He pay.'

Hamish was already pacing when he noticed Bellamy look to him for inspiration.

'Where is Cy Wong?' he said at last.

The two men looked at Foong May.

'Cy Wong no good. She with that *xiong shou*.'

'Murderer,' said Hamish. 'I think she means Sam Hung.'

Bellamy sighed and placed his fingers on his temples.

'Foong May, listen to me. Sam Hung is in a cell, locked up.'

At that moment, Pennyweather crashed into the room, falling over a pile of journals on the floor as he did so.

'Sam Hung's gone,' he said. 'Escaped.'

Bellamy leapt to his feet. 'How the hell did that happen?' He pushed past Hamish and ran with Pennyweather to the empty cell. One of the constables was on the floor holding his head beneath an upended tray. An enamel mug lay on its side in a pool of milky tea.

'Bloody hell.' Bellamy clapped his hand to his forehead.

'He went out the back entrance,' mumbled the constable on the floor.

'Wasn't it locked?'

'No, sir. We leave it unlocked in the mornings for the char lady to come and go. No one knows it is unlocked for that hour, sir.'

'You bloody idiot, the prisoner in this cell knows. He can see her come and go.'

Bellamy turned to Pennyweather. 'Call in all the men. I want Sam Hung found. Tell them to look for Ah Tay while they're at it.'

He turned back to Hamish and saw that Foong May had followed them. She stared at him for a moment before leaving them. Hamish felt the discomfort of the moment so he imagined how uncomfortable it must have been for the sergeant.

'I'm going to pick up Cy Wong,' said Bellamy. 'I'm not sure who poses the greater threat to her, Sam Hung or Ah Tay but I think she'll be safest in custody until we find them.'

'I wouldn't worry about Cy Wong,' said Hamish. 'I wonder if the other two are safe from her.'

They left in a police carriage for the house in George Street. Everything was quiet when they arrived. They checked behind the building; the house was locked up tight and there appeared to be no movement inside.

They entered through the back window as they had done previously and moved slowly and carefully from one room to the next on the ground floor. All was silent. Bellamy nodded toward the staircase, indicating for Hamish to follow him. They made their way up, testing each step for sound. They listened intently, controlling their breathing, for even a minute sound of movement upstairs. Finally, they reached the door of Ah Chit's old bedroom and immediately saw that the safe door was open ... and the safe was empty.

'The gold!' shouted Bellamy.

He turned around, knocking Hamish off his feet as he did so, and flew down the stairs, his feet only making contact twice on the flight. He landed at the bottom with a thud.

'Come on,' he cried back up the staircase. 'We need to get to the wharf and notify the authorities to keep an eye out for that gold.'

Hamish hurried but took a more measured approach to the stairs. They ran down Alice Street alongside Queen's Park to the naval office where a crowd was gathered at the dock. A large clipper was inching its way from the wharf. Men on board were shouting instructions to one another and the crowd left behind on land were bustling about various chests, luggage and other cargo. Another ship had berthed earlier that morning and among the items on board were fifty sheep. A man was valiantly attempting to corral them into a makeshift pen that looked unlikely to hold them even if he could get them into it. Bellamy pushed past the crowd to a naval officer trying to create order from the chaos.

'The ship just setting sail,' he said. 'Where is it headed?'

'Southern China,' yelled the officer over the commotion.

'We must stop her,' shouted Bellamy. 'There is illegal cargo on board.'

The officer lifted both brows. 'That's impossible now, sir. In any case, the customs officers searched the cargo and found naught amiss.'

Bellamy stepped back as others took the attention of the officer.

Hamish knew the gold would be well hidden in the cargo on that ship but it was too late to do anything other than telegram officials at the next port.

'We should return later and find out if any cargo was transported to the ship this morning prior to departure. It should be easy to identify as it would have been taken on board last.'

'Yes,' said Bellamy, 'so we shall. But I don't hold any confidence that officers will be motivated to search energetically for it. It is obviously well-enough hidden to be overlooked by customs here.'

Hamish wondered if it really mattered. He hoped the gold was going to help alleviate the terrible poverty among the peasants in China. He would rather that than have the Australian Government seize it anyway.

'Where do we look for Ah Tay now?' asked Bellamy.

Hamish glanced toward Queen's Park. 'Your men will be covering the city streets. Why don't we search the park?'

It was as good an idea as any. They walked toward the park, surveying the people wandering alone or arm in arm along the main thoroughfare. They passed the fountain and headed toward the river. There didn't appear to be anything amiss in the park. Children darted back and forth while young mothers chatted. A nanny in a starched uniform brushed down a child covered in wattle blossoms. A dog barked hungrily at a blue-tongue lizard standing its ground on a mound of pine needles. Hamish and Bellamy struggled to remain alert – their senses were becoming dulled by the morning sun and the ordinariness of the scenes playing out in the park. It was difficult to imagine anything sinister in the midst of this ideal summer setting. Then Hamish caught a glimpse of the sun bouncing off something in the old trees close to the Point. There was the glint of light bouncing off metal.

'This way.' He led Bellamy toward the trees.

As they drew closer they saw two men in a scuffle. Hamish gasped as he saw one of the men tuck his arm around the other's neck and hold a long knife to his throat. Memories of his own assault rushed back to him and he knew immediately Sam Hung was the attacker. He held Ah Tay in a headlock. Fifty paces to the left of Sam Hung and Ah Tay was a woman, holding her ground, poised, ready to strike.

'Found them,' said Hamish.

KATE

They had stayed in the coffee house as long as could be considered reasonable when Cy Wong slipped quietly from her booth into the street. Kate waited for a few seconds before following. She saw Cy Wong slip in and out of the crowd down Queen Street, then turn right into Albert Street. Cy Wong moved silently, almost imperceptibly like a shadow down the busy street. Then she ducked into the lane alongside the drapery.

She must think the police will have already checked for her at the Pearl, Kate thought. Kate saw Cy Wong's back as she turned into the lane, then she saw her step back into Albert Street. Something was wrong. What she saw wasn't a natural fluid movement. It was a jerking response as though someone had tugged her away. Kate quickened her pace. When she reached the drapery store and stared down the lane alongside, she could see nothing out of the ordinary.

She edged along the wall to the back corner of the building and peered around it. In the distance, she saw a figure dragging Cy Wong behind the row of buildings. They were ducking in and out of view behind ramshackle sheds and outbuildings. Cy Wong's head was covered in a black hood and the figure was forcing her along. She tripped and struggled but could not get free.

Kate continued to follow, remaining far enough back that they would not hear her. Suddenly, as they emerged onto Elizabeth Street, Kate saw Sam Hung appear as if from nowhere and knock down the figure dragging Cy Wong. The figure stumbled and Cy Wong leapt from the ground, swung her body in a full circle and kicked the figure hard in the chest. Finally free of his grip, she ran. Her attacker immediately ran after her. Sam Hung also took off in pursuit. Cy Wong ran past Elizabeth Street and kept going parallel to Albert Street until she reached Queen's Park. At that point Kate lost sight of them. She hurried as quickly as she could behind the old storefront but she couldn't run without drawing attention to herself. Kate rushed through the gates to Queen's Park and looked around.

There were people strolling along the path toward the elaborate fountain but there was no sign of Cy Wong. In the distance, through the branches of the giant fig trees, was the slim figure of Sam Hung as he caught up to Ah Tay. Hung grabbed him from behind and held a sword to his throat. In the same instant, Cy Wong appeared from the George Street end of the gardens running toward the men. She stopped a few yards from them. It was clear they hadn't seen her. Time froze. Kate scanned for cover. Then Hamish and Bellamy crashed in on the scene from the Edward Street end of the park.

Hamish ran to within hearing distance of Ah Tay.

'My friend.'

Sam Hung forced the blade tighter against Ah Tay's neck and turned his attention to Hamish.

Kate held her breath.

'Stop! Whatever your grievance, you can't get away with this. You can't kill a man in public in broad daylight.'

Sam Hung did not release his grip. He appeared to be weighing his options. Cy Wong was tense and still, keeping her distance from the men.

'I apprehend this man in defence of Cy Wong,' shouted Sam Hung, still hedging his bets with the knife tightly against Ah Tay's throat.

'Is this what you want?' Hamish turned toward Cy Wong.

She didn't flinch. Her face was unreadable.

Kate wanted to shout out to her, make her do something to stop this nightmare but her throat constricted.

'This has gone on long enough. It is time for the truth, from everyone. No one else needs to die,' said Hamish.

Bellamy had caught his breath at last. 'You'll be tried for murder,' he warned. 'Make no mistake about it.'

Sam Hung relaxed his hold on Ah Tay who struggled free. Ah Tay looked like he would leap toward Cy Wong even now. Cy Wong struck a warrior's pose, ready for him. They both stood still, staring one another down.

'This is not the way,' said Hamish.

Ah Tay spat on the ground. 'She watched Ah Chit kill my father,' he shouted. 'She said nothing, all these years she said nothing.'

While Hamish held Ah Tay's attention, Bellamy was inching closer to them.

'She was a child, she didn't know …'

'She knew. She came here to work with him. She knew and she did nothing. Then she came here to help him get rich.'

Cy Wong appeared alert and ready to pounce if necessary. 'I didn't want to help your slimy uncle get rich. I came to make money to release my father. Ah Chit wanted no part of it.'

'Is that why you and Sam Hung killed him?' asked Hamish.

Ah Tay lost his focus for only a split second but it was long enough for Sam Hung to move close to him.

'Ah Tay, we will make sure we find the evidence to convict them for the death of your uncle. I promise you will have justice.'

The desperation in Hamish's eyes moved Kate.

Like a bolt from the blue, Sam Hung flew at Ah Tay. Hamish screamed, 'No!'

Sam Hung propelled himself forward and charged at Ah Tay, his sword thrust forward. The sword slid cleanly through Ah Tay's stomach and he fell to the ground.

As Sam Hung plunged the sword through Ah Tay, Bellamy lurched forward and tackled the Chinaman only a second too late. They rolled on the grass together until Bellamy was on top of him holding his arms and body flat to the ground. Sam Hung's right hand still clutched the sword, his knuckles white.

It wasn't until Bellamy had Sam Hung securely held to the ground, one arm behind his back and the bloodied sword removed from his grip that Kate made herself known. She walked up to Cy Wong and stood silent beside her. Though neither woman spoke, Kate felt the bond between them. Men were behaving foolishly and while they claimed their motives were in defence of the women, the men had no idea what it was that was important to them.

HAMISH

Hamish ran to Ah Tay and held his head in his hands, remembering the little boy who had been his friend.

'There will be justice for Ah Chit,' he said, tears forming in his eyes.

'Justice has already been done,' said Ah Tay. 'For my father.'

Ah Tay closed his eyes. 'I killed Ah Chit.'

Hamish held his friend's head against his chest for some time. Tears poured down his cheeks. He didn't want to process the words spoken. He wanted to remember the skinny Chinese boy, older, braver, who had been kind enough to be his friend when he had needed one. Ah Chit and Ah Tay were both gone from this world but they would live in Hamish's memories, as slightly different people, perhaps, than reality had shown them to be.

Cy Wong moved closer. Hamish could see her out of the corner of his eye, standing over Ah Tay. Bystanders, their stroll in the park disturbed by the violence, must have alerted the local constable on the beat because three men in police uniform were rushing toward them. They took hold of Sam Hung and dragged him to a waiting carriage.

Bellamy struggled to his feet and staggered the few steps to where Hamish was still holding Ah Tay. He kneeled beside him and placed his hand on Hamish's back.

'He said he killed Ah Chit,' Hamish croaked, his voice thick with grief.

Bellamy nodded.

Two constables left with Sam Hung but Pennyweather was leaning over his boss's shoulder. Hamish saw his young face and felt older than his years.

'They are waiting for the body, sir,' he said.

Bellamy held Hamish under his arm and lifted him away from Ah Tay. Hamish shook away the policeman's touch but he complied. He turned toward the river and staggered to its edge, where he sat alone, his face in his hands, while the authorities removed Ah Tay's body from the park. Quite a lot of people had gathered to see what was going on. Hamish wanted to be away from them. He looked up and stared out onto the river as the bustle and murmur of the group receded. He concentrated on the permanence of the river, its depth, its infinite movement, its calmness beneath the surface. The mystery had been solved but he felt he had failed. His goal had been to help Ah Tay, now Ah Tay was dead.

Hamish was numb when he became aware someone was beside him. He raised his eyes from the river, surprised to see it was Kate. How long had she been sitting there? Her eyes told him she understood. He couldn't speak and she didn't either. They simply sat there staring at the river, processing their own separate thoughts, retelling their own stories to force them to make sense in their minds and comforted by the presence of another human being. Both of them knew that to keep too close company with the river was dangerous.

Eventually, Wallace arrived, led by his wiry terrier. 'Time to go home,' he said.

Hamish agreed.

'Do you wish me to retain a cab to take you home?' he asked Kate.

'No. I'd prefer to walk. I need time to think about what has happened.' She smiled weakly.

When Wallace and Hamish arrived at the house, Rita was waiting for them. Sergeant Bellamy had alerted both Wallace and Rita of the events of the day. Rita threw her arms around Hamish's neck and held on tight. Hamish clung to her. Her proximity reminded him of all his successes in his life in the colony. He had made friends who loved him and he had a growing practice with patients who relied on him. The police sergeant trusted him, perhaps more than was warranted but he was grateful for his trust, nonetheless.

'You need sleep,' said Rita, stepping back to look at him.

'Hot tea,' she said to Wallace, 'if you please.'

CHAPTER TWENTY-TWO

Many improvements have recently been made for applying gas to a variety of purposes connected with the comforts of and the luxuries of domestic life. By means of a simply constructed apparatus, gas performs the respective processes of roasting, baking, frying, boiling, steaming and broiling, and with a precision that cannot be attained by a common fire. Two or three days' experience is sufficient to enable the servants to conduct any of the above-mentioned operations with success and certainty, whilst the trouble and attention required are less than the ordinary method. Roasting by gas is the very perfection of the culinary art: the meat being cooked uniformly and its juices (on which the nutritious qualities and delicacy of flavour so much depend) being retained and brought to the table.

Gas cooking stoves are made in sizes adapted to the wants of small and large families, and for schools, hotels and other public establishments. As boiling, roasting and baking can be conducted simultaneously as well as separately an ordinary fire in many families will, in summer, be but seldom required. For preserving fruits or for other domestic purposes in which a steady heat easily controlled is of importance, a gas fire is superior to every other. Let it be noticed that, in using gas as fuel, there is no waste of time or materials – no noise or dirt or smoke. The full effect of the heat is obtained and can be applied in an instant just where it is needed, and when it has done its duty, it can be as quickly removed.

Hobart Courier. Friday 29 February, 1856

Three weeks later, Hamish was chopping vegetables and popping them in a massive iron baking dish ready to go into the new gas range he recently had installed for Wallace.

'Far superior for roasting,' declared Wallace. 'The meat cooks through evenly.'

Hamish smiled at the reminder that Wallace was still enthralled by his new stove. They both looked up when Red rushed to the door emitting tiny squeals of excitement. A few seconds later the door opened and closed and Red was yapping with delight.

'Rita,' they both said in unison.

'In here,' called Hamish.

Rita entered the kitchen with the terrier bundled in her arms.

'What's for dinner?' she asked.

'Roast lamb,' said Hamish. 'Wallace is still experimenting with his new stove.'

'It's marvellous,' said Rita. 'I'd like to buy one for Thalia but I fear Cook would be overwhelmed by it. She loves her wood stove.'

Rita set the terrier on the floor and turned to Hamish. Her face and eyes smacked of sympathy leading Hamish to experience an unexpected rush of grief. He tried to speak but his voice cracked.

'Good … ing,' he said.

Rita threw her arms around his neck and held tight. Hamish felt his lips press against her hair and he breathed in the smell of her, her closeness, her touch, while tears welled up behind his eyes. His eyes stung but he held the tears back. Ah Tay was an important part of his childhood, his past. Rita was his present. He held tight to the embrace until he was certain the threat of tears had subsided.

'We all create stories about our childhood and the people who were important to us,' said Wallace, as he placed a lid on the boiling water. 'The stories we create are only a version of the truth. I should know.' He chuckled.

Hamish released his grip on Rita and stepped back. He coughed to cover his embarrassment at the unexpected moment of vulnerability and drawing his fingers through his fringe he pulled it back from his face. He was desperately trying to think of something to say to shift attention away from him when there was a knock at the door.

Wallace wiped his hands on his apron and went to open it. Red accompanied him, eager to find out who else was visiting.

Bellamy strode into the kitchen with Red scuttling about his legs and

Wallace behind him. He shook Hamish's hand, squeezing hard to express his support. Hamish felt the heaviness of the previous moments lift and he smiled.

'It's wonderful to have such friendships,' he said, his eyes fixed mostly on Red. 'Thank you for coming.'

'All of you out of my kitchen,' said Wallace. 'I can't work with this crowd in here. I'll let you know when the food is ready and one of you can help carry it upstairs.'

Hamish, Rita and Bellamy made their way up the staircase with Red ducking and weaving between their legs.

'You've brought out the good china,' said Rita when she saw the dining table set with the lace-work cloth, good English china and silver cutlery.

'Not me,' said Hamish, 'Wallace. He said it's a celebration. We are celebrating the closure of a mystery and the endurance of friendship.'

Rita and Bellamy spread out on the settee while Hamish poured wine. He offered them each a glass and sat down in his blue velvet armchair.

'How is Agatha enjoying her visit with her sister?' asked Rita.

'She's relishing the cooler weather, by all accounts,' replied Bellamy.

'I read in the Courier that the trial of Sam Hung will start tomorrow,' said Rita.

Hamish took a mouthful of wine before commenting. 'Yes.'

Bellamy stuck his chest out to indicate his satisfaction with the way events had turned. 'He is standing charged with the murder of Ah Tay. There was insufficient evidence to link him to the removal of the gold and its illegal dispatch out of the country, more's the pity.'

'What did happen to the gold?' asked Rita. 'Was it intercepted at another port?'

Bellamy looked down at his hands. 'No. It was not recovered. Presumably it made its way to Southern China, where it can only be hoped it did some good.'

'I hope it got Cy Wong's father out of prison,' said Rita. 'What will become of Cy Wong?'

Bellamy laughed. 'Cy Wong has taken over the role of "headman" in the Brisbane chapter of the Sheathed Sword.'

'Bravo,' squealed Rita.

'Apparently, she is the strongest and most respected member of the ancient family line linked to the Society, in Brisbane. I fear if anyone comes up from down south with intent to usurp her, they will come up against a fierce adversary.'

Wallace joined them chuckling. 'Cy Wong will be running the Pearl, then.'

'Yes, and the properties, including the Nine Holes,' said Bellamy.

'I believe she will look after Daisy well,' said Rita.

'What about Kate?' asked Bellamy. 'What has become of her?'

'Kate is still residing at Thalia,' said Rita. 'Her health is improving now she has stopped smoking opium and drinking alcohol. She has three hearty meals a day forced upon her by Cook. Her writing career is taking off nicely. In fact, her piece on the prevention of smallpox was published in The Queenslander this week. Do you have a copy, Hamish?'

Hamish looked about aimlessly while Wallace retrieved the magazine from the sideboard.

Rita perched herself on the arm of the blue velvet armchair and flicked the magazine open to the page she wanted. 'Shall I read it?'

'By all means,' said Bellamy. Hamish and Wallace nodded.

'She interviewed Hamish for the article,' explained Rita. 'Didn't she?' she looked to Hamish for confirmation. 'I'm proud of them both!' cried Rita and she proceeded to read aloud.

In an interview with Dr Hamish Hart, medical officer in practice in rooms on Wickham Terrace and occasional officer of forensic investigation for the Queensland Police, the esteemed doctor expressed his concern at the recent cases of smallpox identified in our fair city. While the Central Board of Health acted quickly, once notified by Dr Hart to quarantine the infected households, and the Queensland Police led by Sergeant Bellamy ensured the quarantine arrangements were enforced, the doctor remains anxious that Brisbane may be on the brink of its first serious outbreak of smallpox.

'Vaccination is the surest tool we have in the prevention of smallpox,' says Dr Hart. 'Yet vaccination and re-vaccination rates are dangerously low in our community.'

Dr Hart acknowledged the fear and reluctance of some parents to expose their children to the process of inoculation; however, he wants to reassure parents that modern methods are far superior to earlier attempts to stem the disease. Dr Hart then went on to explain that the object of vaccination is to produce the mild and harmless disease known as vaccinia. This excites the immune system resulting in protection against the more serious disease. It is known that a direct proportionate response exists between the size of the local scar after inoculation and the degree of immunity. The larger the scar, the higher the immunity. In addition, the protective effect of the first vaccination does not last throughout life. If vaccinated as an infant, a person's immunity is likely to disappear around puberty. It is absolutely essential that re-vaccination should be performed between the ages of ten and twelve years. The protection afforded by vaccination and re-vaccination in almost all cases amounts to immunity.

A major concern expressed by parents has been the accidental transmission of syphilis by vaccination. Dr Hart said this would not be possible as the use of arm-to-arm vaccines has recently been made all but redundant by the availability of vaccines made from calf-lymph. Dr Hart reassures the people of Brisbane that his vaccines are derived from animals rather than children.

When asked what message the doctor would most want to portray to readers, he said this: 'It is absolutely necessary that whole of population vaccination should be achieved across Australia.' He said that as long as any part of the country remains improperly vaccinated, the population, in all parts, is not safe.

Rita looked up from the page. 'Here, here,' she cried.

'Well-written by Kate and well-said by Hamish,' said Wallace.

Bellamy looked thoughtful. 'I wish the government put thought to the number of my officers it takes to enforce household quarantine,' he said. 'Still, I agree in principle.'

'Kate is currently working on a piece on prostitution in Brisbane, from the perspective of a working woman. She wants to highlight the hypocrisy of the Anti-Contagious Diseases Act. Young Bob was instrumental in securing the deal, as a matter of interest. He introduced me to the Editor of the Brisbane Courier and I spoke on Kate's behalf. I think that boy has a future as a reporter himself.'

Hamish clicked his spoon against his empty bowl. 'I believe he will be the editor of one of our esteemed newspapers by the time he is twenty!' he said.

KATE

Kate hesitated on the street in front of the Nine Holes. She was wearing a beige skirt, shorter in length than most of her dresses, just touching the top of her brown, leather boots. She wore a simple linen blouse with mutton chop sleeves and a straw hat. Plain and practical, the outfit had become her work attire as she traipsed through the mud and rubbish of Frog's Hollow in search of people to interview for her newspaper stories. She was becoming comfortable in her respectability. Self-pride had replaced self-loathing. She stared at the makeshift fire pit where the filthy mattresses had burned and was strangely nostalgic when she saw the pile of fresh potato peels and other food scraps near the window. They represented a life continuing inside without her. She hadn't seen Daisy in four weeks. It seemed like a lifetime. How would Daisy react to her unannounced visit? How would she look? What would she say?

Kate felt panic rise and turned to walk away. But something told her it would only become more difficult – until one day it was impossible. She drew in a deep breath and marched through the mud to the back door, knocking loudly before she changed her mind.

The door opened and Daisy's face appeared. Her face was still swollen from sleep and her hair was a mess. She placed a trembling hand on the door and opened it wide.

'Back, are you?' she said.

'I've called for a visit,' said Kate. 'If it's convenient,' she added quickly.

Daisy stared at her through bleary eyes. Kate stared back. She was used to staring down her mother and she had the advantage of not being hungover.

'Humph,' said Daisy at last. 'Yer better come in, then.'

She turned and walked into the cellar as if to indicate she was not bothered either way. But Kate knew she was bothered. She was bothered very much.

She followed her mother and was relieved to see the cellar was still reasonably clean. The night's gowns were scattered about in piles of faded silk and torn lace but the bedding and the floors were clean. The small wooden stove in the corner was lit and there was water boiling. The Chinese man was sitting cross-legged in the corner smoking a pipe, having returned as a somewhat permanent fixture in the room.

Kate sat on the edge of the bed that was once her own. 'Will we have tea?' she asked.

'Tea?' cried Daisy. 'Bloody tea? Are yer the queen of bloody England, are yer?'

Kate smiled. Her mother was scuttling through the pile of chipped crockery in the tin pail by the stove, looking for two mugs.

CHAPTER TWENTY-THREE

At the Ball given by the Mayor and Lady Mayoress in honour of Her Majesty's Jubilee, some exceedingly lovely and novel dresses were worn by the ladies. Lady Carrington wore a magnificent evening dress of white brocaded silk made with a train; on the left side was a falling tablier of silver gauze – the bodice was low and trimmed with silver jet; her Ladyship wore a coronet of diamonds, also a necklace and spray on the bodice. Lord Carrington wore a Windsor costume.

Miss Young appeared as 'Maid of Kent' – a suitable costume, she belonging to a Kentish family. The pretty gown of white net was covered with green leaves and golden hop blossoms. The costume being enhanced by a large hat of white satin trimmed with plumes of ostrich feathers and a border of hop leaves.

Lady Manning wore an evening dress of fawn brocade trimmed with white lace. Mrs Tucker wore a superb gown composed almost entirely of black sequins with a long train having three rows of broad gold tinsel around the edge, a front of old gold satin dotted with large yellow pearls and striped with lines of golden tinsel.

Miss Innes Taylor wore one of the prettiest dresses in the room, a simple white muslin with large, puffed sleeves and white satin hat with waving plumes, such a maid would have shone in any court.

Miss Sharratt wore a striking contrast to the above costume representing 'busy bee', a short dress of black, trimmed in front to indicate the insect, with bands of amber satin, wings of golden gauze, cap of black velvet and gold, with eyes and antennae of the insect sat above flowing golden hair.

Another 'Miss Magpie' was excellent with plumage of black and white silk, skirt of black satin edged with swans down and outspread wings. Veritable magpie's wings fluttered at the back of her gown and a dainty plume waved gracefully over her hair.

Queensland Figaro and Punch. Saturday 7 August, 1886

Four months later Hamish sat alone in his favourite blue armchair. Wallace had provided him with sherry and left him to his thoughts. Sam Hung had been tried and convicted for the murder of Ah Tay and today he hung. It was over. Hamish felt nothing. He searched his soul for something – relief that justice had been done; the sweet-sour taste of vengeance; sorrow for his loss, for the loss of two young men's lives. Nothing. If anything, he had to admit a strange comfort in his wallowing. The whole episode had been too personal, too tied up in childhood memories, too confusing. People had not been who he believed them to be. That was jarring. He was so caught up in his inability to find a sentiment he could rest on he didn't hear Rita come in and climb the stairs. She appeared before him like a mirage.

'Don't you start doing it,' he said.

'Doing what?'

'Appearing out of nowhere.'

'I let myself in as I always do.' She laughed.

Hamish leant further into his chair as if to resist any attempt that might be made to shift him from it.

'It's over,' said Rita. 'Time for you to join the world of the living. You have been morose for months now.'

'I had to give evidence at the inquest into Ah Chit's death and at the trial of Sam Hung for the killing of Ah Tay,' he said. 'It has been a morose time.'

'I am aware of that,' Rita said, her voice softening. 'But now that it is all over you have to put it behind you. Return to your normal level of self-isolation and introspection.'

Hamish looked up under his eyebrows. He thought the accusation unfair. He shifted further into his chair.

'Wallace?' called out Rita. Wallace came in with two fresh glasses of sherry. He gave one to Rita and placed the other on the table beside Hamish.

'Drink,' she said. 'Then we're going out. You too, Wallace.'

Wallace took up the glass behind Hamish and drank it in one mouthful. 'Where are we going?' he said.

'The Queen's Golden Jubilee celebrations,' she said cheerfully. 'The whole city has been lit up.'

'I don't feel like celebrating,' said Hamish.

'Nonetheless.' Rita's tone made it clear that no further discussion would be required.

Hamish knew he would give in to her wishes in the end, so he decided not to waste energy debating the issue.

'Very well,' he said as he uncurled from the armchair.

Hamish, Rita and Wallace made their way to the north end of Victoria Bridge. Long before they arrived, Rita gasped out loud. The words 'South Brisbane Gas Company' blazed around the arch of the bridge like molten gold against the black velvet sky. Hamish's gaze was fixed on the sign until movement in the river below caught his attention. The reflection from the illumination in the inky waters of the river was mesmerizing. It shimmered and danced with the movement of the water. He barely noticed when the crowd gathered around the display. When he decided it was time to move on, he was hemmed in. He and Rita shuffled along with the crowd while he remained intensely aware of Rita's arm in his. He concentrated on not letting her go; if he lost her in the crowd, he would struggle to find her again. The crowd moved as though it were a single entity toward Queen Street with Hamish, Rita and Wallace jostled along in its mass.

The next display to stop them all and invite their gaze was the Town Hall. The building was alight with transparencies of Her Majesty the Queen, the Prince and Princess of Wales and the Mayor and Lady Mayoress standing proudly against the brick. Hundreds of little fairy lamps glistened in a tumble of colours down the façade.

Rita's face shone with delight and Hamish felt the melancholy of the past weeks fall away. It was a truly delightful display. At half-past eight a large attachment of volunteers from Lytton marched over the bridge, along William and George Streets and into Queen. They were headed by the Naval Brigade. Hamish's head swam from the pounding drums and the screeching fife band. Following the Naval Brigade came the artillery and the scarlet coats of the infantry. The parade marched to the music of Red, White and Blue with the backing of a brass band. At the rear, the Boys' Brigade marched proudly in their smart uniforms, a drum corps to rival any in the colony. A passage opened up in the crowd for the parade to pass, then closed around behind them. Hamish, Rita and Wallace continued on their way, pushed along by the crowd.

After the Boys' Brigade marched by, next came His Excellency and Lady Musgrave in their open carriage. The crowd cheered. Hamish and Rita glanced at one another with raised eyebrows, then laughed. Wallace rolled his eyes. Wallace was no fan of pomp and ceremony but he clearly found the spectacle of illuminations a delight.

At the offices of the Telegraph there was a transparency of Her Majesty the Queen and on either side of her, depicted in a very natural way, were two gentlemen ensconced in easy chairs, wearing slippers, sitting by the fireside reading the newspaper. A little further on they passed the Australian and the British Empire Hotels. Faces upward, they marvelled at the millions of tiny coloured lights dripping from every angle of the buildings. The shop of Mr Samuels was next and came as a shock to the senses. The roof of the balcony was festooned with illuminated banana trees, ferns and other tropical plants.

'Good Lord,' cried Hamish, pointing to the roof.

Rita and Wallace looked up to see a group of Aboriginal men and women dancing among the ferns. The crowd in front of the building was overjoyed at the entertainment. It was the first time Hamish had seen such a sight. He had seen Aboriginal people dance, certainly but not for the entertainment of Europeans. He wasn't sure how he felt about it. But there wasn't time to muse over it; the crowd moved him along to the next building. The new opera house, still under construction, was illuminated with a crown of lights comprised of gas-jets spelling out the words 'Victoria Jubilee'. A few yards further along, the crowd were declaring the sight of the evening to be the Queensland National Bank Building on which hung over 5,000 tiny lights of red, white and green from basement to parapet, giving the appearance of a fairy-tale palace.

Hamish was exhausted by the onslaught to his senses. They had made it to the bottom end of Queen Street where the crowd was thinning, so they began making their way uphill toward Wickham Terrace.

'It was a truly magnificent display,' he said as Rita threaded her arm through his.

'I think our little town is coming of age,' said Rita.

Wallace snorted.

'The Chinese Joss House Opening in January and now the Jubilee celebration in July. The citizens of Brisbane have enjoyed an extravagant display of public entertainment this year.'

'There is much to celebrate,' said Rita. 'The pace of building works alone is evidence of the exponential growth of our city in recent months. Brisbane will never be the lazy frontier it was. We are becoming sophisticated!' She laughed.

Hamish lay on his back staring at the ceiling. A small finger of moonlight pointed through the window toward the end of his bed. He was aware of it only out of the corner of his eye. The room, for the most part, blanketed in greyness, lay thick and heavy on his body. Staring at the ceiling trying to clear his mind of the night's conversations, and the previous months' events, he registered the moving mass of flecks that made up the space between himself and the pressed metal ceiling. By his bed, the stand supporting his book and the pipe he'd never used were a shimmering dancing myriad of grey particles, as was the wardrobe against the wall. Light danced and skipped and moved; inanimate objects were no longer solid. Everything was shifting. Hamish let his eyelids close and wondered if he was already asleep, then a sensation of being watched compelled his eyes to open again.

A shadowy figure stood over his bed, silently watching him, poised with one arm raised, as if ready to strike. If the figure had a face, Hamish couldn't make it out. He thought he ought to be afraid but fear wouldn't come. He thought he should flee but he couldn't move. An immeasurably powerful force was pressing down on him. He was caught between light and dark, between wakefulness and sleep, between life and death. In one fluid movement, the figure's arm dropped by its side and it took on a less threatening stance.

'Are you a hungry ghost?' asked Hamish in his mind. Or did he say it aloud?

The shadow transformed from the shape of a man into a large cat, muscular like a tiger but black. It turned away from him and leapt through the window. Hamish felt the weight suddenly lift from his body and he sat upright panting for air.

'Ah Tay,' he whispered. 'One can forgive murder.'

AUTHOR'S NOTES

Like shadowy figures of hungry ghosts in the half-light, the beings that inhabit our past cannot be observed directly. They're shifting shimmering particles that disappear as soon as we look directly at them.

One of the questions I am most often asked is: How much of your stories are true? Are they true or are they fiction? I usually explain that the setting is real but I make up the characters and the murder. There isn't time for nuance when you're chatting with readers at a signing. But the explanation is far too simplistic. The line between truth and fiction in historical writing is blurred because we cannot know anything about the past *directly*. We can only infer from the interpretations of others and from our own experiences.

During my research for *Murder in Frog's Hollow*, I reviewed the traditional reference sources: newspapers, academic articles, novels written and published in the 1880s, government documents, old maps and photographs. But these are artefacts from the past, things we can hold, texts we can read, photographs that seem to capture the hungry ghosts in a chemical chimera. They are not the past. They're merely invitations to imagine the past. Nonetheless, the past, insomuch as it no longer exists, can only be observed through these artefacts. We can hold the broken stem of a pipe in our hands, for example. We can feel its smoothness, we can smell the ash, we can close our eyes and imagine the waxed moustache draped across the pipe's stem, and the piercing eyes of the smoker watching us, watching him. In our minds he is real, like a recalled memory but he isn't real, we imagine him. And we do so within our culturally situated perceptions of what a man who smokes such a pipe would look like, would smell like, would breathe like. Our lives are full of images of the past and every one of them comes together to form the man. Jean-Paul Sartre says that imaginings are relationships we create between images and our consciousness. Our minds seamlessly weave between an object or text, what we already know, and our intention to reach some form of perception, a story about the image in our minds.

In this work, I want to explain to you how this story came to be, from the source to the imagining, from the pipe to the man. I want to show that we shape the past, 'our' past, through a process of re-membering. Kate Mitchell explains in *History and Cultural Memory in Neo-Victorian Fiction*, the historical novel makes something imagined seem like something remembered, as we read and re-read history, we are shaping cultural memory. We are animating the past, lending it life, imagining.

Murder in Frog's Hollow begins, as do all Hamish Hart's adventures, in a place within South-East Queensland in the 1880s. Frog's Hollow was the name used at that time to describe the area roughly defined by Elizabeth Street down to the Botanical Gardens and from George Street down to Edward Street in the Brisbane town centre.

I always walk through the places I describe in my stories. Today, I'm standing at the river's edge, at the bottom corner of the Botanical Gardens where Edward Street begins. It's hot, late January, the same time of year the story takes place. I feel sorry for Hamish in his woollen coat and starched collar. I'm on a pedestrian walkway that skirts the river and offers views back onto the bank and Brisbane beyond. The river flows beneath my feet; I can feel its current through the soles of my sandals, even though it's a good two meters below. Looking back towards the bank, an ancient wall holds the river back and I can see the entrance to a drain carrying water from inland into the river. It's easy to see that a creek once flowed freely down this trajectory. The creek ran vaguely along the line where Creek Street is now. It flooded regularly, not only when the tropical storms made their way south but whenever there was a strong, spring tide. The river is greenish today. I wonder if it was a different colour in 1887, perhaps blue like the sea?

I cross the walkway to re-join the bank and place my hand on the iron gates at the edge of the Botanical Gardens, the same gates that were in place when Hamish was there. This is where he and Sergeant Bellamy entered when they were looking for Sam Hung. For a moment I feel his heart pounding. The anticipation hurts; I feel the pain in my chest. Did Hamish know, somewhere deep in his sub-conscious, how it was all going to end?

Gazing up toward George Street I can see how the land lies, I can see the hollow, I can see how easily it would flood without the great wall holding back the river. I can see how it came to be known as Frog's Hollow. Old Mineral House stands on the corner of Edward Street opposite. Building began in 1888, one year after the story, and I try to picture the corner without the old warehouse. This is the most difficult imagining of all: seeing something not there. There aren't many buildings left that echo the time of the story. Heritage conservation was not a priority in Brisbane during the twentieth century. Most of what I can see is from the building boom that followed the period of *Murder in Frog's Hollow*. Still, heading toward Albert Street, I pass the Port Office Hotel. There's a sculpture on one wall to commemorate a long-gone bridge the convicts once used to cross the creek.

But Albert Street is where I'm headed. Albert Street was the heart of Frog's Hollow. Today it's difficult to manoeuvre because one entire block is barricaded off as construction proceeds on a new railway line and station. Peering through the scaffolding I see a massive hole where the lives of Daisy and Kate played out. I blank out the noise of traffic behind me and the construction works below to remember how Doctor Anastacia Dukovic, of the Queensland Police Museum, describes the Nine Holes: a row of nine houses under one roof, each with a narrow room at the front, used as a shop, and apartments behind that included a cellar. From Doctor Dukovic's words I formed a series of relationships. What sort of people might have lived in such a place? What would their lives have been like? I was less engaged in what it might have looked like than I was in what it must have smelled like. From Doctor Dukovic's description, I imagine the place where Daisy and Kate slept during the daylight hours when they were not working. Now I see only a deep cavern. The Nine Holes would soon be an underground rail line snaking through the dark corners of our past.

Before they began digging the tunnel, archaeologists deployed to excavate the site found thousands of artefacts, broken china, leather boots, coins and sherds of everyday life. One of the finds, a tiny silver pin once used to pick up the sticky substance of opium, captured my imagination and led to a 'deep dive' into the sale, use and regulation of opium in Brisbane in the 1880s. Drawing on this research, I stared at the pin. I imagined the

Chinese man, cross-legged in the corner, dipping the tiny silver pin into a phial of sticky black opium. I watched as the resinous extract adhered to the wire, while he held it over the flame of the lamp until the liquid evaporated. I watched him dip it into the phial again as a new layer of the substance gathered. I saw him transfer the mass into a peculiarly shaped pipe and indulge in the enjoyment he had so patiently prepared. This man is imagined but he is also a cultural memory. An image that has been written and re-written by historians, journalists and novelists.

Archaeologists specialise in building images of the past through inciting relationships between objects and our consciousness. The archaeologists digging up Albert Street found an imprint of dog paws in the cement of a cellar, foundations that were already forty years old when Hamish and Rita visited. The image of a dog, already long passed, scurrying across the foundations of a cellar, screamed of relationships that connect us over time. I included the imprinted dog paws in the scene where Hamish, Rita and Kate are cleaning the mud from the cellar. Somehow the sign of a life now long past in the cement sent them into fits of laughter. Kate cleaned the area thoroughly to make sure she could always see them. The dog paw imprints connect the characters to a past and the story connects them to us.

Leaving the crater-like hole that was once the Nine Holes, I skirt the barricade and walk further along Albert Street to the corner of Elizabeth Street where there was once a drapery store used as a front for a gambling house. It is not there now, it's the entrance to the Myer Centre. There's no record of the name of the store but in my mind, it took on life as the Pearl, the gambling house owned by the Sheathed Sword. The police raid at the Pearl was inspired by an article in the Newcastle Morning Herald. Newcastle is not Brisbane, I know. But the scene triggered my imagination and a similar event at the Pearl developed. The police burst into a gambling house planning to apprehend the patrons 'in the act'. However, the Chinese, finding themselves under raid, began tumbling and vaulting over tables and chairs, and each other's heads. The police had to tie them with rope because the handcuffs slipped off their wrists as soon as they were put on. The police raid in the Pearl is a similar scene, with the addition of a group of larrikins who decide to join in on the excitement.

As I continue my walk along Elizabeth Street, I think about the

Chinese families who lived there in the 1880s. European attitudes toward the Chinese were particularly harsh. This was made clear by the many opinion pieces and cartoons published in the newspapers depicting 'Poor John Chinaman' and describing fear of the 'yellow peril'. The Chinese were different, they looked different, dressed differently and spoke in local dialects. They were also prepared to work for less money at difficult jobs. This made people angry because they were taking jobs white men could have done; at the same time, it validated their inferiority because they worked at the dirtiest jobs for the least money.

But people were most fearful of the potential of the Chinese to seduce their daughters into opium use and prostitution, even though the opium dens were full of the sons of the European and British middle and upper classes. The sale and use of opium was not illegal in 1886. However, the Opium Bill was drafted to regulate its trade. The object of the Opium Bill was to stop the sale and use of opium otherwise than as a drug for medicinal purposes. The Act placed the sale of opium and its compounds into the hands of persons registered under the Pharmacy Act of 1884. Every person had to be licensed and must pledge that he would only sell it for medicinal purposes. The newspapers reporting on the new Bill were at pains to point out that this would mean the selling of opium by the Chinese would be outlawed. The bill, however, was never well policed and opium was sold under the counter in many shops by both Chinese and European businessmen. Today, I see little sign of the Chinese population that once lived in the area. There's one tiny restaurant in Elizabeth Street with faded red lanterns over the door. Could that have been Foong May's teahouse?

Heading uphill, I turn left into George Street. On the corner of George and Margaret Streets, Harris Terrace sits tucked back a little from the road. This is where Ah Chit lived with Cy Wong. A striking example of late Victorian architecture, in a town that lost the majority of its Victorian heritage in the 1970s, this two-story brick row of five terraces seems out of place surrounded by the modern multi-story government precinct. Harris Terraces was built to accommodate politicians near to Parliament House. A Chinese Secret Society such as the Sheathed Sword would never have owned a house in Harris Terraces. The wealthy residents of the other houses would not have allowed it. But the Sheathed Sword certainly had the funds to purchase such a place and Ah Chit would have loved to live there among the city's decision-makers, thumbing his nose at them, while at the same time paying them the compliment of living among them. These are the relationships of imagination. Despite the historical 'unlikeliness', I wanted to give Ah Chit this pleasure.

I had to return to my car and drive across town to the Joss House. Nestled among cement offices in the industrial area of Newstead, it's tucked between the racecourse and the winding motorway. The Joss House is a small building with a lot of attitude; the triple roof is breathtaking. And essentially Chinese.

Sitting inside the Joss House, I absorb the aroma of incense and imagine the Opening in January of 1887. I hear a sound, quiet at first and foreign to my ear – a gentle tapping and clapping of drums. Gradually, the sound becomes louder and there is one deafening clash of the gong. I feel the beating heart of the crowd gathering outside quicken with the sound. More exotic smells fill the air. I feel intoxicated. Around me, the Joss House has filled with images, traditional Chinese costumes, red, gold and green, the pretty courtesans from the roof are dancing and waving fans. Other female figures with faces of porcelain are playing the dizi. I sit in the midst of the celebrations for some time before my consciousness returns to the present. The physicality of the Joss House, a tangible link to the past, has provided the instrument for my time travel. Drawing on research and cultural memory I am able to establish relationships with the past.

Historical writing and historical fiction are not so different. In both modes, writers move from an object or a text to an imagining that is drawn through intent from cultural memory. We build relationships in our minds. Images grow and expand, divide and multiply. What begins with a single image, results in a web of connections that link us in every direction. This is how we imagine the past into being. We read and re-read history; it is not told, it is re-membered.

BIBLIOGRAPHY

Barthes, Roland, *Criticism and Truth*. 1987 Trans. Katrina Pilcher. University Of Minnesota Press.

Barthes, Roland, Historical Discourse, In *The Rustle of Language*. 1967, New York.

Cook, D.P. 1958, *Aspects of Brisbane Society in the 1880's*. Honours Thesis: University of Queensland.

De Groot, Jerome, Consuming History: Historians and Heritage, In *Contemporary Popular Culture*. London: Routledge.

De Groot, Jerome, *The Historical Novel*. 2010 Routledge London.

Derrida, Jacques. Structure, sign and play in the discourse of the human sciences. In Alan Bass (trans.) *Writing and Difference*, London: Routledge. pp 278-94.

Eat, John, W. 2019. The Lost Heritage of Eagle Street: A Case Study in the Commercial Architecture of Brisbane, 1860-1930. Research Report: University of Queensland.

Fitzgerald, John. *Big White Lies: Chinese Australians in White Australia*. 2007. University of NSW: Sydney.

Foucault, Michel, *The Order of Things: An Archaeology of the Human Sciences*. 1966. Travistock: London

Foley, Fiona, *Biting the Clouds: A Badtjala perspective on the Aboriginals Protection and Restriction of the Sale Of Opium Act, 1897*. 2020. University of Queensland Press.

Gandalfo, Enza. Constructing Imaginary Narratives: Practice-led Research and Feminist Practice in Creative Writing. 2012. *Qualitative Research Journal.* Vol.12 No.1 pp.66-74.

Hutcheon, Linda, *The Politics of Postmodernism.* 1989 London: Routledge

Jameson, Bryan. Making 'honest, truthful and industrious men': Newsboys, Rational Recreation and the Construction of the Citizen in Late Victorian and Edwardian Brisbane. Journal of Popular Culture, 1999; 33(1):61-75

Jameson, Frederik, *The Cultural Turn: Selected Writings on the Postmodern,*1998. London: Routledge.

Johnson, Rosemary Erickson, *Contemporary Historical Crime Fiction.* 2006, Palgrave McMillan: New York.

Jenkins, Keith. *Rethinking History.* 2003 London: Routledge.

Lucas, Thomas Pennington. 1894. *The Curse and Its Cure.* JH Reynolds: Brisbane.

Lyotard, Jean-Francois, *The Postmodern Condition,* trans. Geoff Bennington and Brian Massumi. 1984. Manchester University Press.

McGuire, John. 2001, Punishment and Colonial Society: A History of Penal Change in Queensland, 1859-1930's. PhD Thesis: University of Queensland.

Mickel, Emanuel, J. Fictional History and Historical Fiction In *Romance Philology,* Spring 2012, Vol.66, No.1pp.57-96

Miller, Brenda and Suzanne Paola, Chapter 11: The Particular Challenges of Creative Non-Fiction, In *Tell It Slant.* 2019. Mc Graw-Hill.

Mitchell, Kate. *History and Cultural Memory in Neo-Victorian Fiction.* 2010. Pelgrave Macmillan

Mo Yimei (text), Mo Xiangyi (artist), 1988. *Harvest of Endurance: A History of the Chinese in Australia 1788-1988.* Sydney: China Friendship Society.

Munslow, Alun, *Deconstructing History.* 1997. London: Routledge.

Pinto, Sarah. Emotional Histories and Historical Emotions: Looking at the past in historical novels. *Rethinking History.* Vol.14, No.2, June 2010. 189-207.

Piper, Alana (Edit) *Brisbane Diseased: Contagions, Cures and Controversy.* Brisbane History Group Papers No. 25 2016.

Pruitt, Ida. *A Daughter of Han: The Autobiography of a Chinese Working Woman.* 1967, Stanford University Press: California

Rigney, Ann, Imperfect Histories: The Elusive Past and the Legacy of Romantic Historicism. 2018. Cornell University Press.

Rushdie, Salman, *Imaginery Homelands* 1991. London: Granta.

Sanders, Graham (trans.) *Shen Fu: Six Records of a Life Adrift.* Hackett Publishing Company: Cambridge.

Sartre, Jean-Paul *The Psychology of the Imagination* 1948. Routledge: New York.

Sartre, Jean-Paul *Nausea* (trans.) Robert Baldwick 1938 Penguin: New York.

Smith, Hazel and Roger T. Dean (Eds.) *Practice-led Research and Research-led Practice in the Creative Arts.* 1988. Edinburgh University press.

Yen Mar, Adeline, *Falling Leaves Return to their Roots: The True Story of an Unwanted Chinese Daughter.* 1997 Penguin: London.

Shawline Publishing Group Pty Ltd
www.shawlinepublishing.com.au